D0250943

Also by Rhys Bowen

The Molly Murphy Mysteries

City of Darkness and Light

The Family Way

Hush Now, Don't You Cry

Bless the Bride

The Last Illusion

In a Gilded Cage

Tell Me, Pretty Maiden

In Dublin's Fair City

Oh Danny Boy

In Like Flynn

For the Love of Mike

Murphy's Law

The Constable Evans Mysteries

Evanly Bodies

Evan Blessed

Evan's Gate

Evan Only Knows

Evans to Betsy

Evan Can Wait

Evan and Elle

Evanly Choirs

Evan Help Us

Evans Above

Praise for Rhys Bowen's Molly Murphy Series

"Once again Rhys Bowen proves why she's one of the great mystery writers working today. She never, ever falls into formula. And in this latest Molly Murphy novel, she takes her hero away from all the comforts of her New York City home to the bright lights of Gay Paris at the turn of the twentieth century. It's a world of cafés inhabited by Picasso and Degas and Monet. It's a Paris where the Eiffel Tower is still new, Sacré-Cœur a construction site, and the ripples of the Dreyfus affair linger—in the city, and in the murder in which Molly finds herself embroiled. Atmospheric, tightly plotted, heart-pounding, this is Bowen at her best."
—Louise Penny on *City of Darkness and Light*

"What could be more fun than a new Molly Murphy adventure? A Molly Murphy book set in Paris's avant-garde art world just after the turn of the century! A beautifully rendered portrait of the city and the period, seen from Molly's eyes as she deals with one of her most challenging cases yet."
—Deborah Crombie on *City of Darkness and Light*

"Highly entertaining . . . [Molly] pieces together a complicated mystery set against a rich historical backdrop."
—*RT Book Reviews* (4½ stars) on *The Family Way*

"[A] well-paced twelfth mystery featuring feisty and endearing Molly Murphy . . . The usual full-blooded characters will keep readers engaged."
—*Publishers Weekly* on *The Family Way*

"The latest addition to Molly's case files offers a charming combination of history, mystery, and romance."
—*Kirkus Reviews* on *Hush Now, Don't You Cry*

"Engaging . . . Molly's compassion and pluck should attract more readers to this consistently solid historical series."
—*Publishers Weekly* on *Bless the Bride*

"Winning . . . The gutsy Molly, who's no prim Edwardian miss, will appeal to fans of contemporary female detectives."
—*Publishers Weekly* on *The Last Illusion*

"This historical mystery delivers a top-notch, detail-rich story full of intriguing characters. Fans of the 1920s private detective Maisie Dobbs should give this series a try."
—*Booklist* on *The Last Illusion*

"Details of Molly's new cases are knit together with the accoutrements of 1918 New York City life. . . . Don't miss this great period puzzler reminiscent of Dame Agatha's mysteries and Gillian Linscott's Nell Bray series."
—*Booklist* on *In a Gilded Cage*

"Delightful . . . As ever, Bowen does a splendid job of capturing the flavor of early twentieth-century New York and bringing to life its warm and human inhabitants."
—*Publishers Weekly* on *In a Gilded Cage*

"Winning . . . It's all in a day's work for this delightfully spunky heroine."
—*Publishers Weekly* on *Tell Me, Pretty Maiden*

"Sharp historical backgrounds and wacky adventures."
—*Kirkus Reviews* on *Tell Me, Pretty Maiden*

"With a riveting plot capped off by a dramatic conclusion, Bowen captures the passion and struggles of the Irish people at the turn of the twentieth century."
—*Publishers Weekly* on *In Dublin's Fair City*

"Molly is an indomitable creature. . . . The book bounces along in the hands of Ms. Bowen and her Molly, and there is no doubt that she will be back causing trouble."
—*The Washington Times* on *In Dublin's Fair City*

Death of Riley

Rhys Bowen

 Minotaur Books ✹ New York

DEATH OF RILEY. Copyright © 2002 by Rhys Bowen. All rights reserved. Printed in the United States of America. For information, address St. Martin's Press, 175 Fifth Avenue, New York, N.Y. 10010.

www.minotaurbooks.com

The Library of Congress has cataloged the hardcover edition as follows:

Bowen, Rhys.
    Death of Riley / Rhys Bowen. — First edition.
        p. cm.
    ISBN 978-0-312-28211-0 (hardcover)
    ISBN 978-1-4299-0174-1 (e-book)
    1. Murphy, Molly (Fictitious character)—Fiction. 2. Women private investigators—New York (state)—New York—Fiction. 3. Irish American women—Fiction. 4. Women immigrants—Fiction. 5. New York (N.Y.)—Fiction.
    PR6052.O848 D43 2002
    823'.914

                                                    2002032470

ISBN 978-1-250-05391-6 (trade paperback)

Minotaur books may be purchased for educational, business, or promotional use. For information on bulk purchases, please contact the Macmillan Corporate and Premium Sales Department at 1-800-221-7945, extension 5442, or write to specialmarkets@macmillan.com.

First Minotaur Books Paperback Edition: December 2014

10 9 8 7 6 5 4 3 2 1

This book is dedicated to my fairy godmother, Meg Ruley, and to Dorothy Cannell, who was kind enough to introduce us.

Death of Riley

❧ One ❧

"Y ou want me to do what?" I demanded so loudly that a delicate young female walking ahead of us glanced back in
horror and had to reach for her smelling salts. I burst out
laughing. "For the love of Mike, Daniel—can you picture me as a
companion?" Then I looked up at Captain Daniel Sullivan's face.
He wasn't smiling.

He gave me an embarrassed half-smile, half-shrug. "I was only
thinking of you, Molly. You do need a job, and you haven't
exactly been successful in your search so far."

"So I haven't come up with the perfect job yet." I picked up
my skirts to avoid the wet patches around a grand-looking fountain. It had a fine bronze statue of the Angel of the Waters on top,
but at this moment the scene was anything but grand. A host of
little boys, some of them naked as the day they were born, were
scrambling in and out, standing under the curtain of spray before
being evicted again, squealing and yelling as they avoided the
nightstick wielded by an overzealous policeman. It was Sunday
afternoon and we were doing what most New Yorkers did on hot
summer Sundays—we were strolling through Central Park. For
once Daniel's day off had actually fallen on a Sunday, and there
had been no incidents to drag him away with an apologetic peck
on the cheek.

It seemed as if pecks on the cheek were all I was getting these

1

days from Captain Daniel Sullivan. Yes, I know that pecks on the cheek, properly chaperoned, are all that decent young ladies should expect before marriage, but propriety rather went out of the window when I was with Daniel. And I had hoped our romance might have blossomed into something more substantial by now, but as New York's youngest police captain, Daniel threw himself wholeheartedly into his job. I, on the other hand, had no job to keep me occupied.

It wasn't as if I hadn't tried. After my somewhat dramatic arrival in New York, I had looked for something suitable. The saints in heaven will attest that I really put my heart into it. I wouldn't have minded a governess position, in fact I'd have been good at it. But it didn't take me long to discover that an Irish girl, fresh off the boat, and with no references—or at least no references that could be verified (I had made some very convincing forgeries), would not be hired to teach the children of a good family. Nursemaid maybe, but I didn't think I'd last a week as a servant.

After that, I tried my hand at any job I could find, short of gutting fish at the Fulton Street fish market. I did draw the line at standing up to my elbows in fish entrails.

"You have to admit that there have been some rather spectacular disasters." Daniel voiced my thoughts for me, making me wonder whether he could actually read my mind.

"I wouldn't say disasters."

A breeze blew off the boating lake beyond the fountain, sending a fine curtain of spray in our direction. The cool tingles on my hot skin felt wonderful and I was tempted to stand there for a while until Daniel pulled me clear. "Molly—you'll get soaked to the skin."

"But it feels divine."

"It might feel divine," he said, looking down at me with those alarming blue eyes, "but that's a very fine muslin you're wearing, my dear. We wouldn't want other men ogling you, would we?" He led me firmly away from the fountain terrace, along the edge of the boating lake. I paused to look longingly at those rowboats. A couple came gliding by, the girl's face hidden by a deliciously decadent parasol—all frills and lace and froufrou—as she trailed a hand languidly through the water. Her beau, pulling manfully at the oars in rolled-up shirtsleeves, didn't look as if he were enjoying himself quite as much. Undignified rivulets of sweat streaked the beet-red face beneath his boater.

"You wouldn't say disasters?" Daniel repeated, chuckling as he led me away. "The shirtwaist factory?"

"So I got a needle through my thumb. It could have happened to anyone." I tossed my head, almost losing my straw boater into the water.

"And who sewed all those sleeves on inside out?" Those alarming blue eyes were twinkling.

"That wasn't why I was fired and you know it. It was because I stood up to that brute of a foreman and wasn't about to take any of his nonsense. All those unfair rules—docking their workers' pay every time they so much as sneezed. I knew right away that I'd never be able to hold my tongue for long."

"Then there was the café," Daniel reminded me.

I gave him a sheepish grin. "Yes, I suppose that counted as a spectacular disaster."

We had reached the dappled shade of spreading chestnut trees as the path left the lakeside. The effect was instant, like stepping into a pool of cool water. "Ah, that's better," Daniel said. "Look, there's a bench under that tree. Let's sit awhile."

I noticed that Daniel seemed to be feeling the heat more than I. His face was as red as the young man's in the rowboat and his wild black curls were plastered to his forehead under his boater. Of course, gentlemen are at a disadvantage on days like this, having to wear jackets whilst we women can keep cool in muslins. But he was a born New Yorker. I'd have thought he grew up used to this heat. I, on the other hand, had come from the wild west coast of Ireland, where a couple of sunny days in a row counted as a heat wave, and we had the chilly Atlantic at our feet whenever we needed to cool off.

Daniel took out his handkerchief and mopped at his brow. "That's better," he said. "I swear, every summer is hotter than the last. It's those new skyscrapers. They block the cooling breezes from the East River and the Hudson."

"It's certainly hot enough." I fanned myself with the penny fan I had bought from a street vendor last week. It was a pretty little thing from China, made of paper and decorated with a picture of a pagoda and wild mountain scenery. "Here, you look as if you could use this more than me." I turned and fanned Daniel too. He grabbed at my wrist, laughing. "Stop it. You'll be offering me your smelling salts next."

"I've never carried smelling salts in my life and never intend to," I said. "Fainting is for ninnies."

"That's what I like about you, Molly Murphy—" For a long minute Daniel gazed at me in a way that turned my insides to water, his fingers still firmly around my wrist— "Your spirit. That and your trim little waist, of course, and those big green eyes and that adorable little nose." He touched it playfully. Then the smile faded but the look of longing remained. "Oh, Molly. I just wish . . ." He let the rest of the sentence hang in the humid air, making me wonder what exactly he was wishing. He was young and healthy, with great career prospects—and a future that should have included a wife too. But I wasn't going to press him on this one. Who knew how men's minds worked? He could be waiting for a pay raise or saving enough to buy a house before he popped the question—if he did indeed intend to pop it. For once in my life I kept silent.

"I'm pretty content myself," I said gaily. "I have a fine big room of my own and a handsome fellow who comes to call from time to time, and I'm living in a big city, just like I always dreamed I would."

Daniel let his gaze fall and he sat there for a moment silent, his eyes focused on his hands in his lap.

"There's no rush for anything, Daniel," I said. "If I could just find a way to keep myself a respectable job where I wasn't abused or overworked . . ."

"Did I not mention the companion's position?"

I patted his hand. "Daniel—can you see me as a companion to an old lady? Companions are pathetic, down-trodden creatures who cringe when spoken to and spend their days holding knitting wool and combing cats. I tried my hand at being a servant, remember. I wasn't born to be humble. And you know yourself that I can never learn when to hold my tongue."

"But a companion is not a servant, Molly. You'd be expected to read to Miss Van Woekem and take her for strolls around the park—that kind of thing. What could be easier?"

"She'd be crotchety and finickety. Old spinsters always are. I'd lose my patience with her and that would be that." I gave a gay little laugh, but still Daniel didn't smile.

"Molly, I'm sure I don't need to remind you that you do need to find some kind of job soon. I know the alderman gave you a small gift by way of apology for what happened at his house—"

"It was a bribe, Daniel, as you very well know."

"But it won't last forever," Daniel went on, ignoring my statement. It was funny the way the New York policemen seemed to become suddenly deaf at the mention of the word 'bribe.' "And you do have rent to pay, even though it's a modest amount."

"The O'Hallarans are being very kind," I agreed. "I'm sure they could rent out their attic for much more if they chose to." It was Daniel himself who had found me the pleasant top-floor flat owned by a fellow policeman. "And don't forget Seamus shares the rent, and pays for most of the food, too."

"I should think so, considering that you cook it and look after his children for him."

"I'm glad to do it," I said. "They're no trouble, and how would he manage without me, poor man, with his wife back home in Ireland just waiting to die?"

I had brought Seamus's young son and daughter to New York

5

at their mother's request when she found that she had consumption and wasn't allowed to travel. And in case you think I'm some kind of saint, let me assure you that the arrangement suited my own purposes very well.

"You've a good heart, Molly," Daniel said, "but this arrangement can't go on forever. I'm not entirely comfortable with you living up there with a man whose wife is back in Ireland."

I laughed. "Not comfortable, Daniel? Seamus O'Connor is a perfectly harmless individual—you've seen him yourself. Hardly the greatest catch in New York. What's more, we have a kitchen and hallway between us to keep things proper, and Mrs. O'Hallaran downstairs too, keeping an eye on things."

"That's not the point," Daniel said. "People will talk. Do you want them saying you're a kept woman?"

"Certainly not."

"Then may I suggest you listen to me and find a suitable job for yourself that will not end in disaster."

His reminders of my dismal failures in the world of commerce were beginning to rile me. I didn't like to fail at anything. "If you really want to know, I'm still planning to follow my original idea and set myself up as a private investigator." I threw this out more to annoy him than anything.

Daniel rolled his eyes and gave a despairing chuckle. "Molly, women do not become investigators. I thought we'd been through all this before."

"I don't see why not. I thought I was pretty good at it."

"Apart from almost getting yourself killed."

"Right. Apart from that. But I told you. I don't plan to deal with criminal cases. Nothing dangerous. I still keep thinking about all those people when I was leaving Liverpool, Daniel. They were desperate for knowledge of their loved ones who had come to America. I'd be doing good work if I united families again, wouldn't I?"

"Did it ever occur to you that the loved ones might not want to be found?" he asked. "And anyway, how would you set about this—this detective business? You'd need an office to start with, and you'd have to advertise . . ."

"I know that too!"

"And if you discovered that the loved one you were seeking had gone to California, would you take the train to find him? Families of immigrants won't have money to pay."

"So I'd need some capital to get started." I paused to watch an elegant open carriage pass on the road beyond the trees. Lovely women in wide white hats and young men in blazers sat chatting and laughing as if they hadn't a care in the world—which they probably hadn't. "And I'd just have to take some cases that paid well."

Daniel turned to me and took my hands in his. "Molly, please put this foolish idea to rest. You don't need to set yourself up as anything. You need a pleasant, dignified job that pays the rent, for the time being, that's all."

"Maybe I won't be content with a pleasant little job. Maybe I want to make something of myself."

He laughed again, uneasily this time. "It's not as if you're a man and need to be thinking of a future career. Only something to bide your time until some fellow snaps you up."

His eyes were teasing again, all seriousness apparently forgotten.

"Snaps me up? But surely you know I'm a hopeless case? Already turned twenty-three and therefore officially on the shelf."

"You? You'll never find yourself on the shelf, Molly. You'll be just as fascinating at fifty."

"Hardly a comforting thought," I said. "Still a companion at fifty? Shall we go on walking?" I got to my feet. This conversation was definitely not leading where I wanted it to. Daniel had had several chances to state his intentions and failed miserably at all of them. It wasn't as if he were either hesitant or shy. Then he said something that made me realize how his brain might be working.

"I wish you'd give the companion's position a try, Molly. Miss Van Woekem is well respected in New York society. My parents really look up to her. Being with her would give you an introduction into society here."

Then it dawned on me. That was why he was hesitating—he didn't want to marry an Irish peasant girl fresh from the old sod. I'd left Ireland with its snobbery and class prejudice and crossed the Atlantic to find that same snobbery alive and flourishing in the New World. And he with parents who came over with nothing in the great famine! Well, if that was how Daniel Sullivan thought— I opened my mouth to tell him what he could do with his companion's job, and with Miss Van What's-it too. I stopped myself at the last second. He presumably thought he was doing this for my own good. He wanted me to fit in and become acceptable and accepted in society here. What's more, it certainly beat out fish gutting. What did I have to lose? "All right, if you think I should take it, I'm prepared to give it a try."

He stopped and put his hands on my shoulders. "That's my girl," he said, kissing me on the forehead.

"Should we try the Ramble today?" I motioned to the inviting woodland path that disappeared into the undergrowth to my left. The area of Central Park known as the Ramble was made up of a series of winding, intersecting paths through a thickly wooded copse. Only a few steps into the woods and it was hard to believe that you were in the middle of a big city. It was also one of the few places where it was possible to steal a kiss undisturbed.

But Daniel shook his head. "It's too hot for walking today. Why don't we head for that ice cream parlor?"

"Ice cream? That would be wonderful!" On a hot day like this, ice cream won out over kisses with me too. I had only just tasted my first ice cream and was still amazed at a place where such luxuries were available every day.

Daniel smiled at my excitement. "Don't ever change, will you?"

"I might well turn into a severe and snooty spinster when Miss Van Woekem starts to influence me," I retorted.

He laughed and slipped his arm around my waist. In spite of the heat and the fact that this was surely not proper behavior for a park on a Sunday, I wasn't about to stop him. We joined the stream of Sunday strollers on the wide East Drive. Half of New York had to be here. The upper crust passed by in their open carriages, oblivious to the stream of pedestrians beside them. On the sandy footpath it was ordinary people like ourselves, severe Italian mothers dressed all in black with a fleet of noisy bambinos, Jewish families with bearded patriarchs and solemn little boys with skullcaps on their heads, proud fathers pushing tall perambulators—every language under the sun being spoken around us. As we neared the gate the noise level rose—music from a carrousel competed with an Italian hurdy-gurdy man and the shouts of the ice cream seller. I knew that Daniel wouldn't buy ice cream in the park. You never knew what it was made from, he said, and typhoid fever was always a worry in the hot weather.

Suddenly a dapper little man in a dark brown suit and derby hat stepped out in front of us.

"Hold it right there!" he shouted.

"It's all right. He's only taking our photo," Daniel whispered as I started in alarm. "He's one of the park photographers."

I saw then that the man was pointing a little black box at us and we heard a click.

"There you are, sir. Lovely souvenir of the day," he said, nodding seriously. He had a strange accent that seemed to be a mixture of London Cockney and Bowery New York. He came up to Daniel. "Here's my card if you care to stop by the studio and purchase the photo for your lady friend."

As he handed Daniel his card he moved closer and I thought I saw his hand go to Daniel's pocket. It was over in a fraction of a second, so that I didn't know whether to believe my eyes. For a moment I was too startled to act, then, as I grabbed Daniel's arm to warn him, I saw the man's hand move away from Daniel again, and it was empty. I didn't want to make a scene, so I kept quiet until we had walked past the photographer.

"I think that man tried to pick your pocket," I whispered.

"Then he was out of luck," Daniel said, smiling. "I only keep my handkerchief in that pocket."

He slipped his hand into the pocket and I noticed the change in his expression. "Yes, the fellow was unlucky all right," he said, taking my arm. "Come on, let's get that ice cream."

❧ TWO ❧

A crisply starched maid showed me into the refined brick house with wrought-iron balconies on South Gramercy Park.

"Miss Murphy, ma'am," she said and dropped a curtsy before retiring. The old woman who sat in the high-backed chair by the window looked as if she had been chiseled from marble. Her face had shrunk to a living skull but the eyes that fastened on me were still very alive.

"Well, come in, girl. Don't just stand there," she said in a sharp, gravelly voice that sounded as if it had dried out like its owner. "What is your name?"

"Molly. Molly Murphy." Her look was so intense that I was startled.

She sniffed. "Molly—a nickname only suitable for peasants and servants. You were presumably baptized with a Christian name."

"I was baptized Mary Margaret."

"And that is a little too pretentious for someone in your station. Nobody below the middle class needs two names. I shall call you just plain Mary."

"You can call all you like, but I won't answer." I had recovered enough to challenge her stare. "My name's Molly. Always has been. If you don't like it, you can always call me Miss Murphy."

She opened her mouth, went to say something, then shut it again with a "hmmph."

"Let me take a look at you."

I could feel those dark boot-button eyes boring into me. "Are you not wearing a corset, girl?"

"I've never worn one," I said. "Back where I come from, we didn't go in for such things."

She made a disproving tut-tutting noise. "Daniel mentioned that you were newly arrived from Ireland, but he didn't say that you'd come straight from the bogs. When you leave here today I'll give you the money and you'll go to my costumier and have yourself fitted for a corset. And as for the rest of your clothing—I suppose I can't expect you to wear black in this summer heat. Do you possess a plain gray dress?"

"I don't possess much of anything," I said. "I had to leave most of my things behind in Ireland."

I didn't mention the reason I'd had to leave in a hurry. Nobody knew that but me. Nobody was going to know it.

"I'll have my housekeeper see if there is anything suitable for you in the servant's closet," she said.

"I understood that you wanted a companion, not a servant." Again I matched stares with her. With that hooked nose and those black little eyes she reminded me of some kind of bird. A bird of prey, definitely. "I don't get out much anymore," she said. "I like to be surrounded by things that are pleasing to the eye." My gaze followed hers around the room. It was indeed pleasing to the eye—not cluttered with too many knickknacks like other well-to-do rooms I had seen, it managed to be austere and elegant at the same time. The furniture was well-polished mahogany, with lots of silk cushions, a mahogany bookcase filled with rich leather tomes took up most of one wall. There was a lamp with a shade like a miniature stained-glass window and a couple of good, if somber, paintings hung on the walls. Not what one would call a woman's room, but a room of definite good taste.

"The lamp is from Mr. Tiffany," she said, noticing my eyes

falling on it. "My one concession to the latest fads. And the painting over the fireplace—"

"Looks as if it's of the Flemish School," I said, studying the dark and rather too real-looking still life of a dead pheasant and some fruit. "Is it a copy of a Vermeer?"

She snorted. I couldn't tell if the sound was pleased or contemptuous. "It *is* a Vermeer," she said. "And how do you come to know about painting? Are they hanging Vermeers in Irish cottages these days?"

"I'm not uneducated, even though I may not be fashionably dressed. Our governess was a great devotee of art. She had visited all the fine galleries of Europe."

"You had a governess?" She looked at me incredulously.

"I was educated with the land-owner's daughters," I answered, hoping she wouldn't interrogate further on this topic.

She stared at me in a way that could be considered rude among equals, obviously deciding whether I was lying to her or too impudent to keep. "You have a nice enough face," she said at last, "and you carry yourself well, but that outfit has definitely seen better days. I'll have my dressmaker come in and measure you up. Maybe not gray. Doesn't do justice to the hair, which would be quite striking if properly arranged." In deference to my companion's position I had managed to twist my unruly red curls into a severe bun. Not too successfully, I might add. Trying to tame my hair was like trying to hold back the ocean.

"So if you know about art, and you were educated by a governess, you presumably know how to read more than penny dreadfuls."

"There's nothing I like better." I let my eyes wander to the bookcase on the back wall. "I love to read whenever I can."

"In which case maybe you'll turn out to be satisfactory after all, in spite of appearances. You can start by reading to me now. What do you like to read?"

"Oh, the novels of Charles Dickens—"

"Popular sentimental drivel, written for the masses," she said.

"Why does one need to read about squalor when there is already too much on one's doorstep?"

"Jane Austen, then."

"Feminine frippery. You won't find many novels in this house, Miss Murphy. I believe that reading should be for two purposes only—to educate and to uplift. Now if you will pick up that slim volume lying on the sofa, you may read to me from it. It is a newly published account of last year's atrocities in China, written by the sister of a missionary who was beheaded. I am very much afraid there are some races that we shall never succeed in civilizing or Christianizing."

"The Chinese have a very old civilization and they might not have wanted to be Christianized," I pointed out.

"What rubbish you talk, girl. It is our duty to spread the Gospel. But then I suppose you are another of those Holy Romans. You've never learned the lessons of Martin Luther or John Calvin, more's the pity. And now my goddaughter is thinking of marrying one. 'You'd better bring the boy in line before the wedding,' I told her, because I'll not attend any service where they swing incense and pray to idols."

I decided this was a time to keep my mouth shut and went to get the book.

"But Arabella is a headstrong girl and probably doesn't care a fig for anyone's opinion, even mine, though she knows she'll inherit everything from me," she added as I crossed the room.

I realized I was gritting my teeth with a forced smile on my face. I hoped Daniel realized what I was doing for him, because I wasn't sure who was going to break first, I or Miss Van Woekem. A white fur rug was lying behind the sofa. As I went to step on it, it leaped up, yowling, and clawed at me. So there were to be cats, after all.

"Watch what you're doing, clumsy girl," Miss Van Woekem snapped. "Now you've quite upset Princess Yasmin."

I forbore to say that Princess Yasmin had quite upset me as well. The large white Persian sat watching me with a look of utter disdain. I reached carefully past her to get the book. I need not have worried. She turned her back on me and started licking a paw as if I were of no consequence whatever.

At the end of an hour's reading the maid reappeared to announce luncheon.

"I will take mine here, on a tray," Miss Van Woekem announced. "Miss Murphy will eat at the dining table." She nodded for me to close the book. "You read surprisingly well for one of your station. The accent is uncouth, of course, but I am pleasingly surprised. Maybe you'll do after all."

"And maybe I won't," I thought as I followed the maid to the dining room. If Daniel thought this was easy work, he had never tried it.

I spent an uneasy meal sitting alone at a vast polished mahogany table, with the maid waiting attendance behind me. I won't say I didn't enjoy it, however. For one who has always had ideas above her station, according to my mother, this was the way I should have been eating all my life. And the food was delicious—some sort of cold fish mousse and salad, fresh fruit and tiny meringues for dessert and freshly made lemonade to drink. I began to think better of the job, especially when I discovered that Miss Van W. took an afternoon nap and I was free to browse in her library.

After tea taken at the little table in the sitting room, she instructed me to get her bath chair ready. The maid brought it into the front hall—an impressive wicker contraption on wheels—and helped Miss Van W. into it.

"You can wheel me around the gardens, girl. It is the most pleasant place to be at this time of day."

The central square of Gramercy Park was an iron-railed garden filled with trees, shrubs and flowers. I wheeled her across the street to the park's entrance, a wrought-iron gate facing the north side. As I approached, an elderly couple was leaving. The man, with impressive white mustaches, took off his boater, gave a sweeping bow, then held the gate open for us to pass through.

"Good evening, Miss Van Woekem. Seasonably warm again, wouldn't you say?"

Miss Van Woekem nodded to him. "Since it's July, that goes without saying. Good day to you."

As we passed into the gardens, she muttered to me, "Odious man. Just because he knew McKinley in Ohio, he thinks he can forget that his father was a grocer."

I pushed her around the park, enjoying the shade under the trees, the sweet-smelling shrubs and the banks of glorious flowers. I noticed a man in a brown suit and derby standing among those trees, blending into the shade as we passed. I wondered if he was a gardener, but he wasn't doing anything and there was no sign of tools. He just stood there, staring up at a house on the south side of the park, and didn't even notice us.

In the distance a clock struck six. "Time to go," Miss Van Woekem said. "I must change for dinner. My goddaughter may be joining me, if she doesn't get a better offer, that is. She is in town for a few days of shopping. You may push me home."

I wheeled her to the park gate and leaned on it. It remained firmly shut.

"Didn't you bring the key, girl?" she asked in annoyance.

"Key? I didn't know there was a key." I felt my face flushing.

"Of all the stupidity! Of course there's a key. We don't want to admit riffraff, do we?"

"You might have mentioned it before we set off," I said.

"You are most insolent and do not know your place."

"I thought you required a companion, which, by definition, is not a subordinate," I said. "If I don't suit you, then maybe you should look elsewhere."

We stared at each other like two dogs whose territories have overlapped.

"I think I'll manage to whip you into shape eventually," she said with a slight glint that could have been a twinkle in her eyes. "And you had better find a way to get us out of this park before nightfall."

I left the chair in the shade and walked around the gardens, hoping to attract the attention of a passerby outside the railings. But the square was deserted apart from two women servants who hurried along the far side and a carriage that passed me at a brisk trot, too quickly to be hailed. As I approached the southeast corner, which was the most wooded, I remembered the man in brown. I hadn't seen him leave the park, and he would have to have a key for us. But he was no longer standing under the trees. I looked around. No movement except for a squirrel that darted across the lawn.

Just then a large shrub close to the railing rustled. The movement was too big to have been caused by another squirrel. A cat, maybe. I moved closer, then froze when I saw the man in brown crouching down beside the shrub. He turned and looked around, nervously. I managed to shrink back behind a tree trunk just in time. Obviously satisfied that there was nobody to see him, he grasped one of the railings, removed it, slipped through the opening and then replaced the railing. It was all over in a second. I watched him brush himself off and walk down the street whistling.

I was so impressed with what I had seen that it took me a moment to realize I had seen him before. He was the same man who had taken our photograph in Central Park.

❧ Three ❧

I didn't think any more of the strange incident until the next day. I presumed that the man merely wanted to access the gardens without owning a resident's key. The cool shade was certainly tempting on these stifling summer days when the heat rose from the cobblestones and reflected from the brick walls.

I had followed his example and made my exit through the loose railing, then picked up a key from the maid, not disclosing to Miss Van Woekem the details of how I had made my escape. I had, however, noted the railing for future use.

I had arrived home that night to find my landlady very agitated.

"Well, here you are at last, Miss Murphy, and not a moment too soon." She stepped out into the hallway, blocking my passage up the stairs. She had an uncanny habit of doing this, no matter what time of day I came home. She was one of those women my mother used to call "lace-curtain" Irish—nothing better to do than sit behind her lace curtains and snoop at the world.

"Why, what has happened, Mrs. O'Hallaran?" I asked.

"All hell has broken loose up there." She indicated the stairs. "Half the rabble from the Lower East Side, if you ask me."

"Oh, that will be his cousin's family." My heart sank. My least favorite people in the city of New York.

"A fleet of wild children making so much noise that I had to

19

send himself up after them. Any more noise and they're out." She turned back to me. "I was given to understand that Captain Sullivan recommended you as a quiet and sober young woman. Now look what you've brought into the house."

"I'm sorry, Mrs. O'Hallaran," I said, "but I did explain to you about the O'Connors. I felt responsible for those children, packed like sardines into that awful tenement room, and their poor mother dying back home in Ireland."

My landlady's grim expression softened. "Well, you would, wouldn't you. Any decent, God-fearing woman would. Poor little mites in a strange country and their dear mother maybe already up there with the angels." She paused to cross herself. "There's nothing wrong with those two that a firm hand wouldn't mend, but those cousins . . ."

"I couldn't agree more," I muttered. "I'll speak to them myself."

"Yes, you do that, Miss Murphy. I'd be most obliged."

I sighed as I walked up the stairs. Little had I known what I was taking on when I escorted two children across the Atlantic to their father. I had expected to deliver them and vanish from their lives, but I had found that hard to do. They were, as Mrs. O'Hallaran had said, poor little mites. I couldn't leave them jammed into a two-room apartment with that dragon of a cousin Nuala and her terrible family. It had been a case of hate at first sight for both of us when the children and I arrived from Ellis Island. Nuala couldn't have made me less welcome, even though I had nowhere else to go. Which was why I wanted to rescue Seamus and his little family from that squalor as soon as Daniel found me this wonderful attic on East Fourth Street. I had grown very fond of young Seamus, whom I now nicknamed Shameyboy, and little Bridie. Taking care of them seemed the least I could do for their poor mother, Kathleen, who must have been worrying her heart out back home in Ireland. It had been with misgivings that I had left them to go to Miss Van Woekem's. They were so small to be alone all day in such a vast city while their father worked eighteen-hour shifts digging the tunnel for the new underground railway. I had to remind myself that they needed to learn to stand on their own feet. New York was the kind of place where only the strongest survived. And after all, I wasn't related to them. Working for Miss Van Woekem would be a way of easing them into independence, I decided as I mounted the second flight of stairs. It would be up to Seamus to take responsibility for his own children.

The next morning passed quickly and remarkably smoothly as Miss Van Woekem sent me on an errand to match her knitting wool. When I returned from a successful mission, I found her staring out of her window.

"There is a strange man in the gardens," she said, not looking up. "He has been there all morning."

I joined her at the window. It was the man in the brown suit.

"He was there yesterday," I said. "Standing in the same place."

"I don't like the sound of it," Miss Van Woekem said. "Probably a burglar, deciding which house to break into."

"He's taking an awfully long time to decide," I said. "If he's been standing there all morning and yesterday too."

"He's watching our movements and seeing when a house might be unoccupied. Go and find a constable and bring him here."

I did as she asked and returned with a large red-faced constable I had found on the corner of Fourth Avenue and Twenty-first Street.

"A strange man in the gardens, you say, miss?" he asked, slapping his nightstick against his palm to show he was ready for action. "We'll soon take care of him. What exactly was he doing? Making a nuisance of himself?"

"No, just standing there and staring up at one of the houses."

We came into Gramercy Park. "Where exactly was he when you saw him last?" the constable asked in a low voice. I pointed out the southwest corner. He nodded. "We'll stroll by on the other side, casual-like, so that he thinks we haven't noticed him. Then I'll slip into the park and nab him."

"There he is," I whispered. "See, under that big tree."

He gave a quick look, then looked again. "Why, he's nothing to worry about, miss. That's old Paddy. I know him well. Wouldn't harm a fly. I expect he's doing a spot of bird-watching. That's what he'd be doing."

I reported this to Miss Van Woekem. "Bird-watching?" she exclaimed. "I wasn't aware that any birds nested on the second floor of houses. Still, if the police think he's harmless . . . upon their heads be it if there is a break-in."

While she took her nap that afternoon I looked out of the window again. Just what was he doing there? Then I saw the glint of something flashing in the sunlight. Field glasses! The man was using field glasses to watch the house. Then, of course, it hit me. He wasn't a burglar at all. He was some kind of investigator. And the constable must have known what he was doing. He may even have been working with the police . . .

My mind went back to our encounter with him on Sunday afternoon. Daniel's relaxed smile when I told him the man had tried to pick his pocket and then his change of expression when he put his hand into that pocket. How could I have been so blind? The man hadn't tried to take anything from Daniel's pocket. He had put something into it.

I felt a rush of excitement. I had talked to Daniel about setting myself up as an investigator, but I had no idea how to go about it. When I had tried to solve a real crime, I had stumbled over clues by good or bad luck, more than through my own skill. Now here, before my eyes, was the real thing. As soon as I got off work I would go and see Daniel at police headquarters. I'd make him tell me everything he knew about the man in the brown suit. If the man was, indeed, working with the police, and not a gangster, then I'd go and ask him to take me on as an apprentice.

I waited impatiently for the end of the day.

"Stop fidgeting, girl. You're acting as if you're sitting on an anthill," Miss Van Woekem chided. "What is the matter with you?"

"Nothing. I suppose I'm not used to being cooped up in a room all day. I was brought up in the fresh air. Would you like me to take you for a stroll around the park again?"

"No, thank you. I won't have time for that today. In fact, I am meeting my goddaughter at the theater. She insists that I see a new play with her. I know it will be dreadful. It's by a dull young European, and their plays are always middle-class melodramas. As if the middle class could be anything but boring. But I have to humor the child when she comes to town. I don't see her often enough." She gazed out of the window. "You can leave early and go and select yourself some fabric for a dress. Nothing fancy, you understand. A plain, dignified single color—beige or gray would be suitable. Here is the money." She fished into her mesh purse and handed me two dollars. "Bring the fabric tomorrow and I will arrange for my dressmaker to measure you."

I took the money, thinking that I might not be shopping for fabric at all. If I could worm the old man's name and address out of Daniel, then Miss Van Woekem would be looking for a new companion to bully. I set off, my heart racing with anticipation.

I hadn't visited Daniel at police headquarters on Mulberry Street since I had been brought there as a suspect, and I still felt a chill of alarm as I went up those stone steps and along that echoing tiled corridor. Even though reason told me that I was safe on the other side of the Atlantic and that my past could never catch up with me, I still found it hard to breathe.

Daniel's office was at the far end of the hallway and had a front wall and door of frosted glass. I could see the silhouette of a figure seated at his desk. So I was in luck. He wasn't out on a case and he might even have time to take a dinner break with me. I tapped and pushed open the door, all in one movement.

"You'll never guess who I have just seen in Gramercy Park, Dan——" I began, then stopped short in confusion. "Oh, I beg your pardon. I expected to find Captain Sullivan here."

The figure at Daniel's desk was an exquisite young woman in a pink silk dress with a large cameo at her throat. A luxuriant coil of dark hair was piled high over an elfin face and was topped with one of those new little hats, with just a hint of pink veil, perched saucily to the front. Her big blue eyes opened even wider in surprise as she looked at me.

"He is due back momentarily, so I am given to understand." She spoke in a soft, girlish, American-accented voice. "Although with policemen one never knows, does one?" She gave a dimpled smile. "If you have an urgent message to give him, miss, you could write it down and I will make sure he gets it." She was staring at me, trying to sum me up. "You're not a witness to a crime, are you? I always adore hearing about crimes. I should dearly love to be a witness, but nothing ever seems to happen in White Plains."

"No, I'm not a witness. Merely a friend dropping in to give Daniel a message."

"Oh, well, if you're a friend, then you'll have heard all about me."

"I'm afraid not. You are?"

"Daniel's fiancée, Arabella Norton. He hasn't told you about me? Naughty boy." A simpering laugh. "Well, I suppose he doesn't go blabbing about his personal life to everyone he meets in New York."

The world stood still. She was still smiling. "I'm up in town for shopping and theater, so I thought I'd pop in and surprise him."

"Oh, I imagine you'll do that, all right." I fought to keep my face composed. "So if you'll excuse me, Miss Norton, I won't bother you any further. What I have to say can wait for another time."

"Oh, but do leave a message. I'll promise he gets it."

"No message," I said and walked out with steady gait and my head held high.

It was only when I got outside the building that I had to hold on to the railings and remind myself to breathe. Then I started to walk, faster and faster, striding out with no plan and no direction in mind. All I wanted to do was to walk far enough and fast enough to make the hollow pain in my heart disappear. It was approaching the dinner hour and the streets were full of factory girls leaving work, housewives buying last-minute purchases from street carts, children dodging underfoot as they played wild games.

It all passed me by in a blur. I was not even aware of my surroundings or how hot I was until I reached Battery Park, at the tip of Manhattan Island, and felt the cooling breeze from the harbor in my face. Quite a stiff wind had blown up this evening, accompanied by a heavy bank of clouds on the eastern horizon promising rain by nightfall. I stood there letting the wind blow into my face, feeling the chill on my sweat-drenched bodice.

I was so angry I thought I would explode. How could he? How dare he? All this time he had led me on and let me believe that I mattered to him, when he was committed to another woman and knew there could be no future for us. All those times he had taken me in his arms and looked into my eyes with love had been a sham, mere playacting. I was not sure with whom I was angrier—with Daniel or myself. He was a man, after all, and men were out to get all they could from women. I, on the other hand, had been a naive fool. When I thought about it, I realized he had never made me any promises, never even hinted that we might be married someday. In fact, when marriage had been mentioned, he had skirted around the subject or hastily changed it. So he hadn't lied to me—just never told me the truth.

And I? For once in my life I had kept quiet, waiting patiently for him to choose the right moment for a proposal, as any good girl should. If only I had been my normal impatient self I would have demanded to know his intentions right away and I would have known where I stood.

At least I knew where I stood now. I was on my own again. I would have to forge my own future without any prospect of marriage, or even without the support of his friendship. All the more reason to set myself up in a profession as soon as possible. I reached into my pocket and fingered the two dollars. I wouldn't be getting any sensible dresses made, that was for sure, because I wouldn't be going back to work for Miss Van Woekem, I'd rather starve than set foot in that house again. How conveniently Daniel had come up with the companion's position for me. Miss Van Woekem was a family friend, indeed. How conveniently he had omitted to mention that she was also the godmother of his fiancée. Just thinking the word brought a physical stab of pain around my heart. I had never believed that heartache was anything more than a metaphor before. I squeezed my eyes shut to stop tears from forming. I was not going to cry.

At that moment the rain began, fat drops that fell, sizzling, onto the granite of the seawall. I stood without moving, letting the rain wash over me as if I were a marble statue. Only when the first drops turned into a veritable deluge and thunder rumbled nearby did I realize the foolishness of my present position. There was no sense in being struck by lightning. I brushed back the plastered strands of hair from my face and started to walk back up Broadway.

As I passed a tavern, a group of young men was entering it. I braced myself for the usual ribald comments. Instead one of them broke away from the rest.

"Kathleen?" he called.

It was my old friend Michael Larkin, my shipmate from the *Majestic*, my fellow suspect in a murder case. He stood there before me, grinning delightedly. I would hardly have recognized him. I had left a thin, pale-faced boy and here was a well-muscled man with a confident swagger. I had explained to him why I had been using another woman's name when we first met, but I suppose he still thought of me as Kathleen. He corrected himself before I could. "I mean Molly, of course. Silly of me. Molly, it's grand to see you. Whatever are you doing with yourself? You're soaked to the skin."

"I got caught in the storm. I was out at Battery Park."

"Recalling fond memories of Ellis Island?" he asked. "How are you? How are the little ones? Are they still living with you?"

"The children are doing just fine, thank you," I said. "The rest is a long story."

"Could we meet sometime and you could tell it to me?" he said. "Right now I'm just about to have a drink with my mates, and I won't invite you to join us. This is no place to take a lady."

"I'd be delighted, Michael." I even managed a smile. "I'd been wondering about you. You look as if you're doing well for yourself."

"You've no idea how well. This is the land of opportunity, all right. I'm foreman of a team now and we're just starting work on what's going to be the tallest building in the world. The Flatiron Building, they're calling it, on account of it's shaped like one. My, but it will be a sight to behold. I must take you to see it someday."

"I'd like that."

"You better get on home, before we're both washed away." He dragged me out of the way of a downspout that splashed from a rooftop. "Do you have the trolley fare?"

"Yes, thank you." He was as kind and generous as ever—a true friend when I had needed one.

"We'll meet again then," he said. "Oh, and Molly, you'll not believe this, but I've got myself a sweetheart. My landlady's daughter, Maureen. I'd like you to meet her. She's the most lovely creature in God's whole universe. I'm a truly lucky man and I have you to thank for all this. You saved my life. I'll never forget it."

He was standing there, rain running down his boyish face, beaming at me. Suddenly I couldn't take it any longer. "I'm glad for you, Michael," I said. "Now if you'll excuse me . . . ."

"So when will you come and meet her, Molly?"

"Some other time, Michael. There's a trolley coming. I really must go."

I picked up my skirts and sprinted away through the puddles.

❧ Four ❧

I don't think I slept all night. The storm broke with nightfall and the constant rumbling of thunder, along with the rattle of rain on the roof tiles above me, would have kept me awake without the turmoil in my heart. I tried not to think of him, but I couldn't help it. None of it made sense. If only he had been following normal male instincts, then all he would have wanted was to have his way with me. And yet he hadn't. We had come close to passion on occasion, and yet he was the one who had restrained himself and not allowed the passion to continue. He had always treated me with the utmost respect, as if we were waiting for the right time and occasion. Naively I had always thought that the occasion would be marriage.

"Tomorrow I start a new life," I said out loud into the storm. I had come through worse things than this. I wasn't going to let one disappointment, one betrayal break my spirit.

Early in the morning I presented myself outside the house on Gramercy Park. It was an hour earlier than I was supposed to arrive for work, but I had to get it over with as quickly as possible. I rang the bell and inquired before I entered whether Miss Van Woekem's goddaughter was indeed staying there.

"She's here, yes, but she didn't want disturbing before half past nine, if you please," the maid muttered to me. "And she wants her breakfast taken up on a tray. Spoiled rotten, if you ask me."

29

Secure in the knowledge that I wouldn't have to face Arabella Norton, I took a deep breath and went into the dining room, where, I was informed, Miss Van Woekem was currently breakfasting. She looked up in surprise from her boiled egg.

"You are certainly an eager beaver this morning, Miss Murphy," she said. "Do the hours without my company seem too long for you?"

"I came early because I have something to tell you, Miss Van Woekem," I said. "I'm afraid I can no longer work here as your companion."

She looked surprised and disappointed. "I didn't think you'd give up so quickly," she said. "I took you for a creature of spirit. In fact, I was beginning to look forward to the challenge of taming you."

"And I think I might have enjoyed the challenge as well," I replied, "but I'm afraid I can no longer work in this house. It would be too difficult for me. I pray don't ask me to go into details."

I had thought she was sharp. She looked at me, birdlike, head on one side and black button eyes boring into me. Then she nodded. "I understand perfectly," she said. "I always wondered where young Sullivan managed to find a suitable companion for me so quickly." She extended a hand. "Won't you join me for breakfast?"

"No, thank you. I'd prefer to go immediately, before there's any chance of . . ." I glanced at the door.

"So what will you do now?"

"I plan to set myself up in a profession," I said. "I'm thinking of becoming a private investigator."

She gave a surprised laugh. "An investigator? You? But that's not a suitable job for a woman."

"I don't see why not. Women have eyes and ears just as men do. And women are more observant, more patient."

"But the danger, my dear. Have you thought of the danger?"

"Oh, I wouldn't handle criminal cases. I'd like to find lost relatives. There are so many families back in Europe who have lost touch with their loved ones."

"And what makes you think you'd be any good at this kind of thing?"

"I did a little investigating once. I think I'd get the hang of it quickly."

She gave a half-snort, half-laugh. "So how do you plan to set about it? I would imagine you need money to open a business."

"I need to learn more before I can set up on my own. I plan to apprentice myself."

"Apprentice yourself? To whom?"

"I have connections." I wasn't going to betray what my possible future employer had been doing in Gramercy Park.

Miss Wan Woekem held out her hand to me. "You have spunk, I'll say that for you. I wish you well, Molly Murphy. Come and see me from time to time. I'd like to hear of your progress. It would liven up an old woman's tedious days."

"Very well," I said. I reached into my pocket. "Oh, and here are your two dollars back. I won't be needing the suitable dress after all."

She closed my hand around the dollar bills. "Keep them. Your wages."

"Oh, but I couldn't possibly—" I began.

"Wages earned," she insisted. "Good luck to you, Molly Murphy."

Then I was coming down the front steps into Gramercy Park. Last night's storm had dispelled the stifling heat, leaving a crisp blue sky and a fresh breeze. The smell of jasmine wafted from the gardens. A maid was sweeping front steps and the swishing noise echoed from the tall buildings around the square. A milk cart approached with the neat clip-clopping of hooves and then the reassuring clink of milk bottles as the milkman made a delivery. It was strange, but I felt as if I'd stepped into a new world. I ran down those steps, ready for anything.

My first disappointment came as I crossed the street. My future employer was not in the gardens. I slipped through the fence and went around carefully, in case he was hiding behind a shrub, but the only occupants were two nursemaids who walked side by side pushing their charges in high wicker prams. After a careful search I had to admit to myself that he wasn't there. I sat on a bench and waited. It was, after all, early in the day. Maybe his vigilance didn't start until after a hearty breakfast. I waited and waited. The cool morning melted into uncomfortable midday sun. At last I admitted to myself that he wasn't coming.

I left the garden by the way I had entered and went to find the constable on Fourth Avenue. He was standing under the awning of a corner grocery shop, looking red-faced and sweaty.

"Not more trouble, miss, I hope?" He brought up his night-stick to touch his helmet to me.

"Not at all, officer. The man, Paddy, you called him, hasn't appeared today. I was wondering if you knew where I could find him."

"And what would you be needing to find him for, I'd like to know, miss? Not to lodge a complaint, I hope. I did tell you he was harmless."

I leaned closer. "I understand he is a private investigator."

The constable glanced around worriedly, as if I had given out this information to the world and not just to him. "You're not thinking of making trouble for him, miss? I swear to God the man wasn't doing any harm."

"I might have work for him." I gave him something close to a wink. This was an outright lie, but I'd become so good at lying recently that it seemed a shame to let the skill get rusty.

He leaned closer to me now. His breath smelled of onions and I wondered if he'd had them for breakfast. "If Paddy doesn't want to be found, then nobody's going to find him, although I believe he operates out of a place on lower Fifth Avenue."

"Fifth Avenue!" I had been here long enough to know that Fifth Avenue was the haunt of swells.

"A man in his job needs an address where the clients won't be afraid to visit him, doesn't he?" the constable said. "But in truth Paddy's on the lower part of it—the part that's seen better days."

He stared out across the street. "Of course I remember it when Fifth Avenue *was* Fifth Avenue, right down to Washington Square. Only the real nobs lived there."

"You wouldn't happen to know where on Fifth Avenue?" I asked hopefully. The day was heating up by the minute and I, of course, had come out without my hat again.

He shook his head. "That's not part of my beat, miss. Below Fourteenth, anyway."

"Thank you, officer. You've been very helpful," I said.

"Always glad to send business in Paddy's direction," he said. "Tell him Constable Hanna sends his regards."

I was glad that Fifth Avenue wasn't too far away. I'd already worn out one pair of soles in this city and it was always a big decision whether to squander five cents on the trolley or the elevated railway when the distances were great and the weather was too hot for walking. I continued down Fourth Avenue until I reached Union Square and then intended to cut across on Fourteenth Street. I was only halfway across the street when I realized I had made a bad decision. With its bell clanging furiously, a trolley car bore down on me, coming at a speed I had thought impossible for trolley cars. I had to pick up my skirts and sprint for it as the trolley swung around the sharp curve. I glimpsed the startled faces of its passengers as it passed me with inches to spare. When I reached the sidewalk and stood catching my breath, I heard laughter and spun around. A group of men was sitting outside Brubacker's Café and they were obviously enjoying themselves at my expense.

"Jesus, Mary and Joseph," I muttered, giving those men a haughty stare.

"My, but you're fleet of foot, young lady. We were wagering two to one that you wouldn't make it," one of them called to me, an inane grin on his unshaven face.

"You must have a death wish, young lady," another, more sympathetic-looking man said. "Only fools or those who are tired of this life cross at Dead Man's Curve."

"Dead Man's Curve?" I wondered if they were pulling my leg.

"The trolleys have to speed up around the curve because they lose the cable if they don't. I reckon there's a near miss here every day . . ."

"And a fatality every week," the annoying man added.

"And you sit here making bets on it?" I snapped. "Have you nothing better to do with your lives?" Then I stalked on with my head held high.

As I turned onto Fifth Avenue and saw it stretching ahead of me with the arch on Washington Square just a mirage in the heat haze, I realized what a task I had set myself. I couldn't possibly check every building for seven or eight blocks. Even if Paddy had a brass plate outside his front door, I didn't know his last name, so that wasn't going to help me much. I walked slowly down the first block, examining the buildings on either side of me. They were big and imposing. If Constable Hanna thought that lower Fifth Avenue had seen better days, then the better days must have been grand indeed. These were still clearly the homes of the well-to-do. There were carriages with uniformed coachmen waiting outside and even a couple of automobiles. Surely Paddy wouldn't be found in one of these houses?

As I continued southward there were indeed signs that the tone of the area was slipping. Some of the bigger houses had been divided up into flats, to judge from the many plates beside the front door. I began by examining them, one by one, but soon gave it up as impossible. Paddy was an Irish nickname, but the man hadn't sounded Irish. If anything, he had sounded English—so there was no point in searching for an Irish surname.

Then I came up with a bright idea—I'd ask at the local cafés. He'd have to eat somewhere, wouldn't he? The only problem was that there were no eating houses on Fifth Avenue. It was all respectably residential, with the odd church thrown in. I tried Eleventh Street going west and then east, but with no luck. By this time my feet were tired, I was hot and thirsty and ready to give up. Did I really want to be an investigator so badly?

I continued along East Eleventh in the hope of finding a soda fountain. With Miss Van Woekem's two dollars in my pocket I could certainly treat myself to a cool soda. There was a drugstore on the corner of University and I was about to go in when I heard the voice.

"'Ere, watch what you're doing with them clippers! Do you think I want to wind up bald?"

A barber's pole hung outside a small dark shop beside the drugstore. I peered inside. He was facing away from the street, so I couldn't get a good look, but a brown derby hat was hanging from the hatstand. I moved out of sight and stood on the street, wondering what to do next. I could wait on the street for him to come out, introduce myself and tell him my plan, or I could follow him back to his office so that I could demonstrate that I had aptitude for the job. The latter appealed to me more. I stood under the drugstore awning pretending to be examining the display of foot powders and patent medicines in the window until I heard a cheerful "Thanks, Al. Cheerio, then, until next time." Again I noted that strange accent that was a mixture of Cockney and New York.

Out of the corner of my eye I watched him leave the barber's. I let him get a good way down the street before I followed him. He was walking fast and I had to run to catch up as he headed onto Fifth Avenue, going south. I turned the corner after him, then shrank back as he stopped to buy a newspaper. He set off again. I followed. I was doing rather well at this, I decided. It was a pity there weren't shop fronts to duck into, but I managed to blend into the shade every time he stopped, pausing as if I were checking the numbers on the houses.

He crossed Tenth Street, then Ninth, then Eighth. The arch on Washington Square was now clearly visible, blocking the end of the avenue, its marble facade glinting in the sunlight. I paused to admire it and when I looked back, Paddy was no longer ahead of me. I ran. He couldn't have gone into any of the houses—it would have taken time to mount the steps to the front doors. And he surely hadn't reached Washington Square. Then I noticed a narrow alley going off to my right. I ran down it and found myself in a cobbled court that must have formerly been a mews. Some of the low buildings still had stable doors. Some had been converted into living quarters. I spun around as I heard the sound of a door closing. It had come from above my head. Then I noticed a flight of rickety steps going up the side of the first mews cottage. I went up. The door was not properly latched. I tapped on it. "Hello? Paddy?" I called.

The door swung open and I peered in. I saw a large untidy room, a desk buried under mounds of paper and a half-eaten sandwich. But the room was empty. Cautiously I stepped inside.

"Hello. Anyone here?" I called again.

Suddenly I was grabbed from behind and a hand clamped over my mouth.

❧ Five ❧

A
ll right," a voice hissed in my ear, "out with it. Who sent you?"

"Let go of me." I tried to force the words through his fingers around my mouth. I jerked my elbow backward in what I hoped was the region of his stomach and heard a satisfying exhale. Not for nothing had I grown up with three brothers. I wrenched myself out of his grasp and spun around on him. "Holy Mother of God! Is this the way you always greet prospective clients? It's a wonder you do any business."

"Go on with yer," he said, eyeing me suspiciously. "You're no more a prospective client than I'm the man in the moon."

"And how can you tell that?"

"By the clothes, love. There's no quality in the fabric. It takes money to hire my services." Now that I had time to study him I reconfirmed my first impression of dapper. He was well turned out in a suit that had seen better days. His shirt had a clean starched collar. His face must have been quite handsome once but now sagged so that he had a bloodhoundlike mournful appearance. This disappeared as he gave me a cheeky grin, then the wary look returned. "So come on, out with it. Who sent you? If it's the Five Points Gang using their womenfolk to deliver messages again . . ."

"If you think I look like a gangster's messenger, then you must have poor eyesight or be a very poor judge of character," I said coldly. I was rapidly making up my mind that this man would make a worse employer than Miss Van Woekem.

"Sorry, miss. No offense meant," he said. "You can't be too careful in my business. The last lady who came on a friendly call from a gang had a six-inch blade down her boot—and she intended to use it as soon as my back was turned." He was squinting at me with narrowed eyes set in a hollow, pinched face. "Wait a second. I've seen you before, haven't I? I've got a good memory for faces. It will come to me in a tick." He held up a finger. "Hold on, it's coming. Central Park."

"With Captain Sullivan," I added. "You were pretending to be a photographer."

"Whatcha mean, pretending?" he asked, but he had relaxed now. "I supplement my income from time to time."

"And conveniently pass messages to Captain Sullivan," I added triumphantly.

"Well, I'll be blowed. I must be slipping in my old age." He nodded approvingly. "You've got good eyes in your head, I'll say that for you."

"I have. And my good eyes noticed you slipping out of Gramercy Park by way of a loose iron railing on Monday, and standing in the same gardens on Tuesday, watching a house through binoculars."

The suspicious look had returned. "Surely Captain Sullivan didn't send you? No, he'd never involve women when it comes to work."

"You're right. He didn't send me."

"Then what do you want from me? You don't work for Miss Le Grange, do you?"

"Who?"

"Kitty Le Grange. The lady whose house I was watching. Pfew, that's a relief. That would be three days' work down the drain if they knew I'd been keeping a record."

"A record of what?"

"None of your business." He touched his finger to the side of his nose. "Mum's the word. So they didn't send you?"

"I don't work for anybody," I finally managed to interrupt, "and if you'll shut up for a second, I'll tell you why I came here."

He looked rather surprised at being spoken to this way. "All right, keep your hair on. Go on then."

"I think you and I can help each other."

"Information? You've got information that's worth money?"

"Holy Mother, it's hard to get a word in edgewise around here. And my mother always told me I had the gift of the gab. I want you to hire me."

"As what?"

"An assistant," I said. "Look at this room. It's a disaster. I could keep things clean and neat for you and you could teach me the business."

"What business?" The suspicious look had returned.

"*Your* business. I want to learn to be an investigator."

He started laughing silently, his scrawny body shaking with mirth. "That's a good one. A woman investigator. Now I've heard everything."

"And why not, I'd like to know?" I faced him with my hands on my hips. "I'm sharp, I'm obviously more observant than you, and I think I've got a knack for it."

"Oh, you do, do you?"

"I tailed you all the way from the barbershop."

"You wouldn't get two yards, tailing somebody like that," he said. "I spotted you as I came out of the barbershop door and my sixth sense told me you were hanging about for no good reason. So I kept tabs on you all the way down Fifth. Why else do you think I stopped to buy a paper?"

"Oh." This was somewhat deflating, but I wasn't going to let him see that. "So I need practice. I'll get better with good instruction."

"Not from me, you won't. There's no way on God's earth I'd employ a woman."

"So you like working in a pigsty, do you?"

This made him pause for a moment and scan the room with his eyes. "I didn't say I couldn't use help from time to time. In fact, if you could find me a bright and willing young lad, I wouldn't mind taking on an apprentice. But no woman. This can be dangerous work, my dear. You'd get us both killed first time you opened your mouth."

He left me and walked across the room to his desk. "Go on, run along home. I've got work to do." He pulled out a rickety chair, sat down and began writing notes.

I had no alternative but to leave. This time I noted the grimy brass plate at the foot of the stairs. P. RILEY DISCREET INVESTIGATIONS. An Irish name. Then why did he sound like an English Cockney with a touch of the Bowery thrown in? It seemed as if I'd never know now.

I left the mews and started back across town to East Fourth and my attic apartment. Exactly what was I going to do now? I wondered. Money was, indeed, a factor. I supposed, as a last resort, I could always go back to Miss Van Woekem and tell her that I'd made a mistake. I considered this for a second before I decided that starvation was preferable to having to see Miss Arabella Norton or her despicable fiancé ever again.

When I spied a café on the corner of University Place and West Fourth, I threw frugality to the winds and decided on coffee and a bun to cheer myself up. It was almost midday now and the coffee house was crowded. The noise level was intense and I looked with interest at the clientele. They were all young and dressed in an interesting diversity of styles, from flowing capes to well-patched tweed. It took me a moment to register that they were all students and the building opposite was New York University. I took my coffee and bun to a stool at the counter which ran around the wall and sat there, listening in on as many conversations as possible. After a life that had been so solitary I gazed in envy at these tight-knit groups of people not much younger than me. There was even a sprinkling of women among the men—

serious-looking girls in dark colors and glasses, who were not afraid to speak their opinions and enter fully into the debates. If only that could have been me, I'd have liked nothing better. I sat listening, long after the coffee and bun had disappeared, then followed them out when a bell tolled and they hurried back across the street, clutching piles of books.

The walk home along Fourth seemed particularly long and empty.

Mrs. O'Halloran appeared by magic as I let myself in through the front door.

"You had a visitor," she said. "Captain Sullivan." She must have noticed the color draining from my face because she went on hurriedly, "Don't worry. I told him you were not at home, just like you wanted."

"Thank you."

"Has there been a falling-out between you and the good captain?" she asked, blocking my way as I sought to go up the stairs. "Such a lovely man, I've always thought. Made me wish I was younger and single."

"Captain Sullivan and I were nothing more than acquaintances. He was kind enough to help a fellow Irishwoman get established in a new country. Nothing more than that," I said. "Good day to you, Mrs. O'Hallaran."

She looked disappointed, then suspicious, as I attempted to hurry past before she thought up any more questions. I wasn't quick enough.

"Just a minute," she said, grabbing at my arm. "I've been doing a spot of cleaning out and I've come across some old clothes that maybe the young boy upstairs can use. He's beginning to look like a ragbag with no mother to keep an eye on him, and our son Jack was always very careful with his clothes. Not a harum-scarum like most boys."

She darted into her sitting room and reappeared with a neatly folded pile of clothing that smelled strongly of mothballs. "Here you are."

"Thank you. Seamus can certainly use them."

I carried them upstairs. "Shameyboy? Look what I've got for you," I called. No answer. Usually the children came rushing out when they heard my feet on the stairs. I opened the door of their room and found it empty. That must mean that they were off with their cousins again, swimming in the East River. I found this latest pastime rather dangerous and I'd expressed my worries to their father, but he didn't seem to mind. He seemed to think their cousins would keep an eye on them. Children did need to find ways to keep cool and have fun during the long summer days, and half the ragamuffins on the Lower East Side did it. Also, girls weren't permitted to strip off and swim like the boys, so my only worries for Bridie were that she'd fall in by mistake, be run over by a delivery cart or crushed under a pile of dockland freight. As I reminded myself yet again, they weren't my children.

I stood in the hallway that served as our communal kitchen, staring down at the pile of clothing. On the top of the pile was a boy's cloth cap—the kind of cap worn by every newsboy in the city of New York. A rather preposterous idea was forming in my head. I went straight into my room and tried on the cap. It took a while to get all my hair tucked into it, but once it was finished, an impish, cheeky face looked back at me from the glass on the wall. Excited now, I examined the rest of the pile. The knickers looked as if they might fit. I discarded my skirt and petticoat, then struggled into them. They were tighter than I'd hoped and came only to my knees instead of around midcalf, which was where most boys wore them, but they might do. There was no jacket big enough for me, but there was a white Sunday shirt. I tried that with the knickers and the cap. The result wasn't bad. I thanked providence for my boyish figure, usually so despised by fashion and connoisseurs of beauty.

Of course, I looked too clean for a boy. I've never met a boy yet who can fail to get dirty within half an hour of getting dressed. But that could be remedied. I'd wait until twilight and pay another visit on P. Riley, Discreet Investigations!

❧ Six ❧

A s I prepared myself that evening, I realized that I had another problem—my feet. No boy would ever wear a pair of pointed button boots, and they were my only footwear. It was no use trying to borrow from Shameyboy next door. He only had one pair of boots and they were on his feet. I'd have to do what many poor youngsters did—go barefoot.

The hardest part of the assignment was sneaking out of the house undetected. Luckily Sergeant O'Hallaran had returned home for his dinner. I heard them talking in their kitchen as I slunk past. Once outside, it wasn't hard to find a puddle and get myself good and grimy. I set off for Washington Mews, my swagger marred by the hard cobblestones on my bare feet. I'd run barefoot as a child, but that was a while ago now and my feet were sore and throbbing by the time I reached Washington Square. My first tap on P. Riley's door brought no answer. I was angry and frustrated at having gone to such trouble and walked so far for nothing. But I hung around in the mews, listening to life in the city going on around me until darkness began to fall. I was just about to give up and go home, defeated, when I saw him. He came around the corner, clutching a cardboard box which, judging by the greasy stains already appearing on it, contained his dinner.

I took a deep breath, then stepped out to greet him as he

started to climb the steps. I didn't want to risk surprising him and being attacked again. "Evening, mister."

He stopped and turned to look at me.

Another deep breath. I forced my voice as low as it would go. "The lady next door says you need a 'prentice. I'm bright and willing, mister."

"And your name is?"

I hadn't thought of that one. "Uh—Michael, sir. My friends call me Mike." The first name that came into my head.

"Then you'd better come upstairs, Mike," he said, giving me the cheeky grin.

He was smiling, pleased to see me. I couldn't wait to reveal my true identity to him and watch his astonishment.

I followed him into the dark room and waited while he lit the gas bracket on the wall. "Now then, uh, Michael," he said, still grinning. "What makes you think I'd want to employ you?"

"I told you, mister. I'm willing and ready to learn. And honest, too."

"Not quite honest," he said, clearing off an area of his desk and putting the box down on some newspapers. "What was your name earlier today, Michael?" He took a sudden step toward me and yanked off the cap. Red hair spilled over my shoulders.

"I'll give you top marks for persistence," he said. "Now, for the love of Pete, would you go away and leave me alone? Don't try any more stupid charades with me. I'm losing my patience and my good humor."

"How did you know?" I asked. "I thought I looked quite real."

"You thought you looked quite real?" He started that soundless chuckling, his body shaking silently. "Let me point out a couple of minor details, my dear. Look at your hands, to start with. Have you ever met a boy who didn't have dirt under his fingernails? And your feet? Oh, you've got them nice and dirty, but see how the little toe is pressed against the next one? That comes from years of wearing pointed shoes. Ever see a boy wearing pointed toed shoes? And then there's the smell of mothballs. Very odd that your clothes were stored away until this very moment, don't you think?"

I nodded. "So I have a lot to learn, I know. That's why I want you to teach me."

"Do you think what I know can be taught?" he demanded. "If you hadn't slipped up with those details, I'd still have caught you out. You know why? Because you didn't think and react like a boy. You came up the steps daintily, one hand on the rail. A boy would have taken them two at a time, probably, and he'd always be alert. A boy in the city is used to being on the lookout for danger. He's had plenty of cuffs around the head and he doesn't want another one. And when he's on an errand like this, trying to convince me that he can do a man's job, he'd show a touch of bravado. You can't just dress the part. You have to get inside the head."

"How did you learn all this?" I asked.

"Me? I've had a lifetime on the streets, my dear. Nothing sharpens skills like survival." He brushed off his greasy hands. "Let me give you a little demonstration."

He went through into a back room I hadn't noticed before and closed the door behind him. While I was waiting, I looked around. Under the clutter was a sparsely furnished room, the table being the only piece of real furniture. I went across to look out of the back window, which opened onto more outbuildings and another alleyway filled with garbage cans. I jumped when I heard a tap at the front door.

"Mr. Riley?" I called. "Someone at the door." Then I went to answer it.

An elderly Jewish man stood there, bearded, dressed in the long black coat and tall black hat I had seen so often on the Lower East Side. "Mr. Riley? Is he, perchance, at home?" His voice was little more than a whisper and there was a touch of European accent. "It is a matter of great urgency, great delicacy, you understand."

"Just a minute. I'll go and get him," I said.

I went and tapped on the door to the inner room. "Mr. Riley. Someone for you."

"I don't think you'll find him in there," the Jewish man said. Before I could answer, he'd peeled off the long straggly beard and Riley himself stood there grinning at me.

"That was truly amazing. And so quick, too. I never suspected . . ."

"Of course you didn't. However, if I was using that character on Essex or Delancey, I'd have to play my cards right. I don't speak much Yiddish, you see. I'd soon be caught out." He took off the hat and coat and hung them on a peg on the wall.

"But how did you learn all this? Who taught you how to do the makeup?"

"A long story, my dear." He looked at me, long and hard. "Tell you what. After all the trouble you've gone to, the least I can do is offer to share my supper with you."

"Thank you. You're very kind." I'd have stayed if it had been tripe or pig's feet—my two least favorite foods. Anything to keep me there a moment longer.

He spread out a piece of newspaper in front of me on the desk and motioned for me to pull up a packing case. "Got a bit behind with the paperwork," he said.

"Which is why you need an assistant," I reminded him.

"Hmmph," he said, cutting the meat pie in half and putting some on a piece of newspaper for me. "Have to use your fingers. Sorry about that."

"Your name," I began. "It's not really Riley, is it? You're a Londoner, not from Ireland."

"That's where you're wrong. I was born in Killarney."

"Then the accent is a fake? It's very convincing."

He chuckled. "No, the accent's real enough. I was born in Killarney but we left when I was two. My parents were clever enough to use the little they'd saved to get out during the Great Famine. They got as far as London. Maybe they'd have done all right there, but they didn't hold up long enough. They were both dead by the time I was ten. So I was out on my own on the streets."

"That's terrible. What did you do?"

He took a big bite of pie and wiped the gravy from his chin with the back of his hand. "What did I do? I learned to survive, that's what." He leaned over confidentially. "Did you read that famous book by Charles Dickens? *Oliver Twist*—that's its name. Know the Artful Dodger?—that was me. I turned myself into one of the best pickpockets in London. They used to say that I could take away a toff's handkerchief in mid-sneeze and he'd not notice."

"So you were a criminal. What brought you to the other side of the law?"

"Fate, I suppose you could say. In the end I got caught, as most criminals do. I would have been put away for life, only this American gentleman was visiting London prisons, wanting to see how he could improve the lot of the poor prisoners. I suppose I must have looked young and angelic, because he took a fancy to me. He persuaded them to give me a second chance and let him take me to America. So that's how I got here. He had me taught a trade—printing, it was, but I never really took to it. So when I finished my apprenticeship, I tried my hand at a lot of things, including going on the stage. I wasn't much good at it, to tell you the truth, didn't have the voice, but I liked the theater. I worked as a dresser for a while—that's where I learned about makeup and disguises. Then I decided it was a pity that I couldn't put all the tricks I'd learned on the London streets to good use."

"You went back into crime?" I asked.

He shook his head. "I'd promised Mr. Schlessinger when he brought me to America. A proper Bible-fearing gentleman he was. He made me swear on the Bible that I'd never resort to crime again. I couldn't go against that, could I? But I decided I could use my knowledge on the right side of the law. I do a bit of under-cover work for the police from time to time, and I've got my own nice little business here. It's not for everyone, but it suits me fine." He broke off, staring at me with his head tilted to one side. "I can't think why a pretty girl like you would want to do it, though. About time you got married and settled down, isn't it?"

I looked down at the remains of the meat pie. "I came over here alone. I have no one. I want to be dependent on no one."

"I saw you with Captain Sullivan . . ."

"He's just a friend, and he can't be anything more," I said. "I think I could do this job well if you'd give me a chance."

"There are plenty of other jobs you could do. It's a big city."

"I've tried some of them. I don't want to work in a factory. I don't want to be a servant. I'm not very good at taking orders and being humble, I'm afraid."

"So what put this stupid idea in your head?"

"When I left Ireland, there were all these people who wanted to know what had become of their loved ones. A woman gave me a letter, in case I should meet her boy. I thought I could trace some of those lost loved ones for them."

"And if they didn't want to be traced?"

"It would be up to them if they got in touch again."

"Never make any money doing that," he said.

"Oh, so you do think I could make money doing other kinds of detective work?"

"I didn't say that. Women are bad news. They talk too much. They can't keep secrets and they let their hearts rule their heads."

"So did you, just now," I said. "You demonstrated your skill to me, instead of throwing me out. So you must have a soft spot in that hard heart of yours."

"Irish blarney," he said, but he didn't look too upset.

I got up and picked up the box and newspapers, depositing them in the can in the corner. "I could make this place look really nice for you," I said. "I've kept house all my life. I could handle your appointments so that you wouldn't miss any clients when you were out on a job. And you could teach me what you know."

"I knew I should never have let you in through this door," he said.

"I'll make you a proposition." I perched on the packing case opposite him again. "Give me a week's trial. You don't have to pay me. If you are not satisfied with me at the end of a week, you show me the door. I'll go and never trouble you again."

"You are a persistent young woman," he said. "What did you say your name was?"

It was dark by the time I left Paddy Riley's place. As I crossed from west to east on Eighth Street, I began to appreciate the advantages of being dressed as a male. A woman out alone in the dark is constantly on guard, ready for drunken men staggering out of saloons, ribald comments from layabouts on street corners, or worse. Nobody paid any attention to a barefoot lad coming home from his day's labor. I remembered what Riley had told me and tried to think like a boy. I shoved my hands into my pockets, swaggered a little and even attempted to whistle.

By the time I was close to home my feet were really aching again and those cobblestones dug into every soft spot on my soles. I'd have to practice going barefoot more often, somehow, and thus toughen up my feet again if I wanted to make use of this disguise. I had just trodden in an unexpected pile of horse droppings when I looked up to see Daniel Sullivan coming toward me. He must have been to my house again. I was in no mood to confront him. I ignored the warm horse manure that clung to my feet, resumed the swagger and the whistle and walked toward him. He passed me within a couple of feet and didn't look at me twice. I didn't look back until I reached my front stoop. Then I stopped to clean off my feet, as best I could, on the scraper. My heart was still racing as I ran up the steps. If I could fool Daniel, then I had the feeling that I might be pretty good at this one day!

It was only when I had washed the grime from my person and

stood at the open window in my camisole, letting the cool night air caress my bare arms and neck, that the negative aspect of my encounter with Daniel struck me. There would be no more visits to look forward to, no more Sunday strolls in the park, no more times when he took me in his arms and set me on fire with his kisses. I was going to have to throw myself into my work so intensely that I had no time to think or to feel.

❧ Seven ❧

The first week came and went and there was no mention of terminating my services; in fact, Paddy even agreed to pay me a very modest amount. But as the days went by I was no closer to finding out how a private investigator actually worked. I understood that most of his business came from divorce cases and involved standing around for long hours, watching and waiting to witness assignations with "the other woman." If he was lucky, he'd capture the two of them together on camera. He owned one of those new Kodak Brownies—neat little contraptions, no bigger than a cigar box, that could take pictures without ever having to go under a hood. I couldn't vouch for the quality of the pictures. He kept them well away from me, as he did all the details of his cases. I didn't ask questions and bided my time. The trick would be to make myself indispensable first.

During that first week, I swept and scrubbed out the place—and believe me, it took some scrubbing! I tidied his papers into neat piles, threw away mountains of rubbish, and then attempted to file the papers away. I had discovered that the back room contained a big oak filing cabinet. I opened it and tried to get a sense of Riley's filing-system. Before I had a chance even to look at the file headings, there came a great roar behind me.

"What the bleedin' hell do you think you're doing, woman?"

I jumped up and spun around. I had never seen Paddy Riley look angry before.

For once even I couldn't think of a smart answer. "I—I was just trying to see how your filing system worked, so that I could file your papers for you."

"Snooping, that's what you were doing."

"Absolutely not. You've got a tower of papers the size of a skyscraper on your desk and they should be filed away somewhere. This is a filing cabinet. I was trying to be helpful, that's all."

We stood there, glaring at each other.

"That filing cabinet is off-limits," he said, but more calmly now. "That's where I keep the information on my cases. It is all strictly confidential, you understand. The top families in New York come to me on the understanding that what I find is between me and them."

"I don't see the point in having an assistant if you don't want any help," I said. "How am I supposed to be any use to you if you won't share any information on your cases with me?"

"The answer to that is simple. You won't be any use to me— not beyond what you're already doing. Clean up and run errands, that I can tolerate, I suppose, but I'm not sharing my cases with you. You'd have me out of business in a week. Women can't keep their mouths shut to save their souls."

"You have a very poor opinion of women," I said. "Is that why you've never married?"

"Who said I'd never married?" He walked past me and slammed the open file drawer shut. "I was married once. Pretty little thing. Actress. She ran off with another guy."

"Aha. So that's it!" I smiled triumphantly. "That's why you're down on all women—because you couldn't trust one of them. Well, I've had bad enough experiences with certain men, but it doesn't make me think that all men are scoundrels."

"Hmmph." This seemed to be his standard expression when I'd gotten the better of him. "I'd be obliged if you'd stay out of this room." He motioned me to the door. "This is my inner sanctum, so to speak. Tidy up the outer office all you like, but leave my inner sanctum alone."

"You had a weeks'-old pork pie in here," I commented over my shoulder as I swept out. "You'll be attracting mice."

"Speaking of pork pies"—he reached into his vest pocket— "You can go to the delicatessen on Broadway and bring me a liverwurst sandwich for lunch. Get yourself something too. And while you're out, find a locksmith and tell him to come round this afternoon. I'll have a lock put on that filing cabinet, for my own peace of mind. Go on, move them plates of meat."

I looked around, confused. "What plates of meat?"

"Plates of meat—feet. Cockney rhyming slang," he said, grinning at my discomfort. "Blimey, you'd never have lasted two minutes in London if you didn't speak the language."

"Since I've never been to London, the matter has never arisen," I said haughtily, "and I would have made sure I only mixed with higher-class people who didn't have to use slang."

Instead of being annoyed, he laughed out loud. "You're a rum one, I'll say that for you. Plenty of spunk. Go on then. Take them plates of meat down the apples and pears."

I smiled too as I went down the stairs. I had the feeling that Paddy might even learn to like me someday.

I was coming out of Katz's Delicatessen with liverwurst for Riley and cold roast beef for myself when I stood aside to let an automobile go past. I swear they were becoming more common in the city every day, making crossing the streets even more hazardous. As if streetcars and galloping hansom cabs weren't hazards enough! But instead of roaring past, this automobile screeched to a halt and Daniel jumped from the driver's seat. He was wearing a cap and motoring goggles and I didn't recognize him until he yelled out my name.

I thought about running, but there was no point in it. I had to face him sometime, and maybe a busy street was better than at home.

"Where on earth have you got to these past days?" he demanded, removing the goggles as he approached me. "I've been worried about you. All Mrs. O'Hallaran would say was that you were out, and Miss Van Woekem told me you'd changed your mind and no longer worked for her. And you didn't answer the notes I left for you. What is going on?"

"Maybe I misunderstood the nature of our friendship, sir," I said, "but in the circumstances I feel it wiser that we should have no further communication with each other."

"What are you talking about? What have I done to offend you?"

"Maybe I found the small matter of an undisclosed fiancée somewhat offensive," I said. "I am sure Miss Norton would not wish you to waste any more of your time with me. Now I must return to work or my employer will wonder what has happened to me. Good day."

I started to walk away.

"Molly, wait, don't go, please," he called after me. "Let me explain."

"What do you think I might not understand about the word fiancée?" I asked. I had been so controlled until now and was shocked to hear my voice crack. If I stayed here any longer I would let myself down and start to cry. "There is only one meaning to it, as far as I know. I may be a common peasant girl, but I was educated in French."

I started to run.

"Molly, please!" I heard him call after me.

"Go away and stop following me," I shouted back. "I wish never to see you again."

He didn't attempt to pursue me any further.

I worked like a crazy woman for the rest of the day. I thought Paddy would be pleased with the way his place was looking, but he didn't respond with anything more than a grunt until late in the afternoon he finally exploded. "Will you stop for a moment, woman, you're exhausting me just looking at you. If you polish that floor any harder you'll have us both going arse over tip every time we cross the room."

"I need to be busy," I said.

"Well, you're in my way. I have to get myself dressed for my appointment at Delmonico's."

"Delmonico's, eh? You do move in elevated circles."

"I'm not planning to eat there," he said. "A certain gentleman will be dining there tonight in one of the private dining rooms. Delmonico's will have an extra waiter on duty. You can watch me transform myself. Wait here."

He disappeared into the back room and reappeared wearing a waiter's tuxedo and white apron. "Now all it needs is the application of the finishing touches."

He opened a box and took out a neat black toupee, parted in the middle, which he placed on his head.

"Now for some facial hair," he muttered and held up a waxed black mustache. "Trick of the trade, my dear, is to have one distinguishing feature—a beard, a mustache, a monocle, an unusual hat, even a flower in the buttonhole. That is all that people will remember about you. He squeezed out a ribbon of spirit gum and applied the mustache. The transformation was most impressive. He had gone from a colorless old man to a rather flamboyant and younger waiter.

"How can you get away with something like this? Surely they know all their waiters?"

He grinned—that cheeky Cockney grin. "Those poor devils are so run off their feet that they haven't got time to notice a new face. I've done it enough times to know how to make myself unobtrusive. The secret is to look busy. Look as if you're supposed to be there and you've got an important job to do. I pick up something like a candle, or a vase of flowers, or a couple of glasses, cross the floor with them, into the private room. Diners never notice what the waiter is doing, especially not these diners. They'll be too engrossed in each other. I'll fiddle about in one corner, take a picture if I can, and then depart."

"How exciting. I'd like to try that."

"They don't have women waiters."

"They have slim young men and you've just shown me how to apply facial hair."

"Over my dead body." He looked up and glanced at me from the mirror. "Now go on, clear off home. I've got work to do."

On the way home the despair I had been keeping at bay since my afternoon encounter with Daniel finally threatened to engulf me. I would not be seeing Daniel ever again. I suppose until that moment I had hoped that the whole thing was a ghastly mistake. At the back of my mind was a fragile hope that I had somehow misunderstood, that Daniel would laugh and say, "What fiancée? I have no fiancée." But he hadn't.

All I wanted to do now was to crawl into my bed, pull the covers over my head and escape into sleep. I opened the front door, tiptoed up the stairs without attracting the attention of Mrs. O'Hallaran and was about to open the door to my room when I froze on the landing. Someone was moving around inside my room.

I flung open the door. Two guilty faces looked up, holding my pillows with which they had obviously just been fighting.

"Seamus, Bridie, what is going on here?" I demanded. "What do you think you're doing in my room?"

"Auntie Nuala told us to come in here," Bridie said in a small voice. "She said we had to stay with you cos Daddy can't take care of us."

"What's wrong with your father?"

"He got buried," young Seamus said matter-of-factly.

At that moment the door to the O'Connors' room opened and Nuala herself came out, putting her finger to her lips. "Not so much noise over here. Can't the poor man rest in peace?"

"Seamus is dead?" I gasped.

"Not yet, but he will be if he's not allowed his rest." She stood there, meaty hands on her big hips. "Did the children not tell you then? The tunnel caved in and the poor man was buried alive. He was lucky—they saw his hand sticking out of the muck and they

56

got to him in time. Any longer and it would have been too late. As it is the doctors don't know. He's got a nasty concussion and they say his lungs are full of dirt. If he doesn't get pneumonia it will be a miracle. He's in the hands of the Blessed Virgin now."

"Oh, no. That's terrible. Why is he home here and not in the hospital?"

She was still looking at me with that offensive sneer. "Hospitals cost money, so unless you've got yourself a fancy man on the side and you're offering to pay, it's home here the poor man will be staying. The doctor says there's nothing they can do for him anyway. Either he gets better or he doesn't. But it's no concern of yours. He's our responsibility. That's why I've come over to look after him myself. I've left Finbar to take care of my boys and I'll stay here until poor Seamus is on the mend."

"Oh, but you really don't have to," I exclaimed, trying to disguise my look of horror. "I'm sure between myself and Mrs. O'Hallaran we can take care of him."

"What else are families for?" she said. "We take care of our own."

"But your boys will be needing you. And what about your job at the fish market?"

"Family troubles come first," she said. "Always have. And it's slack season at the market. So I'll be moving in for a while, until the poor man recovers, God and all his saints willing."

"It's very good of you," I said with a sinking heart.

She gave me a condescending smile. "He'll be needing someone with experience to nurse him. But he must have absolute quiet, the doctor says, so the little ones will have to stay in there with you."

"Yes, of course." I could hardly say no without seeming completely hard-hearted.

"They'll be wanting their tea." Nuala turned to go back into Seamus's room.

* * *

So it seemed I was to be mother to two small children again. Not that I objected. In fact, now I saw them as a blessing in disguise. I would be too busy to have time to sit around and mope. That night I made up beds for them on the floor in my room, but in the middle of the night Bridie crawled into bed beside me, just as she used to do on the ship. "I don't want my daddy to die," she whispered.

"Of course he won't die, sweetheart," I said, stroking back her soft hair. "He'll be as right as rain before you know it."

"Aunt Nuala says he might die."

"Your Aunt Nuala says a lot of stupid things," I said. "We'll say a little prayer for him together and put him in the Blessed Mother's hands, all right?"

We were in the middle of our prayer when Shamus crawled into bed with us. "I want to pray for my daddy too," he said.

I fell asleep with an arm around each of them. In the morning I gave them bread and jam and tea and left for work with strict instructions that they weren't to make noise, they weren't to touch anything and they weren't to try cooking on my gas ring. Actually I was more concerned about Nuala. I didn't doubt for a moment that she'd be going through my possessions, if she hadn't done so already. Fine. Let her. It wasn't as if I had anything of any value, except for some letters Daniel had written me—I would have to burn them as soon as I got a chance.

As soon as I reached Riley's place I explained that I might need to be spending more time at home because someone had to care for the children. I had expected that he'd see this as an opportunity to point out another reason why women were no use to him in business, but he merely nodded distractedly. "Go on then. Clear off."

I stood there, staring at him. He hadn't looked up from a notebook on his desk in which he was doodling a lot of angry black spikes.

"Hold on a minute. This doesn't mean you're firing me, does it?" I asked. "I mean, I've done a good job for you here. This place looks clean as a whistle and I've run your errands . . . and I didn't mean I wasn't coming to work at all. Just that I'd like to check in on the little ones from time to time."

"Yes, I suppose you haven't done too badly, considering," he said grudgingly, "but I've got some serious work to do. I don't need someone hanging around me, polishing and scrubbing around my feet. Things have taken a very unexpected turn."

He started thumbing through the small black notebook, scowling in concentration. "You found out something last night at Delmonico's?" I asked excitedly.

"Not Delmonico's. Afterward. In the saloon. They didn't recognize me, see, because I was still in my waiter's gear. They didn't think anyone could overhear them." He was clearly rattled, otherwise he'd never have babbled on to me like this. "I can't really believe . . . I mean, him of all people, and I never took it seriously." He looked up, almost surprised to see me still standing there. "Look, why don't you clear off. I've got work to do. This is no time to have a woman around the place."

"Should I pop in later to see if there are any errands you want run?"

"I won't need errands run. I'll be out and about."

"I could keep an eye on the office for you and greet potential clients."

"I don't want you poking around when I'm not here. Go on. Hop it. Oh, and if you see your friend Captain Sullivan, you might tell him that Paddy would like a word with him, on the quiet, so to speak. I'll be at the usual place this evening."

I was dismissed. The thought of going back to the room with two lively children and Nuala next door was not appealing, but I had nowhere else to go. The weather didn't encourage strolling the boulevards. If I'd had my way, I'd have been swimming in the East River with the boys, but the only swimming ladies were allowed to do was out at Coney Island, where Daniel had taken me one Sunday. And that wasn't what I'd call swimming—a little discreet bobbing at the edge of the waves in bathing suits with so many frills that they weighed a ton.

Little boys were splashing one another with water from a horse trough on Broadway. A few drops came in my direction. "Whoops. Sorry, miss," the boys called, grinning. I smiled back.

It seemed that boys were allowed to get away with anything. My mind went back to my adventure in boy's costume and the way I had passed through the streets as if invisible. I liked that. Sometime I'd use it again, when Paddy Riley finally trusted me enough to send me out on a job. He obviously didn't trust me with anything yet, though, or he'd have wanted me around today when he had important work to do. I wondered exactly what he had overheard last night that had disturbed him so.

I checked on Seamus when I got home. He was still drifting in and out of consciousness while Nuala applied cold flannels to his forehead, his face ashen-gray. What on earth would happen to those children if he died? Would it be better to send them back to Ireland to a mother who was dying of consumption, or leave them here with that dragon of a cousin? I tried not to think about it as I took the children to St. Patrick's Cathedral to light a candle for their da, then we rode the trolley up to Central Park, where they had a grand old time for the rest of the day. I had quite a grand old time myself. There is something about grass and trees and water that makes the world seem all right again.

The next day Seamus was awake but still looking as pale as a ghost. Nuala asked me to run some errands for her. Calves'-foot jelly and marrow-bone soup would be nourishing, she said. This brought up the matter of money. I was down to almost nothing myself, except for the pittance Paddy was paying me and Miss Van Woekem's two dollars. I was willing to spend that, but what would happen if Seamus was out of work for a while? I certainly couldn't afford to support a whole family.

My head was filled with troubled thoughts as I bought the calves' feet and barley for barley water, started a good soup cooking and set the children some lessons to keep them occupied.

They seemed to like playing at school and told me I wasn't strict enough to be the schoolmistress and that I needed a cane. I left them practicing their penmanship on their slates and decided to go and see whether Paddy Riley was back in his office and in need of my services.

It was late afternoon and the August heat was intense. The poor horses were flecked with foam as they dragged their delivery wagons and hansom cabs. One was lying in the gutter, cut free of its shafts, dying. People walked past, unconcerned. The horse's owner stood by the wagon looking bewildered. I hurried on by, wanting to do something but knowing there was nothing that could be done. Dying horses were too frequent a sight in this city.

My white blouse was sticking to my back as I reached the mews. The alleyway was cooler, nestled in the shadow of taller buildings, and I dragged myself wearily up Paddy's steps, praying he was there, and looking forward to a drink of water. It seemed I was in luck. The door swung open to my touch. Paddy himself was taking a snooze at the table.

"So this is how you've been working hard . . ." I began. Then I stopped. The room was in complete disarray. In fact, it looked as if a whirlwind had been through it—papers strewn all over the floor, wastebasket tipped upside down.

"Paddy? What on earth's been—" I broke off as I heard a noise in the back room. I didn't stop to think. I went over and opened the door. This room was in equal disarray and someone was crouched on the floor, bent over the toppled file cabinet. It was a man, dressed head to toe in black. He looked up, startled. For a second our eyes met, then, before I could say anything sensible or let out any sort of sound, he leaped at me. A fist came flying at my face. I went reeling backward and collapsed on the floor, darkness singing in my head, as the dark shape leaped over me, ran to the open back window and jumped out. Still dizzy and feeling I was about to vomit, I staggered to my feet and made it to the window. I couldn't call out—my jaw hurt to move. I could only watch helplessly as an agile dark shadow dodged between garages and out of sight.

I stood there clutching the windowsill, fighting the nausea, and then I remembered Paddy. I ran over to him and tried to rouse him. As I attempted to lift him, his head lolled back, and I saw the ugly red stain on his chest. But he was still warm. There was still hope. I looked around for something to stop the bleeding, found a towel and clamped it over the wound. As I did so he opened his eyes. He looked around in a bewildered way, then focused on me.

"It's all right, Paddy," I managed to say, although it hurt to speak. "You're going to be all right. I'll go for help."

He clutched at my arm, his bony fingers digging into my flesh. "Too . . . big . . . for . . . me." The whisper was so faint I could hardly hear the words.

"Who did this, Paddy? Who did it to you?" I asked.

"Didn't think he . . ." he muttered, then the tension left his face and I could tell that he had slipped away.

❧ Eight ❧

I stayed with him until a constable arrived. I had dispatched a ragamuffin playing in the alley below to find a policeman and stood, supporting Paddy, not wanting to let go of him. My own hurts were forgotten as rage and impotence surged through me. If I had come earlier, I might have been able to save him. I might, at least, have done something—scared off the intruder, raised an alarm. Instead all I had done was to let him die in my arms. I hadn't been with Paddy long enough to form a strong bond, but I had truly liked him. Maybe I recognized myself in him—loner, outspoken, not afraid of much. I suspected that he liked me too, in his own gruff way. If he had lived, we might have become good friends, partners, maybe.

I looked up at the clatter of feet on the outside steps. A young constable poked his head in through the door, took one look at Paddy and me and crossed himself. "Saints preserve us," he muttered. "Should I get a doctor?"

"Too late for that," I said.

"What happened?"

I put my hand up to my face and felt the stickiness. "It was an intruder. He hit me," I said, "but I'm all right."

"Then stay where you are. I'll go for help."

He ran down the steps again. The ragamuffin stood gaping at the door. I could hear the murmur of a crowd gathering down

63

below. It wasn't long before I heard a voice bark, "All right then, move on. No loitering. Go on, back to your homes," and heavy steps came up the stairway. A young man came into the room. He was fair-haired with light eyes and eyebrows and a sort of pale pastiness that I had never seen at home in Ireland, where most of us had healthy red cheeks and a sprinkling of freckles. He was dressed formally in a dark suit that made him look even more washed-out. He glanced swiftly around the room with a look of distaste, then his gaze focused on me.

"Sergeant Wolski," he said in a clipped voice. "What have we got here?"

A New York policeman who wasn't Irish. That was unusual to start with. I looked down at the dead man in my arms. "He's dead. The murderer got away through the back window."

"Paddy Riley, right?" The young man strolled around the room.

"That's right. Shouldn't you be sending men out to find the murderer?"

"You're a neighbor, presumably." Those pale blue eyes eyed me coldly. "Name?"

"Molly Murphy. I am Mr. Riley's business associate." Even in the midst of my shock and grief I savored my choice of the word—much better than assistant.

"Paddy never worked with anyone."

"Well, he does now. Did now." I had already taken a dislike to the aloof and rather arrogant young man. "He was training me in the business, if you must know." A slight exaggeration, but warranted.

A disbelieving smile crossed his face. "Paddy must have been getting soft in his old age."

"Look, why are we talking when there is a murderer on the loose?" I snapped. "You might still have a chance at finding him if you act quickly."

"I'm the law around here," he said. "You shut up until you're asked a question."

I opened my mouth to tell him that Captain Sullivan would have something to say if he talked to me like that. Then I realized I couldn't call on Daniel as my protector any longer.

"Are you always this rude?" I asked.

"Only to people who don't know when to keep quiet," he said. "I could take you down to police headquarters for questioning if you don't watch your manners."

Again it was so tempting. I let myself relish in the fantasy of this young upstart dragging me into police headquarters only to meet Daniel, but again my pride won out.

Sergeant Wolski pushed me aside, examined Paddy briefly, then turned to the constable who was waiting in the doorway. "Stabbed. Neat little blade—stiletto, by the look of it. He's probably taken it with him, but search around the place for it anyway. And the area outside. He may have tossed it through the window, or dropped it when he ran." He pushed open the door to the back room. That was in equal chaos, with the filing cabinet lying on its side, still locked.

"Could have been a robbery attempt," Wolski said. "Although I can't think that anyone believed Paddy had anything worth stealing."

He went over to the filing cabinet and motioned for the constable to help him right it. "What's in here?" he asked me.

"His case notes, I think. That was private. He didn't want me touching it."

"Any idea where the key is?"

"None at all."

He came back to me. "So how is it that you've escaped with only a scratch or two and yet a wily old guy like Paddy gets killed?"

I could tell what he was thinking—that somehow I was in cahoots with the murderer.

"The answer to that is simple," I said. "I arrived here to find Paddy slumped over the table and the place looking like this. I heard a noise in the back room and went to investigate—"

"With Paddy lying dead? That was either brave or stupid."

"I didn't know he was dead, did I? I thought he was sleeping. It never occurred to me that . . ." I let the sentence trail off. "As I opened the door to the back room I surprised the intruder. He leaped up and swung a fist at me. I was knocked to the ground with considerable force. He jumped over me and got away through that window."

"So did you get a good look at him? Anyone you've seen before?"

I shook my head. "I hardly had a chance to look at him before I was knocked over backward. I saw his back as he was running away—a slim young man, dressed in black. Dark hair, I think, and maybe a black cap on his head. Very agile, the way he moved." I shrugged. "That's all I can tell you."

"Send word to HQ with that description," Sergeant Wolski called to the constable. "Tell them I'll need backup and the morgue wagon. And tell them to hurry up. He won't last long in this heat."

"The young lady is hurt," the constable said, eyeing the sergeant with obvious dislike. "Shouldn't she be attended to? I could have her taken home."

"When I've finished questioning her," Wolski said. "I'm still not satisfied about what she was doing here." He pulled out a notebook. "I'll need your full name and an address."

"As to that, I live with the O'Hallarans." For the first time I was allowed to score a point. "You know Sergeant O'Hallaran? Captain Sullivan persuaded them to let me have their attic." I couldn't resist that one. It obviously registered with Wolski too.

"So you say you were working for Paddy?"

"I just started recently." I wasn't going to say how recently.

"Do you know what cases he was working on? Any ideas on who might have wanted to shut him up?"

"I'm afraid Mr. Riley didn't share his most sensitive cases with me. I know he was handling a couple of divorces, but that's all I can tell you."

"I can't say I'm surprised," Wolski said. He paced around the room, kicking idly at the papers on the floor. "He was asking for it, wasn't he?"

"What are you saying?"

Wolski grinned. He had an unpleasant, supercilious grin that made me want to slap his face. "What can you expect when he tried to play on both sides of the fence?"

"Meaning what?"

"Meaning he'd work for both sides, the police and the gangs—whoever would pay him. That's what I call living dangerously. Someone was bound to get him in the end." He turned to me. "You're lucky he didn't take you into his confidence or you wouldn't have lasted long yourself. All right. You can go home now. Have that cut lip taken care of."

"So what will happen now?" I asked.

"We'll look for the man you described. We'll ask our informants with the gangs, but I'm not hopeful anyone will squeal."

"And what about me? I'm still employed here, as far as I'm concerned. There are loose ends in his business I should tidy up if I can. When can I get back in here to clean up?"

He shrugged. "As soon as we've had the police photographer take pictures and we've removed the body."

"What about all these papers?' I blurted out, then wished I hadn't. "Shouldn't someone go through them? It's fairly obvious that the intruder was searching for something and didn't find it, or he'd not have been lingering in the back room after he killed Paddy."

For the first time Wolski looked at me as if I was a human being and not a creature of a lower order. He nodded. "I'll have a man go through everything. But it's probably not worth the effort. You said yourself he was involved with several cases. We have no way of knowing what particular piece of information might be important enough to somebody that they had to kill for it. I'm still going on the assumption that it was a hired killer. Whoever killed him knew what he was doing—thin blade, through the heart.

That's assassin's work." He kicked up another flurry of papers. "It'll turn out to be one of the gangs—you'll see. They think that Paddy passed on information to the police and this is how they repay that kind of thing. Too bad."

"Yes," I said, looking down at Paddy's body. "Too bad." It was fast becoming obvious that this supercilious sergeant wasn't going to put himself out to find Paddy's killer.

"And you'll be looking for fingerprints, no doubt?" I couldn't resist adding.

The icy stare returned. "Are you trying to teach me my job?"

I returned to my humble female mode. "I'm sorry, I didn't mean to imply—"

"Not much point really," he said. "If the man knew what he was doing, he'd be careful not to leave any prints."

I tried to recall whether the hand that swung at me had been wearing gloves, but it had all happened too quickly. However, I wasn't going to give up too lightly on this. "But he could have left a print on the window ledge on his way out."

"You're persistent, aren't you. I suggest you take yourself off home and leave the detective work to trained professionals."

He wasn't asking for my prints, which I would have done, if I'd been in charge of the case. I looked around the room. "I'll be happy to help you go through the papers myself," I said. "Maybe something might strike me."

"We'll call you if we need you. And you'll be notified when we're through with our investigation so that you can come and clean up the place."

So I was to be confined to the role of charwoman. "If I'm to get back in to clean up the place, I'll need a key."

"Where are the keys kept, do you know?"

"In one of his pockets, I think. I could take it and have a copy made, so that you keep the original, in case you need to get back in."

"I'll have one of my men do it. His pocket, you say?" Paddy's jacket was hanging on the hook on the wall, along with his brown derby. Wolski went over to it and fished through the pockets. Then I remembered Paddy producing money from his vest pocket. It was just possible that . . . Cautiously I slipped my fingers into the vest pocket. Luckily it was on the side away from his wound. I felt several coins and then my fingers closed around something sharp and metal.

"I think I've—" I began when Wolski exclaimed. "Ah, here we are. This must be it," and held up a large door key. I looked down at the object in my hand. A much smaller key, shiny, new. My fingers closed around it again. The key to the file cabinet. The intruder had tipped it on its side, maybe in a frustrated attempt to get it open. No doubt the police would find a way to open it, if they were interested. If they weren't, then I'd take a look for myself

❧ Nine ❧

More policemen had arrived by the time Sergeant Wolski let me go. One of them was setting up a tripod and a flash holder to take pictures of the scene with an old-fashioned hooded camera.

"Poor old Paddy," I heard one of them mutter. "Who'd a thunk it. He was the type who knew how to take care of himself."

Watching them made me remember Paddy's camera. He would surely have taken it to capture evidence that night at Delmonico's. Might it contain a vital clue? I thought of looking around for it quietly, without mentioning it to the police, then my better side won out.

"Paddy had a camera," I told Wolski. "A little box Brownie. It might be important."

Wolski's eyes registered instant interest. "A camera, you say? Any idea where?"

I shook my head. "Who can say in all this mess?"

He gave a little nod. "Thank you. We'll bear that in mind. Good day to you, Miss Murphy. Constable, show Miss Murphy out."

I made my way down the steps carefully, as the nausea and dizziness had returned. My jaw was starting to throb alarmingly. If this was what a private investigator could expect, I wasn't sure that

I wanted the job after all. Of course, I didn't have the job anymore. I was unemployed yet again. Back to square one.

I didn't want to go home to face yelling youngsters and the nosy Nuala. In truth, I didn't feel up to walking home yet. I turned south out of the mews and went to sit in the shade of a big elm tree in Washington Square. A fountain was playing in the center of the square and an evening breeze blew cooling spray in my direction. Children were playing hopscotch and kick the can. An Italian ice cream vendor pushed his barrow, ringing a small bell as he went. Students were sitting on benches, engaged in earnest discussion. Life was going on exactly as it had before Paddy died. Nobody paid any attention to me or my swollen lip. I took out a hankie, went over to dip it in the fountain and cleaned away the blood, then held it against my face until the coolness of the water reduced the angry throbbing.

What should I do now? Go home and find myself a steady, sensible job where my employer was not likely to be murdered? That was obviously the rational answer. Enough of dabbling in a world about which I knew nothing. I knew I should leave Paddy's death well alone, but I had the feeling that the obnoxious Sergeant Wolski wasn't going to put himself out to find Paddy's killer. Why couldn't Daniel have been summoned instead? Maybe I could tell him and—I broke off this thought. I was not going to tell Daniel Sullivan. I would just have to find Paddy's killer myself. I paused at the enormity of this idea. How could I possibly find a murderer? I had none of Paddy's skills, no idea where to start. But I had let my mouth run away with me enough times, claiming that I wanted to be an investigator. Well, now was the moment to put my money where my mouth was, as I'd heard the gamblers on the transatlantic liner say. Besides, Paddy's murderer had hit me. I had a personal score to settle. Tomorrow I would come back to Paddy's office and go through his file cabinet. Somewhere among those cases was a piece of information worth killing for.

I looked up as a group of people passed me and I heard a languid, aristocratic English voice saying, "Now do be good chaps and leave me alone. Even I don't know what the new play is about yet. I'll probably have the main points done by the time it opens in the fall. If not, the actors will all just have to ad-lib. Now, do run along and leave us in peace."

My eyes were riveted on to the speaker, who was the most beautiful man I had ever seen. I suppose it's strange to be describing a man as beautiful, but this one was. He was like a figure from an old painting or statue—tall, elegant, dark curly hair worn longer than fashionable, dark eyes, a long straight nose and a strong angular chin. Perfection, in fact. I just couldn't stop looking at him. As the reporters who had been following him finally left, he said something to one of his companions and they broke into laughter. His face was even more delightful when he was smiling. Now if ever I met a man like that, I could be persuaded to give up any notion about having a career and be content to serve him breakfast in bed every day for the rest of my life.

With a smile at my own foolishness I got up and made my way home.

I managed to creep past Mrs. O'Hallaran successfully, but I wasn't so lucky upstairs. Nuala was sitting in my room with the two little ones.

"Saint Michael and all angels, what happened to your face?" she demanded as she caught sight of me.

"Molly, your mouth is all funny," Shameyboy added, staring at me in wonder. Bridie came over to me. "Does it hurt a lot? Did you cry?"

"It's all right. It feels much better already."

"So your fancy man finally beat you up, did he?" Nuala was smirking. "I knew it would happen in the end. Always does."

"For your information, I have no fancy man. And I don't believe I invited you into my room either."

"Just keeping an eye on the children while you were out and about, up to God knows what." That unpleasant smirk again. "And

73

it's no good denying it. I have it from Mrs. O'Hallaran that there's a certain police captain who comes visiting. And someone has to be paying the rent, seeing as how you have no honest job."

"Well, for once Mrs. O'Hallaran doesn't have her facts straight," I said. "The police captain was a friend, nothing more, and we've parted company. And as to an honest job—I'll have you know I'm a private investigator. I got this fat lip trying to apprehend a murderer."

"Go on, pull the other one, it's got bells on," she said, chuckling.

"You can read all about it in the papers tomorrow, I expect. It was my partner, Paddy Riley, who was murdered."

"Saints preserve us." She crossed herself. "What kind of job is that for a woman?"

"More interesting than fish-gutting," I said. "Now why don't you go and look after Seamus while I get these youngsters their tea."

I put cold tea compresses on my face all night and by morning it looked almost normal again. At least I didn't look like a woman whose fancy man has just beaten her up! I checked on Seamus, who was now sitting up and had some color in his cheeks. Thank heavens for small mercies. Maybe Nuala would be going home soon and I'd have some peace and privacy again.

I had been doing some thinking during the night. I found it hard enough to sleep in the heat anyway, and with a throbbing face and two restless children, it was nearly impossible. So I had lain there going through things in my mind. I had told Nuala that I was a private investigator yesterday, so now I was truly committed to going back to Paddy's place and proving to myself that I could do the job. And if I was an investigator, a woman of business, then I should look like one. Nobody would take me seriously if I looked like any factory girl in my white blouse and cheap cotton skirt. I still had Miss Van Woekem's two dollars. If I were sensible I would keep them for necessities, but I wasn't going to be sensible. I was going to find a dressmaker and have a costume befitting a serious businesswoman made for me.

And then I was going to solve Paddy's murder. I had no idea how, or where I was going to start, but I was confident that something would come to me as I cleaned up his rooms. The more I thought about it, the more I was convinced that it wasn't a gangland killing. If a gang had wanted Paddy paid back and silenced, then the stabbing would have been enough. There would have been no need for the desperate search through his papers. And there would have been no need to do it in his office. A quick stab with a stiletto on a busy street would have been more efficient. Someone had been looking for evidence Paddy had gathered recently.

Start with what you know—I almost heard Paddy's voice saying the words. What did I know? Precious little, really—that he had passed something to Daniel in the park, then stood observing a house in Gramercy Park for three days. That would be worth following up. I knew he had gone to Delmonico's, presumably to witness an assignation in a private room; it should be possible to check on that also. Then something happened on the way back from Delmonico's—he had overheard something that had rattled him enough to send me away and start him investigating in a new direction. That would be the key.

I closed my eyes and was close to drifting off to sleep when I remembered the other fact that I knew—Paddy's words to me before he died. "Too big for me." What was too big for him?

I drifted into uneasy sleep and dreamed of Paddy wearing a coat that came down to his ankles. "This is too big for me," he was saying. "You'll have to wear it."

In the morning I helped the children to wash and dress, impatient to be off and get started. They were painfully slow, with lots of bickering and Bridie crying, before I finally packed them off to find their cousins and set out on my own errands. My first call was to Wanamaker's Dry Goods on Broadway, where I decided that black would be unbearably hot for summer wear and chose a soft beige fabric instead. Then I located a dressmaker, conveniently only a block away, and ordered a double-breasted suit pattern in a manly style. The dressmaker assured me that this was favored by women in commerce. I could come in for a fitting that afternoon and she could have it ready for me by the close of the next day, if I paid fifty cents extra for the rush job. It was worth the fifty cents, even though I probably wouldn't be eating by next week.

Then, deciding it was in for a penny, in for a pound, I spied a printer's shop opposite and went in to have calling cards made. They were also promised for the end of the following day. It seemed that by tomorrow night, I'd be a fully fledged woman of commerce. I tossed back my head and practiced walking down Broadway the way a woman of commerce might stride. I even had to restrain myself from hailing a passing hansom cab!

It was with reluctance that I presented myself to Sergeant Wolski at police headquarters to pick up my own key to Paddy's door. I was dying to ask if he'd found out anything new, but then reasoned that he'd be hardly likely to tell me if he had.

It felt strange to go up those steps to Paddy's place again. My mind kept replaying the picture of what I had seen when I opened the door yesterday. What if the murderer had come back and was waiting in the back room to finish me off? That thought had never struck me until now—that I, too, might be in danger. Surely nobody knew that Paddy had taken on an assistant. It wasn't the kind of thing he'd have gone around boasting about to his pals, of that I was sure. The man who struck at me yesterday could hardly have gotten a better view of me than I did of him. So I should be safe enough. Even so, I tapped on the door and called, "Is anyone in there?" before I turned the key in the lock and went in.

If anything, the place was in more disarray than I had left it. So much for the police taking Paddy's papers to look through. My eyes went to the empty chair at the table. I half expected to see him still slumped over and was surprised by the physical jolt of loss. I hadn't expected to become fond of him.

"Don't worry, Paddy," I said out loud. "I'll find out who did this and bring him to justice, I promise. I'll show you that I was worth training."

I started picking up papers, glancing at them before putting them on the table or throwing them into the trash. It was hard to know what to keep. There were newspaper clippings that seemed of no significance to me, posters advertising prize fights and new plays, and Paddy's recent correspondence I had so neatly stacked for filing. As I moved the chair, I noticed the dark brown stains on the seat—Paddy's blood. I bent to pick up some blood-spattered papers under the chair, touching them with distaste, and found I was looking at Paddy's little black notebook. I couldn't believe that the police hadn't even wanted that! I opened it excitedly and then saw why it had been discarded. It was written in a foreign language that I didn't recognize. This was a shock. How an Irishman who grew up in London had acquired facility in a strange foreign tongue, I had no idea. But I put the notebook into my bag for future study.

In the back room the file cabinet still stood there, righted again, but unopened. I took out the little silver key, put it into the lock and turned it. Then I saw why the police hadn't managed to open it, if they had indeed tried. It was a complicated lock attached to a rod which went down through all the file drawers. The locksmith had done a good job. I pulled out the rod and slid the top drawer open.

I took out the first folder. "Client Edgemont" was written across the top of it. That was the only clear word in the entire file. The pages inside were full of cryptic notes. "July 28th: LE observed leaving A at 10.45 am. LE observed entering GP. LE observed at MSG, Rooftop Restaurant, with KL."

Obviously I had work ahead of me.

I flipped through the first few folders. Divorce cases, by the look of them. Then I came to a folder with a big red stamp across the front of it—CASE CLOSED. FEE PAID IN FULL. Only a few current cases then. Not an overwhelming number. If the case had been closed, then Paddy had already shared any damaging information—unless it was as Sergeant Wolski suggested, a revenge killing. In which case, the killer wouldn't have been searching so desperately, would he? If only Paddy had trusted me enough to share information with me—but then I, too, might have been dead by now, I reminded myself.

I went back to the first folder. Client Edgemont had an address in England. In the depths of the folder I found the client's letter. There was a crest embossed on the envelope. The address was Eaton Square, London, and the sender was a Lady Clarissa Edgemont. She wanted Paddy to check into the activities of her husband, the roving Lord Edgemont, whom she believed to be in New York.

That must have been the assignment in Gramercy Park. "LE observed entering GP. House of K"—Paddy had mentioned Kitty Le Grange, whose house he had been observing. This wasn't going to be as complicated as I had feared. I had some facts to start on—I could visit the famous Kitty and find the roving Lord Edgemont. Although I couldn't see that this kind of case might lead to murder. Would a roving English lord feel it necessary to hire an assassin to stop news of his assignation with an actress from getting back to London? If she was well-known and they had been seen together, it was probably common knowledge. This sort of thing happened all the time, if one were to believe the daily papers—look at the Prince of Wales, now the new King Edward. The whole world knew of his lady loves, but his wife didn't seem to mind. At least it gave me somewhere to begin.

I looked at the second folder. Similar to the first but with a New York address. A Mrs. Angus McDonald wishing to bring divorce proceedings against her husband. The name was vaguely familiar. Another name I had read in the papers. Wait a minute. Wasn't McDonald the railroad baron? But he was an old man with whiskers. A relative, maybe. Also easy enough to check into and not a likely motive for murder. New York millionaires were hopping in and out of marriage every day.

The third was a little more promising. The owner of a big import and export business had noticed profits were not as high as they should have been and suspected one of his clerks of embezzling. Now we were moving into more turbulent waters. The threat of losing a job and going to jail might drive a hitherto respectable young man into a desperate act. The only question was—would he have killed so neatly and efficiently? There was nothing for it but to wade through the papers and see what evidence Paddy had managed to come up with.

I was squatting on the back-room floor, looking through the case folders, one by one, when I heard a sound. Someone was coming up the steps. I scrambled to my feet, cursing as my shoes got themselves tangled up in my skirts, then stood, ready for action. Probably the police coming back to look for more clues. Not necessarily the police, however—anyone could have been watching this place and seen me go back inside. And that someone could have been waiting for a chance to find the door unlocked. Until now I had felt angry and upset about Paddy's death, but I hadn't felt personally threatened. Now I realized my folly. I had not locked the front door behind me, if, indeed it could be locked from the inside. I hadn't checked the window to see if it also was locked. I was a sitting duck.

The tread on the stairs was not the heavy plod of police boots. I waited. A moment of silence. Then the slightest click as the door handle began to turn. I looked around for something I could use as a weapon. No cane in sight, not even a vase I might break over his head. Nothing except clothing hanging in a neat row on hooks. Paddy's disguises, obviously. I looked to see if I could hide myself behind them, but they hung well clear of the floor.

A squeak sounded as the door opened slowly. Through the crack in the door to the inner room I saw a dark shape enter, silent and stealthy. I could hear his breath. I held my own and shrank back against the wall, out of sight. I stared at a cloak on the wall. I inched my hands toward it and lifted it down. Then all I could do was stand there, waiting. He would come in here in the end. If I was in luck and he had left the front door half-open, I might be able to startle him enough to make my escape past him. If not . . .

I tried to let my breath out with no sound. It was becoming hard to breathe at all. I could hear his footsteps and the rustle of papers as he examined the piles I had made in the other room. I heard the footsteps cross the floor and a rattle as he checked the window—opening it for a second escape route if necessary, I concluded. It might also provide a second escape route for me, if I was bold enough and agile enough to cross a couple of rooftops and leap down like the young man had done. I could have done it back home in Ireland when I had run around barefoot and kept up with the boys. Now I was out of practice and hampered by petticoats and pointed shoes. Still, it might be worth a try.

The footsteps left the window again and came closer. He was coming into this room. I held the cape ready. A dark shape filled the doorway. A surprised intake of breath and a muttered exclamation as he saw the open file cabinet. As he reached out for the folders I had left on the floor, I seized my chance. I threw the cape over his head, gave him a hefty shove and pushed past him. He gave a grunt and lurched forward. I was out, free, making for the door, but not fast enough. He lunged at my feet and felled me like a tree. This time was not as painful or violent as yesterday's attack had been, but I went over, unable to stop myself and he was instantly on me, pinning me to the floor with horrible strength.

"Okay, let's get a look at you, scum," he growled in a terrifying voice, wrenching my hand up behind my back and grabbing at my hair to force my face from the floor.

"Let go of me or you'll be sorry." I tried bravado. "The police will be coming back here any minute. They know I'm here."

The pressure that was wrenching up my arm relaxed instantly.

"Molly, what the devil are you doing here?" Daniel Sullivan asked.

❧ Ten ❧

Daniel's face was ashen as he took my arm and helped me to my feet. "I could have killed you," he muttered. "Are you all right?'

"I think so. Once my heart starts beating again, I'll be fine."

"And just what do you think you are doing here?" He sounded angry now.

I was so flooded with relief and the sheer joy of being close to him again that I didn't know whether to laugh or cry. "Cleaning up," I said. "I came to clean up the place."

"Clean up the place? So it's a Mrs. Mop service you're running now, is it? Who asked you to clean up the place, I'd like to know?"

"The police, if you must know." I started brushing myself down. A lot of dirt had accumulated on that floor in the past couple of days. Also brushing down my skirt meant that I didn't have to look at him.

"And why would they have asked you in particular?" He came to stand very close to me, his presence still unnerving. But I wasn't going to be unnerved.

"I worked for Paddy," I said. "I kept the place clean for him. I was just doing my job."

Daniel looked amused. "You worked for Paddy?"

"I did indeed. I was fast becoming his right-hand woman."

"Now I've heard everything. Paddy hated women. He wouldn't touch one with a ten-foot pole."

"Ah, well, he didn't actually touch me," I said, "but he liked me well enough. I was helping him around the office. He was showing me the tricks of the trade."

I could see this sinking in. "So it was Paddy who taught you how to throw that cape over someone's head?"

"No, I invented that for myself when I couldn't find anything I could use as a weapon."

"It was quite effective."

"Not effective enough. You still got me."

Daniel stared at me long and hard, then shook his head. "So you were serious when you said you were going to be an investigator."

"I'm always serious. And I don't toy with other people's affections either." I had recovered my equilibrium enough to remember that I shouldn't be glad to be talking to Daniel.

"Molly, I'm really sorry," he said. He reached out to touch my arm. I shrank away. "I wasn't trifling with your affections. Everything I felt for you—feel for you—was genuine."

"And yet you're betrothed to another woman. So what were you waiting for, enough money to set me up in a quiet little flat somewhere as your mistress? I hear it's all the rage in polite society. But I wouldn't know. I'm only a peasant girl. Where I come from, if you dally with a woman's affections, you're expected to marry her."

"Damn it, Molly. You know it's not like that." He reached out to grab my arm. I neatly sidestepped away.

"What other choices are there? Unless you're about to drag me out west with the Mormons where they can have two wives, although I can't see Miss Arabella Norton in a covered wagon, somehow."

I thought I saw the twitch of a smile on his lips. "If you'd let me try to explain."

I brushed him away. "Either you're betrothed or you're not. It's

82

as simple as that. And if you are betrothed to another woman, then there is no place for me in your life." He tried to say something but I held up my hand. "If you want to explain something, you might tell me why you were creeping in here like a thief in the night, frightening me out of my wits."

"Ah, good question," he said.

"And the good answer is?"

He looked at my face and laughed. "All right, you've caught me. I was snooping. Paddy was doing a spot of work for me, on the quiet. I was distressed to hear he had been killed, so I thought I'd come by to take a look for myself. Wolski doesn't take kindly to interference."

"But you're his superior officer. Why didn't you take the case yourself?"

"I'm in the middle of another investigation and I wasn't on the spot, so Wolski was assigned to this one. I can't officially step on his toes."

"I wish you would," I said. I pulled out the chair and was about to sit on it when I remembered the blood and hastily stood up again. "Sergeant Wolski seems to think that Paddy deserved to be killed because he worked with both the police and the gangs. He thinks it was a revenge killing."

"He confided all this to you? You've become *his* right-hand woman too?"

"I happened to be here when he arrived. I was the one who found Paddy."

"You found him dead?"

"Dying. The killer was still here, hidden in the back room, just like I was just now."

"Holy Mother," Daniel muttered. "He could have killed you too."

"Easily. I thought Paddy was asleep, you see. I heard a noise and went to investigate. He knocked me over, like you did, only a little more violently, as you can see from the bruise on my face, and made his getaway through that window."

He reacted as if he had only just noticed the bruises. He took my chin in his hand and turned the discolored side toward him, wincing as he touched the swollen area around my lip. "I seem to make a habit of meeting you after men have beaten you up. You live a charmed life, my dear."

I moved hastily out of reach of his touch. "I must have been a cat in a former existence," I said breezily. "Don't they say cats have nine lives?"

"You've already used up several of yours," he said. "Be careful."

He was looking at me tenderly again, which I found distinctly unnerving. "Don't worry. I plan to be." I brushed a last speck from my skirt and straightened my blouse. "So what is it you were looking for?"

"I don't know, really. I just wanted to take a look for myself, to see if Paddy had left any notes on—" He broke off.

"On what?"

"On the little matter I'd asked him to check into."

"His cases are all in that file cabinet. The police didn't bother to try to open it."

He looked at the open cabinet, the files on the floor and then at me. "Oh, no," he said. "You weren't getting any stupid ideas about investigating this yourself, were you?"

"I just thought I'd see if there was anything the police had overlooked and they should know about. That's all."

He took a step closer and loomed over me. "Stay out of this, Molly. This is not child's play. Paddy was a cunning old man who knew how to take care of himself. If someone managed to kill him—"

"Wolski thinks it was a hired assassin," I said.

Daniel nodded. "Could be."

I looked around the room, remembering the chaos, the file cabinet on its side. "But not a revenge killing. If you were hired to kill someone in revenge, you'd stab them and go. The killer was still here, remember. He was still looking for something."

"And you were having your own little snoop to find out what?"

"And what if I was? Someone has to use their brains around here. That pale, arrogant Wolski wasn't making much effort to get to the truth. Couldn't you get someone else assigned to the case?"

"Ah, well, that wouldn't be easy. Take an officer off a case and you're saying essentially that he's not up to the job. One day you may need that officer to cover your back. And I don't think I could drum up much enthusiasm for a full-scale investigation anyway. Everyone at Mulberry Street HQ expected to find Paddy's body floating in the Hudson one day, given the life he led."

"But you—you must think it's worth investigating, or you wouldn't be here."

"As I said, Paddy was doing a little business for me. If he had managed to come up with the facts I wanted—they might be around here somewhere and I'd sure like to have them."

"What kind of facts?"

"I'm sorry, I can't tell you anything at all. More than my job's worth. It was strictly hush-hush, between Paddy and me." He glanced around the room.

I remembered something I had forgotten until now. "The day before he was killed he told me he'd like to speak to you."

"And you didn't pass on the message?" he demanded angrily.

"It wasn't put like that. He just mentioned, casually, as I was going out of the door, 'Oh, and if you happen to see Captain Sullivan, you might tell him I'd like a word with him.' Something like that. Of course, he didn't know that it wasn't likely I'd be seeing you in the future. I didn't think any more of it at the time."

"Damn," he muttered, then cleared his throat. "Sorry for the bad language. It just slips out occasionally. So he *had* found something."

"He certainly had," I said. "He spent the evening at Delmonico's, spying on a couple in a private dining room, I think. But then, on his way home he overheard something that really rattled him. He babbled on to me, which wasn't like him. Usually he wouldn't discuss his cases with me."

"Did he say what it was that had rattled him?"

I shook my head. "I can't even remember the words he used now. I got the impression he'd seen someone he recognized, but the person hadn't recognized him because he was in one of his disguises. And the person didn't think he could be overheard. I think he said 'he.' That's right. He said 'Him of all people.' He said things had taken an unexpected turn and he'd need to look into it further. He sent me away. He didn't want me around."

"He was on to something dangerous then," Daniel said, and nodded as if confirming his own suspicions. "He wanted you to stay away and I'm telling you the same thing now. I want you to go home now and stay there. No more thoughts of snooping, or even of cleaning up until we know what we're dealing with."

"So you will be looking into this yourself?"

"I'm going to have my own little snoop around here, ask some discreet questions in the right places, but it's still Sergeant Wolksi's investigation, and he certainly wouldn't take kindly to any interference from a woman."

"Sergeant Wolski couldn't detect his own nose on a foggy day. He didn't even bother to search the room properly."

"May not have been necessary. The police have feelers in a lot of places. If it was anything to do with the gangs, one of our informants will tip us off."

"And then what will you do?"

"Probably just let it go. No, don't look like that—we probably don't have a hope in Hades of pinning it on anyone."

"And if it wasn't a gang killing?"

"We'll look into it. In our own way. In our own time." He grabbed me suddenly by the shoulders. "Either way you are to stay out of it. It's police business, do you hear me?"

I shook myself free from him. "You can't tell me what to do. I work here. I have every right to come and clean up this office as soon as the police have released it as a crime scene. And they took one evening to do that. They didn't even bother to pick up the papers on the floor. They are not going to take the trouble to find his killer, Daniel."

"And neither are you!" His voice had been getting louder and angrier. "Go home, Molly. That's an order." He grabbed my shoulders again. "My God, I'd never forgive myself if anything happened to you."

"You don't care a damn about me!" I shouted back.

Then, without warning, he pulled me to him and kissed me hungrily. I had a moment of pure delight at the feel of his mouth crushing against mine again, until I came to my senses and wrenched myself free. "Just leave me alone, Daniel Sullivan. I can take care of myself," I shouted, dangerously close to tears now. I picked up my skirts and ran for the door.

"Molly, please, listen to me," he called after me.

"Thank heavens I never was your wife," I retorted. "You'd have made an awful bossy husband."

As I ran down the steps I was conscious of him standing at the top, watching me go. I fought to appear calm. He wasn't going to see how badly he affected me.

"And make sure you lock that door behind you when you leave," I called up to him before I strode off down the mews.

❧ Eleven ❧

I turned onto Fifth Avenue but I'd only gone as far as the sidewalk café outside the Brevoort Hotel before I stopped. I wasn't just going to go home like a good girl. I could remember most of the details of Paddy's most recent cases, but I wanted to take them all down, just in case. I decided to go back and keep watch on the mews—good experience for my professional future. When Daniel left I'd go back in. I'd be able to see which case folders he'd taken with him and which he'd left. Maybe I'd get a clue from that the way his mind was working. And as to my own safety—what safer time to be in the place than right after a policeman?

I went back cautiously and passed the alleyway, crossing into Washington Square itself. I positioned myself in the shadow of the great marble arch where I could see the entrance to the mews. I waited and waited. It was hot, and what seemed like an eternity was, on hearing a neighboring clock chime, only half an hour. Maybe I wasn't going to be any good at this job after all. I couldn't see myself standing for three days like a statue, as Paddy had done in Gramercy Park. My mother said I was born impatient, along with all my other faults.

My attention began to wander. I watched some little girls turning a jump rope and chanting as they took turns to run in and out. "She made a drip drop. Dripping in the sea. Please turn the rope for me . . ." It was almost the same as the nonsense rhyme we had chanted at home and I listened, entranced. Luckily I remembered my mission in time and looked back to see Daniel striding out along the north side of the square, then crossing University Place. He didn't seem to be carrying anything. I waited until he was out of sight then headed back to Paddy's. For a moment it all seemed like a great lark, until I remembered that Paddy was dead and that the man I had been spying on was the one I had loved and lost.

Daniel had, indeed, locked the door behind him. I turned my key in the lock and went back inside. From what I could see, he hadn't moved anything. The folders from the file cabinet still lay on the floor. I picked them up and placed them on the table, ready to take them home with me. Then I went through the rest of the top drawer. Farther back I found several folders stamped CASE CLOSED. EVIDENCE DELIVERED, and a date. BILL SUBMITTED, and a date, but no stamp saying PAID IN FULL.

So not all of these big nobs were speedy about paying their accounts, I decided. Then something else struck me. I still worked here until somebody told me I didn't. There was no reason these people should get away without paying their bills just because Paddy was dead. P. Riley, Discreet Investigations still existed. It was up to the junior partner to collect what was owed.

I spent some time in a rather fruitless attempt at cleaning Paddy's chair, then I placed a towel on it before I sat. It didn't seem right to be sitting on his bloodstains, but there was no other chair in the place. I found clean writing paper and wrote, in my best penmanship, "It has come to our attention that our business with you was concluded three months ago and that the account is outstanding. We would appreciate payment at your earliest convenience." I signed it "M. Murphy, junior partner, P. Riley Investigations."

I completed seven of these and put them ready for mailing when I left. I felt rather pleased with myself. If any of this money came in, I could keep this business running and, if Paddy's death was not broadcast to the world, nobody would be any the wiser.

As I was rearranging the files I had taken out of the cabinet, I had a second, even bigger, pleasant surprise. Something was lying on the bottom of the drawer, under the files. It was a slim leather pouch, rather like a pencil case. I took it out, opened it and stared in amazement. I had never seen so much money in my life. There were some silver dollars, but a great wad of bank notes, too. I had no way of knowing if there was a hundred dollars in the roll, or a thousand. The first thought that came into my head was that I should turn it over to the police instantly. That lasted for approximately a second. The New York Police Department didn't exactly have a reputation for honesty. The officer who took the money from me would thank me kindly and it would never be seen again. There was only one New York policeman I could trust, and he had forbidden me to go anywhere near Paddy's place.

I stood there, turning it over in my hand. I was trembling a little at the audacity of what I was thinking. As far as I knew, Paddy had no next of kin. If they turned up, then they could claim it, plus anything else in here that they wanted. Until then I was an employee of the firm, so I was taking it home with me, for safe-keeping. I stuffed it into my purse and locked the file cabinet behind me.

I stopped on the way home for the fitting of my costume, then I decided to give myself a modest advance on wages and get Seamus some nourishing treats—grapes and peaches, eggs and a small bottle of brandy to go with them. I was looking forward to his face when he saw them, but I came up the stairs to find chaos. Nuala's three boys had come to visit and the place was like a monkey house.

"I was missing them something terrible," she said, when I suggested that Seamus needed peace and quiet. "They came over to cheer up their kin, and boys will be boys, won't they?"

"They can be boys down in the street," I said. "Go on, out you go, the lot of you." I reached into my purse. "Here, go and treat yourselves to a soda."

They snatched the coins from me and were gone. Nuala eyed

me suspiciously. "I got a raise at work. They're pleased with me," I said, before she could make any remarks about my fancy man. I sent her to get more milk and bread so that Seamus could get his rest. He looked washed-out and weary, but perked up when I offered him the grapes and heated a little milk with some egg and brandy in it.

"You're a good woman, Molly," he said. "If only my Kathleen were here. I miss her so badly. While I've been lying here, I'm thinking all the time of going home. I mean, what would happen to these children if I died out here?"

"You're not going to die," I said. "You'll be as right as rain soon."

"Maybe this time, but it's a dangerous job I'm in and I know it. Four men dead, they say, in that cave-in. Who knows how many in the next? And no compensation for their families either. They weren't even about to pay for the doctor until some young fellow insisted. He's been trying to form a union. Hadn't had much luck until now, just like me back in Ireland. Most men are scared in case they lose their jobs. If I get back on my feet again, maybe I'll help him. I know a thing or two about unions."

"You're a born troublemaker," I said, laughing.

"Oh, and you're not yourself?" A weary smile crossed his face. "I had a letter from Kathleen," he whispered. "She's not doing too badly. Not any worse, anyway. Says she feels fine when she's out in the fresh air. Who knows, maybe she'll beat it yet."

"Maybe she will." I patted his hand, trying to look as if I believed a person might recover from consumption. "Now why don't you fall asleep in a hurry, so that I can keep the heathen hordes out of your room?"

He chuckled as he sank back onto his pillow.

When I was safely in my own room I took out the money pouch and looked at it again. I didn't dare count that money. I got out my needle and thread and made a crude pocket out of my oldest petticoat, then pinned it to my waistband, where it could hang, under my skirts. It was safe enough there for the time being.

When I went to bed, I put it under my pillow. But during the night I got an acute attack of conscience. That strict Catholic upbringing, those straps on the backside for lying or cheating, those embarrassing encounters with the priest in the confessional started playing on my mind. It wasn't my money. Not that I had any intention of keeping it, nor of helping myself to anything more than my wages, but I shouldn't have brought it home with me. What if there was a next of kin Paddy had never mentioned— a frail, crippled daughter who could have used that money for the operation to make her walk, or even a bright but poverty-stricken nephew who wanted to become a doctor but was working as a servant?

Next morning I went straight to Mulberry Street to police headquarters and asked to see Sergeant Wolski. He didn't look particularly pleased to see me.

"What is it, Miss Murphy? I'm busy."

"I was wondering if you'd traced Paddy Riley's next of kin yet? I'm cleaning up the place today, and just in case I come across any little trinkets the family might like to have . . ."

Did I see those pale eyes flicker at the mention of trinkets? "If you happen to come across something you think might be valuable, Miss Murphy, you can bring it to me. I'll make sure it's passed along to the appropriate person—should one come forth."

"So you've not located any kin as yet?"

"Unless he left behind family in Ireland when he came here."

"He came from England," I said. "From London. Didn't you pick up the accent? He might have been born in Ireland but he was raised a Cockney."

"Ah. So that accounts for it. I always wondered about him."

"And he was left an orphan at a young age."

"It seems that he told you his entire life history," Wolski said. "He didn't perhaps confide in you who might have wanted him dead?"

"When it came to business, he shut up like a clam," I said. "I have no idea who wanted him dead. I'd rather hoped you might have found that out by now."

"We're asking around," he said. "If it was one of the gangs, they'll probably let us know eventually." The eyes turned to me again. It was rather like being stared at by a snake. "I wouldn't have thought Paddy was the kind of man who owned 'trinkets.' What sort of thing were you thinking of?"

"He had a pocket watch," I said. "You probably found it. And he had that little camera. I can't seem to find that anywhere."

"Really?"

"I wondered if the police had taken it to get the film developed as evidence. It could be important, I'd imagine."

"We found no camera."

I couldn't tell from his face whether he was lying or whether the murderer had walked off with the camera. I tried to remember if he had anything in his hand when he leaped out of the window. One hand had been employed to hit me, of course. Had he bulging pockets in his jacket, or a bag over his back? My fleeting impression was of slim and lithe. No bulges. But of course I couldn't be sure. I was seeing stars at the time.

"Thank you for your time." I bobbed a small bow. "I won't be troubling you again, unless I come up with something important."

Did he look disappointed as I made my exit—as if he could somehow sense those dollars hiding under my skirt?

So it looked as if I was going to be custodian of the fortune after all. I didn't want the worry of carrying it around all the time, so I popped into the public convenience in Washington Square Park, removed the money from my skirt, then went up the steps of the first grand-looking bank I encountered, past the uniformed doormen, across the marble floor. It was like walking into Buckingham Palace. I was conscious of stares, and realized that I was the only woman in the place.

The clerk behind the grille was a snooty young man with slicked-down hair and a perfect mustache. "You want to open an account with us?" A most supercilious smile. "I hardly think—"

"What's the matter, isn't my money good enough for you?" I produced the wad of notes. "Because if not, let me know. There are plenty of other banks in this city that would just love to have me as a customer."

I noticed the clerk's Adam's apple going up and down nervously. "Forgive me, madam. Your appearance is deceiving. I thought that—"

"I'm a woman of commerce," I said, glad that I would soon be dressing the part, if my costume was ready today, as promised. "It's the business money that I'll be banking here."

"What kind of business, may I ask?" The Adam's apple danced again.

What did he think I was—a woman of the streets? "A respectable business," I replied. "And a flourishing business."

He looked curious but said no more as he counted the notes. "I make it eight hundred and fifty dollars," he said. "Does that agree with your count?"

I nodded, too stunned to answer. Almost a thousand dollars. In Ireland that was the wealth of dreams and fantasies. Of course, it wasn't mine, but it was certainly enough to kill for. Who knew it was there? Had anyone seen Paddy hiding it away? Was it possible that he had mentioned it to anyone? Paddy, who didn't give away a single useful detail to me, his assistant? But then I realized I knew little of what he did outside of work. From the way he ate his dinner in the office, I concluded that work was pretty much his life. But what if he drank with his cronies afterward, and became loose-lipped in his cups? That was something I should check into.

I waited patiently while the clerk took down the details. I gave him the office address. "P. Riley Associates," I said, changing the firm's name to suit the occasion. "I am Miss Murphy, junior partner." My, but I was rising quickly through the ranks! I could see this made an impression on the clerk. He wrote everything down in a neat flowing script and eventually handed me a receipt with a bow. "The very best fortune in your business, whatever it may be." He gave me an oily smile. I nodded graciously to the uniformed doorman as I swept past him.

I was feeling so pleased with myself that it called for a celebration. So I went into a little French bakery on Bleecker Street for a cup of coffee and a kind of flaky pastry they called a croissant. I was just discovering that the world is full of delicious new things and I aimed to try them all. As I pulled out the money to pay, I noticed Paddy's black notebook, still lying in the bottom of my bag. I should have handed it over to the police, of course. Maybe someone clever at Mulberry Street could have worked out what language it was written in; but then again, maybe Sergeant Wolski would have tossed it into the nearest wastebasket. I took a long sip of milky coffee and flicked through it idly. Why didn't I recognize it? I had a grounding in French and Latin. I'd even been exposed to a little German. This resembled none of those languages. I turned to the last page. Paddy's sharp black doodles decorated the left side of the page, along with some hurried writing.

At the top of the page the writing was still even, as if the writer had taken time. "Was LK htiw EL ta SLED."

Even here he was using initials. I shook my head and put it back in frustration. I'd have to pay a visit to the languages department at the university and see if a professor there could decipher this gibberish. But in the meantime I had other leads to follow. I turned to the back of the notebook and used a blank page for my own notes. What I should do was try to work backward. Paddy had gone to Delmonico's on the night before he died. Then he had stopped off somewhere on his way home. I wrote down the order in the little black book: Del's, trace his route home, visit his apartment. Maybe he'd left some clue there. It would be interesting to see if the police had bothered to search it.

I was impatient to get going, but I couldn't do a thing until my costume was ready. I'd already noted the reception I got at the bank. While I looked like a factory girl, I'd be treated as one. I had another cup of coffee and copied down the names from Paddy's last cases. Kitty Le Grange—I knew where she lived, next door to Miss Van Woekem. Lord Edgemont—he should be easy enough to trace. His wife Lady Clarissa in England was the client, so it would have been in her interest to keep Paddy alive until he had come up with evidence for her.

Next case involved a couple named MacDonald. Wife Elizabeth wanting evidence against husband Angus. I wasn't so sure how I'd find out about them. I wasn't even sure how I'd approach the likes of Lord Edgemont and Kitty Le Grange. I could hardly demand an audience and then cross-examine them about killing my employer, could I? For one thing, if any of them had ordered the killing and they thought I was nosing around, then I'd be next. I'd already had more than my share of luck, blundering around in an investigation. I couldn't expect to repeat that luck indefinitely. So this would take careful thought and planning. I finished my coffee, paid the bill and went for a walk.

I always find that walking in the fresh air clears the brain. The problem was finding any fresh air. New York in August stank. Even on posh streets like Fifth Avenue the smell of drains, plus the piles of horse manure in the street, created a subtle odor which was not conducive to a clear head. I could have taken the trolley or the Sixth Avenue El up to Central Park, but I wasn't anxious to go back there. Too many memories of happy times with Daniel. Instead I walked west to the Hudson and followed West Street along the docks. A big ocean liner was coming in and myriad little craft had come out to greet her. Tugboats tooted their horns and flags were flying.

"The new German ship. She's just beaten the Atlantic Record," I heard someone saying. "Now the English will have to build a faster boat to get it back."

Was it only a few months ago that I had come across the Atlantic in such a ship? Already it seemed a lifetime away. I felt that I belonged to this big, vibrant city, and my past life in Ireland was like a dream. I breathed in the brisk, salty wind off the Atlantic and felt a pang of longing for my home. Only one brief pang, though. Now back to the case in hand, I told myself severely. How was I going to find out more about these people and how was I going to approach them?

Then I had a flash of inspiration. Miss Van Woekem! If anyone knew about New York society, it was she. And she had asked
me to pay a call on her from time to time. Now that her goddaughter would be long gone back to White Plains, thus avoiding
any embarrassing encounters, this might be a perfect opportunity.

The next morning, dressed in my smart new costume, new shoes,
my hair pinned back under a jaunty new beige hat I had bought
on a whim after seeing it in Wanamaker's window, I presented my
calling card to Miss Van Woekem's maid. I was invited into the
hallway and soon summoned to the sitting room on the first floor.

"Well, this is a pleasant surprise," the old lady greeted me. "I
hardly recognized you. Quite an improvement on those dreadful
garments you were wearing the last time I saw you. So you've
managed to establish yourself in business? Well done." She nodded, then glanced again at my card. "Already a junior partner too.
My, my." There was amusement in her voice, as if she sensed that
the junior partner title had been of my own creation. "Most kind
of you to take time out of your busy schedule to visit an old
woman. You'll take tea, of course?"

A tray was brought. For the first time in my life I sat in the
home of a patrician being treated as an equal.

"So tell me"—she leaned forward confidentially—"are you
working on any interesting cases?"

"I am, as a matter of fact." I leaned toward her and lowered my
voice. "One involving your next-door neighbor, in fact."

"That woman? I'm not at all surprised. An actress, she calls
herself." Miss Van Woekem snorted. "Actress, my foot. The procession of men up and down those stairs requires a new stair car-
pet at least once a year. Which one is it now?"

"I'm not really at liberty to say," I said. "Client confidentiality,
you know."

"I shouldn't think there is anything in the least confidential
about that woman's activities. She flaunts herself around town

with half the male population. Why, when I was at the theater last week, she was sitting at the front of a box with that English lord, giggling and talking loudly so as to attract attention to herself."

"Would that be Lord Edgemont?" I asked casually.

"That's the one. Of course those two deserve each other. He'd chase anything in skirts. They say he's gone through the entire family fortune. Hardly ever goes home to administer his estates. And his father was such a good man too. Funny how there is always a throwback."

"So he spends all his time in New York these days, does he?" I took a delicate bite of watercress sandwich.

"Keeps a permanent suite at the Waldorf Astoria, so I understand, although how long before he gets thrown out for not paying his bills, I couldn't say. And when he's finally bankrupt you can bet that Miss Kitty next door will drop him like a hot coal." She gave a satisfied chuckle.

So far, so good. I took another bite of watercress sandwich and was emboldened to ask, "What do you know of Angus Mac-Donald?"

She looked surprised. "His name hasn't come up in connection with Kitty Le Grange, surely?"

"Oh, no. This is something quite different."

"Thank God for that. The old man would drop dead of a heart attack if he heard that his son was involved with actresses."

"The old man?"

"Angus MacDonald is the son of J.P. Surely you knew that? J.P. MacDonald, the shipping and railway magnate? I've no time for him myself. J.P. likes to think that he's now one of the Four Hundred. Of course he's not. He might be rich as Croesus, but he's still the son of a Scottish peasant. He's actually proud of coming over here with nothing and working his way to a fortune. He's kept those dreadful Scottish peasant Calvinist values, too. Won't touch alcohol. Won't accept any social invitations on Sundays. So young Angus has been misbehaving, has he? Papa won't like that at all."

I left the house on Gramercy Park some half hour later with all the information I needed and a possible motive for murder too. If Angus MacDonald was the only son of a strict Calvinist millionaire and about to be sued for divorce, he might do anything to keep the evidence from getting to his father.

❧ Twelve ❧

Now I had plenty of leads to follow up. It made sense that my first visit should be to Delmonico's, and from there I could trace Paddy's route home. I stood in Gramercy Park feeling the sun on my face. The twitter of birds and the heady scent of flowers wafted to me from the gardens. I remembered my bleak despair and determination the last time I left this address. My grief over Daniel and Paddy had receded so that it no longer threatened to consume me. Now it felt good to be alive. I strode out along Twenty-first Street like a racehorse released from the starting gate.

It was still too early in the day for anything to be happening at Delmonico's. A man in a dirty apron was swabbing down the front steps, and a woman was working on the brass on the open front doors. From inside came the clatter of dishes.

The man washing the steps looked up and saw me. "We're closed," he growled.

"Is there someone I could talk to? A head waiter, perhaps?"

"They don't show up for hours yet."

"Anyone who might have been on duty at night earlier this week? It's a very important matter."

An evil grin crossed his face. "Wassamatter—leave some telltale evidence in a private room, didja? Don't worry, no one at Del's ever blabs." He put down the mop. "I'll see if Mr. Carlo is around."

He led me inside, then shuffled off into the kitchen area. I relished my chance to stand alone, taking in the scene. At this time of day it was like being in a vast cavern. The only light came through the open front doors and from doorways leading out to the kitchens, but gradually my eyes became used to the darkness and I gaped at what I was seeing. Such elegance! The polished wood and the sparkling chandeliers, the potted palms, the soft plush of the booths, the doors to private rooms now enticingly open—this was how the other half lived all right. Someday I'd dine here myself, if I ever came up with a suitable escort. That was a bad afterthought. Immediately I pictured Daniel sitting in that corner booth with Miss Norton, and I made myself walk around examining the flower arrangements to stop any further thoughts from escaping.

"Yes, miss, may I help you?" The gray-haired man looked haggard and hollow-eyed, as if he hadn't been to sleep in a while.

"Sorry to disturb you. I know you must be busy." I handed him my card. "My senior partner was conducting an investigation on a couple who may have dined here in a private room last Monday night. I wondered if you keep a record of your customers."

He looked at me as if I'd suggested he show me his underwear. "Reveal the names of our customers? My dear young lady, it would be more than my job was worth."

Was that a hint that he wanted a bribe? It could be some of Paddy's money well spent. I regretted that I had been so modest with the amount I had allotted myself for expenses.

"If there is anything I could do to make you change your mind . . ." I wasn't sure how this bribery business worked. I opened my purse and went to reach inside.

"Not for all the tea in china," he said firmly.

"And would it compromise your job if you just happened to mention where I might find the reservation book and take a peek for myself?"

"My dear young—" he began again.

"Look, it's very important, or I wouldn't be here," I said. "My partner has been killed. I know he came here on Monday night."

"Your partner?" Did I detect a flicker of interest?

"He was—" I was about to say "conducting an investigation." I swallowed back the words at the last second. I didn't think this man would take kindly to the news that one of his waiters on Monday night had been a detective in disguise. "He was here to meet a business associate," I finished lamely. "And the business associate was with a young woman, in a private dining room, so I wondered . . ."

Mr. Carlo still shook his head firmly. "Our confidentiality is as golden as the seal of the confessional in the church. We have never divulged the name of a private customer and never will. Good day to you, miss. We open for luncheon in just over an hour."

So far my investigation techniques weren't exactly impressive. I left Delmonico's more subdued than I had entered it. I could come back, maybe, and attempt to squeeze more information out of the waiters. But then again, it might be more than their jobs were worth to divulge restaurant secrets. I couldn't even see myself sneaking back to take a peek at the reservation book. Maybe Riley had all this information down in his little black book. My next task should be to go to the library, or even to New York University, and find someone who could interpret the unknown language. That would have to wait until next week, however. I didn't think there were classes on Saturdays. So there probably wasn't too much more I could do until Monday—except to follow Paddy's route home.

Delmonico's is located on the corner of Twenty-sixth Street and Fifth Avenue. It was unlikely that Paddy would have spent money on a cab—I hadn't seen any evidence of his wasting money on anything—and it was too far to walk comfortably, which meant he had probably taken the Sixth Avenue elevated railway. I consulted my notes. His home address was a boardinghouse on

Barrow Street, a disreputable neighborhood down by the docks, according to his own description. I knew it was on the far west of the area they call Greenwich Village. I tried to picture the area in my mind. If he had taken the Sixth Avenue El, where would he have alighted? This would be crucial. Somewhere on that route home he had stopped off for a drink and overheard something so shattering that it may have brought about his death.

As I walked down Twenty-sixth Street toward the El station, I heard a clock on a nearby tower chiming eleven. This made me pause and think. I was already halfway to the high society areas of Upper Manhattan. My frugal upbringing reminded me that I should save the expense of an extra train ride whenever possible, even though I apparently had an endless supply of money to play with. Eleven o'clock might be just the sort of time when a man-about-town might be bestirring himself. If I were sensible, I'd go first to the Waldorf Astoria and interview the wayward English lord.

Thus I turned back and set off up Fifth Avenue. I knew where the Waldorf Astoria was. Daniel had pointed it out to me on one of our Sunday walks. "That's where the real nobs stay," he had told me. "It costs more to stay a week there than you could earn in a whole year."

I should never have thought of Sunday walks with Daniel. I reminded myself that M. Murphy, junior partner and business-woman, had better use her brain to come up with a plan of campaign for meeting Lord Edgemont.

I must tread carefully. I could be blundering into a murderer's den, although I didn't think so. I tried to analyze whether Lord Edgemont would make a likely killer. Not personally, of course. The young man who had punched me and leaped from the window in no way resembled the English aristocracy, as I had witnessed them in my childhood. But then men of Lord Edgemont's standing could afford to hire a killer to do their dirty work—if he needed to hire a killer, that was. I had been told he was in financial difficulties, which Miss Van Woekem hinted would bring the relationship with Kitty Le Grange to an end anyway. If his money ran out in New York, he'd have to go home to his wife and estate in England, so she'd get him back—if that was what she wanted.

So no real motive for murder there, even if she planned to drain his coffers to the last penny with alimony demands. Since working with Paddy I had come to learn that marriages among the rich were more like business deals and that some women became considerably richer by divorcing several husbands. What a strange world. When I married, it would only be for love.

I reached the imposing facade of the big hotel and stood on the sidewalk staring up at the high colonnade, collecting my thoughts before I tackled the doorman at the front door. Then I decided that nothing ventured was nothing gained. I was perfectly safe in a hotel, surely, when a cry could bring any number of servants running to my aid.

So I held my head erect and nodded to the doorman as I swept past him.

"I am afraid that Lord Edgemont does not reside here," I was told when I presented myself at the reception desk.

I felt this was a poor attempt to brush me aside and I wasn't about to be brushed. I tried my hand at an English accent, as I had heard it spoken by my aristocratic playmates. "Oh, but I have it on the best of authority that his lordship resides here at the moment. Is this establishment no longer to his liking?"

If a man could bristle, this one did. "This is the Waldorf madam. I believe you want the Astoria, next door."

"It's not the same hotel?"

"Oh no, madam. Two quite separate hotels, each owned by a member of the Astor family."

"You're telling me that two members of the same family run two different hotels in this building?"

He nodded. "Two separate hotels. The Astor cousins were not on speaking terms when the two hotels were built."

Well, if that didn't take the cake. I wondered if Daniel knew that interesting fact. Next time I saw him I'd have to—I mur-

mured my thanks to the man at the desk and went next door, where a matching glass door was opened by a matching grand doorman.

"Lord Edgemont?" the young man at the reception desk asked suspiciously. "May one inquire what this concerns?"

"Some business that the senior partner in my establishment was conducting with him. I wish merely to appraise him of the current status of the situation." Truly my way with words was improving by the minute. I was amazed at myself.

"I'm not sure if he is in occupation of his room at the present. Is he expecting you?"

"No. As I said. He was dealing with my senior partner, who is regrettably indisposed. But I have received an important communication from England and he may not wish to wait until Monday . . ."

That did the trick. "Very well, miss. I'll have one of our bell hops escort you up to his room. Frederick." He snapped his fingers and a young boy with hair as red as mine and a face so freckled that he looked like an orange sprung into action.

"Lord Edgemont?" He gave me a saucy grin as soon as we were out of the elevator and walking down the plushly carpeted hallway. "You don't seem his type."

"And you don't seem smart enough to hold a job for long if you make remarks like that to the customers," I replied, but with a smile.

"Go on," he said, "you're not a swell."

Obviously the two-dollar suit was not as expensive-looking as I had thought. I would have to observe and practice getting inside other characters, as Paddy had said. It was no use dressing like another person if you didn't feel like that other person inside. One little wrong gesture and the cover was blown. I still had a lot of learning to do. Too bad Paddy wouldn't be around to teach me.

The cheeky bellhop tapped on the polished wood door at the far end of the hallway. The man who opened it was not what I had been expecting. He was old, with a bald pate and wisps of white hair around it. He had the serene, innocent face of an elderly monk, not in any way that of a famous seducer.

"A young lady to discuss business with his lordship," the boy said jauntily.

The elderly man looked me up and down.

"His lordship is currently breakfasting," he said. "Does the young lady have an appointment?"

"No, but the matter is of the highest importance." This time I tried to think snooty thoughts as I spoke. I saw those apparently gentle old eyes sizing up that my costume was not of the finest Irish linen but of the thirty-nine-cent-a-yard variety of locally made broadcloth.

"Please wait here and I will inform his lordship." The elderly man bowed and disappeared, leaving us standing in the hallway. I heard a loud, hearty voice demand, "Who did you say it was, Carstairs?"

"A young woman, m'lord."

"Of our acquaintance?"

"I think not, m'lord."

"Pretty?"

"I would say so, although not your lordship's type."

I saw the boy beside me smirk. I gave him my newly acquired haughty stare. "I think you may go now," I said to him. "You'll be needed downstairs and I can find my own way down."

The boy looked at me doubtfully but went under the intensity of my gaze.

"Oh, bring her in, Carstairs," the hearty voice boomed. "A nice glimpse of ankle should liven up what has been a gloomy morning until now."

The door was opened. "His lordship will see you, Miss—"

"Murphy," I said.

He led me through an ornate sitting room with a large red plush sofa and two leather armchairs. The room beyond was a bedroom, thus a completely unsuitable place to receive a young lady, but it seemed his lordship didn't abide by the rules. He was sitting at a small table by the window with a silver salver before him, on which a single boiled egg sat in solitary splendor. His lordship was engrossed in dipping thin slices of bread and butter into a soft-boiled egg. He was instantly identifiable as an English gentleman—long, lanky, with a thin, lugubrious face, hooked nose and nondescript-color hair. He looked up when he saw me, appraised me for a second and nodded with approval.

"Miss Murphy, m'lord," Carstairs said.

"Ah, Miss Murphy, do take a seat. I'd offer you coffee, but they've only sent up one cup. But do feel free to join in the egg-dipping, should hunger strike." Carstairs pulled out the chair opposite for me and I perched at the edge of it.

"I always start the day with my boiled egg and fingers. Nanny thought I had a delicate stomach, y'know. She used to call them soldiers." He waved one of the thin strips of bread at me before dunking it in the yolk and popping it into his mouth. "To what do I owe this delightful visit?"

"A small matter of business, m'lord. And I'm sorry to trouble you on a Saturday morning, but I wanted you to be apprised of a delicate situation."

"Oh, weally?" I noticed he didn't pronounce his *R*'s correctly. "Of what delicate situation are we speaking?" He dipped another finger of bread and butter into his egg.

"I have just taken over the running of a small business, m'lord—"

"If it's money that's owed you, then you'll have to wait like everybody else." He looked up defiantly.

"I assure you it's nothing to do with money, m'lord. As I said, I have just taken over this small business, owing to the sad demise of the senior partner. On going through our books, I find that one of our clients is your wife, the Lady Clarissa."

"Good lord. Clarissa? What on earth does she want?"

"A divorce, it would seem. I thought you should know."

He looked startled for a moment, then burst into laughter. "Oh, she's playing that game again, is she? Stupid female."

"Again?" I asked.

"She does it every time I stay away too long. Doesn't really want a divorce, of course. She only married me for the title. If the divorce went through, she'd be back to being plain old Aggie Sugg—which was her name before she went on the music hall stage—and that wouldn't suit her at all. So don't worry your pretty little head, my dear. I'll send her a telegram promising to come home like a good boy on the next boat, and all will be forgiven." He leaned confidentially toward me. "Between the two of us, I rather fear that I've outstayed my welcome in New York. Too many creditors knocking on the door, if you know what I mean."

"So we may consider your case closed and not proceed any further with it?" I got to my feet.

"Oh, absolutely. I'm running home to Nanny to be a good boy again." He gave me an endearing grin.

"May I ask your lordship one small question, if you don't think it impertinent of me?" He nodded and wiped egg from his chin with a large damask napkin.

"Would your lordship confirm, confidentially, of course, that you were in a private dining room at Delmonico's with Miss Kitty Le Grange on Monday last?"

The genial countenance changed. He got to his feet too. He was tall—at least six feet—and he towered over me. "What the devil do you want? Blackmail, is that what it's all about? Because you've come to the wrong place if it is. For one thing, I have no funds to pay you and for another, my recent dalliance with Miss Le Grange is common knowledge among the gossipmongers of New York."

"I assure you that I am not a blackmailer," I said. "I came here to spare you embarrassment, not to cause it."

"Then what in blazes do you want?" He was still rattled.

"I am merely trying to put together the pieces of a puzzle that is only coincidentally to do with you and Miss Le Grange. My senior partner went to observe a couple in a private dining room last Monday. Something significant happened to him after he left.

So if I knew you were the couple seen at Delmonico's, it would be a great help."

He ran his hand through his thinning hair. "I can't wemember if we were actually there on Monday night, but it is a place we frequently dine together. So let's assume that we were there. Then what?"

"Then one piece of my puzzle falls into place. I am so sorry to have troubled you, m'lord. I thank you for granting me the interview."

"Oh, not at all. The pleasure was entirely mine." He gave a stiff little bow. "Carstairs will show you out."

As I descended in the elevator I decided that I could cross Lord Edgemont off my list of suspects. He had no motive to kill. He was right: his dalliance with Miss Kitty Le Grange was well-known among New York society. He had run through his money and was about to retreat back to England with his tail between his legs. So nothing Paddy Riley could have discovered would have been a matter of life or death to him—unless, of course, he was a good actor and there was something that I, the bumbling newcomer, had not managed to uncover. Too late now, I decided as the elevator opened on the ground floor and the operator slid back the folding ironwork door for me. I had put my cards on the table. It was now up to Lord Edgemont to make the next move.

❧ Thirteen ❧

I walked down Thirty-fourth Street to the El station, climbed
the steps and waited on the platform. It was almost deserted at
this late-morning hour, in contrast to the jostling crowds at the
stations of Lower Manhattan. Most people here would not deign
to take the El. Either they had carriages of their own, or they took
a hansom. Apart from me and an elderly gentleman half hidden
behind *The New York Times*, there were a couple of ladies in smart
silk outfits, parasols open against the sun, probably traveling
downtown to the Ladies' Mile and a spot of Saturday shopping.
The platform vibrated, announcing the arrival of a train, and it
came into view, gliding effortlessly into the station. The Sixth
Avenue line was one of the few that had switched to electric loco-
motives that year. What a wonderful invention, indeed. No longer
were passengers to be blackened by soot from the engine as they
rode or pedestrians to be peppered with hot coals as they stood
on the sidewalks beneath the rails.

I climbed in and we headed south. To tell the truth, I always
feel uncomfortable riding in the El. Such intimate glimpses into
other people's lives as the train passes second-floor windows. In
one house a child was sitting on a chamber pot, in another, a
mother was breast-feeding her baby. Neither looked up as the
train rattled past. But it started me thinking again—what exactly
had Paddy said to me when I had come in on him to find him

1 1 1

scribbling in his black book? Not at Delmonico's. Later. Was it possible that he had witnessed something in a lighted window from this very train? No, I was sure that he had said it was a tavern and that it was something he had overheard rather than seen.

I alighted at Jefferson Market, just to the north of Washington Square and Greenwich Village. This would have been the first possible station that Paddy could have left the train. I came down the steps to find the Saturday-morning market in full swing. A woman passed me holding a live chicken, which flapped and squawked in protest. A man wheeled a barrow of oranges and bananas. Such luxuries to be bought for pennies! Back home in Ireland, oranges were a treat in the Christmas stocking and bananas such a novelty that most of us had never seen one!

I passed the market, lifting my new skirts to avoid the debris in the street, and stood on the corner trying to work out which route Paddy would have taken to his home. It appeared that Christopher Street would be the straightest shot at the docks, although it was hard to tell. Unlike the rest of New York City, where avenues ran from north to south and streets from east to west, this little section south of the Washington Square Arch was a higgledy-piggledy mess. Alleys and narrow backstreets went off in all directions. And every one, it seemed, contained some kind of tavern or café. I would just have to be methodical and explore them one by one.

At that moment a bell began to toll above my head. I thought it must be ringing the hour until a voice behind me commented, "Six strokes. That will be Bleecker Street then."

Before I could turn to ask what his cryptic remark meant, a fire truck burst forth from somewhere in the market complex, scattering crowds with pounding hooves and clanging bells.

After it had disappeared, I set off in an attempt to crisscross the area, first down Sixth Avenue, until I struck Fourth Street. This should take me straight across to the Hudson, I thought. I kept walking with no river in sight until the position of the sun told me

I was heading due north. I had come across the one numbered street in New York that did not play by the rules.

Not that I was in a panic, as I might have been about becoming lost in certain areas of the city. This was all rather quiet and tranquil, with sidewalk cafés, bakeries and houses that looked as if they had been built in other cities and carted to New York. There were no faceless rows here. Every house had its own character, from wrought-iron balconies reminiscent of the South to severe New England clapboard. And between and behind the streets were narrow back alleys, likewise filled with dwellings. It was definitely an area worth exploring, but most frustrating for my present quest. How was I to guess which of those narrow backstreets might contain the very tavern where Riley had sat that night?

I gave up on the search and decided it would make more sense to locate his boardinghouse first, then work backward from there. Maybe his landlady and other tenants could give me more information on his drinking habits. I kept going until, by sheer luck, I stumbled across Barrow Street and followed it westward to the Hudson River. It, too, wound around and it was several long blocks before the salty tang in the air announced that my quest was nearing an end.

The boardinghouse was most unprepossessing, in fact not the kind of place I would have entered willingly. As I approached the front door, a sailor exited with a brightly painted girl on his arm, making me double-check on the house number. Mrs. O'Shaunessey's, Riley had said, and there was the name on a faded wooden sign above the front door. O'SHAUNESSEY'S BOARDINGHOUSE. WEEKLY AND MONTHLY RATES. I rang the doorbell and waited. The door was opened by a large, untidy-looking woman with a dirty dish towel in her hands. "Yes?" she demanded sharply.

"Are you Mrs. O'Shaunessey?" I asked politely.

"And who wants to know?"

"I understand that Mr. Paddy Riley used to live here," I said.

"He did. God rest his poor soul." She crossed herself, the dish towel still in her hand.

"I'm Molly Murphy." I held out my hand, even though I wasn't too keen on touching her wet and greasy one. "I used to work for Paddy. I wonder if I might have a word with you."

"I'm doing the washing-up from breakfast," she said. "I got behindhand today. Had to call in the police to get a drunken layabout evicted, but you can come in if you want." She led me down a narrow dark hallway that smelled of boiled cabbage and drains and into a dark, dank kitchen beyond.

"So what sort of work was it you were doing for Mr. Riley?" she asked, picking up a large saucepan to dry.

"I was his business associate. He was training me."

"You? A young woman?" She laughed uneasily. "I thought he couldn't stand the sight of women. Me excepted, of course."

"I understand he thought very highly of you."

The stern expression softened. "He did indeed. I always took good care of him—I did his laundry and cooked his breakfast every day. Kept his room clean for him. He told me he never remembered his own mother, but I was as close as he'd ever come to having a mother look after him."

"So he was with you for a long time then?"

She sucked through her teeth. "Must be at least twenty-five years. I was a young woman and Mr. O'Shaunessey was working on the docks when he first came to us. Himself has been long departed, God rest his soul."

"Mr. Riley also thought highly of me, as I did of him." I paused, wondering which tack was best to take. "The police are looking into his murder, of course. I take it they've been round here."

"Yes, some young whippersnapper demanded to search the place. I don't know what he was looking for, but he didn't find nothing. Only stayed a couple of minutes. He told me to touch nothing in Paddy's room because they might be back, but when— that's what I'd like to know. I'd like to get his stuff cleared out of there, so that I can rent out the room again."

So much for Paddy's substitute mother.

"I presume he paid his rent through to the end of the month?" I couldn't help inquiring.

"Always paid up regular. A real gentleman."

"So the room is officially his until the end of the month anyway."

She gave me a strange sideways look, as if I were a sweet puppy that had just bitten her. "That's right, I suppose," she admitted. "But it's going to take time for me to clear out his things."

"I'll be happy to come over and help you, when the police give you permission," I said. "And if you don't mind, I'd like to take a look at his room now."

"What for?"

"Now that I'm left alone to run the business, there are certain papers I can't find at his office," I said. "I just wondered if he'd left them here. Things like bills I am supposed to pay."

"I don't recall seeing any papers, but you're welcome to take a look if you like. I just need to do the last of this washing-up, then I'll take you there."

I offered to help, was rejected and waited until the last pot had been hung on the hook over the stove. Then I followed Mrs. O'Shaunessey as she huffed and puffed her way up the narrow staircase. Paddy's room was as dark and depressing as the kitchen had been. The window opened onto a narrow courtyard. It was over-furnished with a heavy wardrobe and a chest of drawers that took up most of one wall. There was also a small desk against the far wall and a single bed, unmade and untidy. I stood there, looking around, trying to take in the fact that Paddy had chosen to stay in this place for more than twenty years, when he could have afforded better. Maybe his bond with Mrs. O'Shaunessey was real. Maybe—I allowed myself to go further—there had been some mutual comforting going on, Mr. O'Shaunessey being dead these many years now, God rest his soul. Otherwise I saw no reason for him to stay.

As I started to examine the room in detail, something else struck me. There was nothing personal in this room at all—no photos, no mementoes, not even a picture on the wall. Paddy Riley had lived in that room for more than twenty years and not bothered to put his mark of identity into it. At that moment it finally hit me that this had been a person who really was alone in the world. No ties, no family, nothing. And on the heels of that thought came a second. This case will not warrant a proper investigation. There is nobody who will make sure justice is served, unless I do it.

I opened drawers aimlessly. The first one contained neatly arranged pairs of socks, the second neatly stacked underwear. Since Paddy himself was obviously not a neat person, the drawers must have been arranged by Mrs. O'Shaunessey—which would account for why he had hidden his savings at his office.

"Not found any papers yet, have you?" she asked, eyeing me suspiciously as I closed a drawer that obviously could not have been expected to contain papers.

"Not yet," I said. "Tell me—you must have a pretty good idea of what Paddy kept in here—" Bad mistake. She bristled. "If you think I have time to go snooping through my guests' belongings . . ."

"Oh, I wasn't implying that at all, Mrs. O'Shaunessey. I merely meant that you did his laundry, so you'd obviously be in and out of this room with piles of washing."

"Well, yes. I'd be in and out all the time. And I tried to keep his clothing neat as best I could. Not the tidiest of gentlemen."

"You should have seen the mess at the office when I first arrived." I smiled like a fellow conspirator. "Took me a full week to get the papers in order. So I wondered if you could tell me if the police actually found anything of importance here and took it away with them?"

She considered, then shook her head. "I can't think that they did. You know, the young officer was only here a few minutes and I'd swear he wasn't carrying anything when he left."

"So there is nothing missing? This is how his room always looked?"

"Except that I usually made the bed when I had a chance. But the policeman said to leave everything exactly as it was, so I did."

I went through the desk. There was a new roll of film in one drawer, plus some packets of negatives. I'd take those when I could. No sign of the camera, though. And not much else of interest. A receipt from a cleaner's, an out-of-date calendar, some postcards and a map of Manhattan, which I'd also appropriate.

I closed the desk and went over to the wardrobe, feeling Mrs. O'Shaunessey's eyes boring into my back. A good dark suit, a heavy winter coat and several items that must have been for disguises—a long flowing cape, a top hat. I lifted a box down from the top shelf and found it to contain wigs and makeup. I'd have to make sure I got my hands on that when the room was finally cleaned out.

I closed the wardrobe again and handed Mrs. O'Shaunessey my card. "Please send someone round to let me know when the police say you can clean out the room. I'll come and give you a hand. It's too much work for one person. Some of this stuff, like the wigs and makeup, really belongs at the office, but I should think there's probably some items here that you could sell—make yourself a bit of extra money."

She was as readable as a book. "Mercy me, I'd never thought of that. Happen you're right." She looked pink and pleased.

"Did Mr. Riley have many visitors?" I asked as we descended the stairs again.

"Visitors? I can't say I ever recall visitors. A private person, Mr. Riley was. Kept himself to himself. Only lived for his work, didn't he?"

"He seemed to. Such a sad life."

"Yes, I suppose you could say that."

We reached the ground floor. "So you don't happen to know if there was anywhere he met up with friends—a particular tavern he liked?"

"Mr. Riley was not what you'd call a heavy drinker," she said firmly. "He liked the occasional tot, though. I believe he stopped off at O'Connor's on the way home from time to time."

"O'Connor's?" My heart beat faster. "And where would that be?"

"Oh, just around the block. Corner of Greenwich and Christopher."

"You wouldn't happen to remember if he told you he stopped off at O'Connor's two nights before he was killed?"

She shook her head. "He came in very late, both that night and the last night of his life. I was already in bed when I heard his key in the lock. I called out, 'Is that you, Mr. Riley?' and he said it was."

"Did he sound quite—normal?"

"If you mean was he drunk, Mr. Riley hardly ever overindulged. But, now that you mention it, he was quite short with me that first night. Usually we had a pleasant little exchange as he passed my room on the stairs. But that night I called out, 'Is that you, Mr. Riley?' and he said, 'What? Oh, yes. Yes, it's me.' And that's all he said. No good night. No nothing. And that was unusual for him. Always had good manners around me, Mr. Riley did."

I opened the front door. "Thank you, Mrs. O'Shaunessey. You've been most helpful. I'll look forward to coming to give you a hand getting that room cleaned out, so that you can relet it as quickly as possible."

"Most kind, my dear. I'd appreciate that."

I left her waving after me in a most motherly fashion. I was learning, slowly but surely, how to keep my mouth from running away with me!

I came to the end of the block and turned left, up Greenwich Street. Another elevated track ran along it and the noise of a train, rumbling overhead, drowned out the city noises beneath. I passed storefronts until I came to O'Connor's saloon on the corner. Even at midday it sounded pretty lively inside. I hesitated on the threshold. No woman of any reputation would go into a tavern alone. The last time I had tried it, seeking information, I had been subjected to ribald comments and forced to deliver a few kicks to the shins before I made my getaway. I wasn't anxious to go through that again. I steeled myself, wishing that I had a spare hatpin about my person for defense, and went in. The fug of smoke made it difficult to see in a poorly lit room, but I could make out groups sitting around several of the tables.

Two young men, interestingly attired in student garb—one in an Oriental smoking jacket, the other in a peasant smock—were being served at the bar. I waited patiently in the shadow for them to be served before approaching the landlord. As I stood there, a voice to my right exclaimed, "But darling, I thought you knew all the time it was I!" and the group around him burst into noisy laughter.

I looked across to see the same beautiful young man I had noticed in Washington Square.

❧ Fourteen ❧

Paddy Riley?" The genial smile faded from the landlord's
face in response to my question. He had heard the news of
Mr. Riley's demise—such a shame. Of course he had been
a regular. He visited the tavern most evenings for a shot of Irish
whiskey. Always the one drink, though. Sometimes he sat with
other customers, sometimes alone. I tried to take his mind back to
Monday last, but he shook his head. "Every day's pretty much like
another. As you can see, we're a popular place, especially with the
young crowd these days. We're always run off our feet until closing time. No chance to notice who is here and who isn't."

I asked about Paddy's friends and acquaintances, but again he
shook his head. "He chatted with other regulars. Just generally
joined in the conversation, if you know what I mean. There was
nobody you'd say was his special crony."

That pretty much summed up Paddy's life.

"Did he sometimes come here in one of his disguises?" I asked.

"I suppose he might have done." Quite the most unobservant
landlord in New York City.

"He would have been dressed as a waiter, last Monday night."

The landlord pursed his lips in concentration. "He might
have done. But again, Mr. Riley wasn't one to draw attention to
himself."

"And you didn't happen to notice anyone special in here when

Mr. Riley came in dressed as a waiter? No unusual people who might have upset Mr. Riley?"

He shook his head. "I'd have noticed any kind of upset. I don't allow any fighting. Look, miss. Like I say, we always get a good crowd. It's noisy, but there's no harm in it, if you get my meaning. Rarely have to throw anyone out."

I glanced back at the table where the beautiful young man was holding court, waving his hands in the air while he described something and those around him howled with laughter. I was interested to see that the table contained both men and women. This was unusual in itself. The tavern was normally the province of men, and yet Mr. Riley, the famous woman hater, had chosen this one to take his evening drink.

"I see you allow women to drink with men in here," I commented.

"Oh, yes. It's only recently, since all the artists and intellectuals started moving into the area. Only a certain type of young woman, mind you. No painted hussies off the streets. The ones we get are very respectable—regular bluestockings, most of 'em."

I made the mistake of glancing around again and caught the beautiful young man's eye. To my mortification, he winked. As winks go, it was wonderful—as if we two alone were sharing a private joke. But I found myself blushing like a schoolgirl and hastily turned away.

I leaned across to the bartender. "That man. The one at the table in the corner who is talking so loudly. Who is he?"

The landlord laughed. "You must be the one person in New York who doesn't know him. That's Ryan O'Hare, the playwright. One of your countrymen. Surely you've heard of him?"

Not wanting to appear a fool, I replied, "Ryan O'Hare. Of course."

"He comes in here quite often when he's in the Village. They say he has a play opening at the Daley Theater—it was to have been the Victoria, but he thought that would have been a bad omen, considering . . ."

"Considering what?"

"Why—the reason he left England, of course." He looked at me as if I was stupid and I didn't like to question him further. If Mr. Ryan O'Hare was as famous as indicated, I could find out everything I needed to know about him in the back editions of the New York newspapers. I added that mentally to the list of things to do at the library on Monday.

Like all good Christians, I observed Sunday as a day of rest. The fact that I couldn't proceed with any of my investigations on a Sunday also had something to do with it. I could visit neither of Paddy's outstanding cases until Monday morning. A long weekend stretched ahead of me, with no Sunday strolls in the park to look forward to. Before Seamus's accident I had always accompanied the little family to mass, even though I wasn't the most religious person in the world.

On this particular Sunday I had planned to take the two little ones to church in their father's absence, then maybe out for an ice cream. Those plans were thwarted when I arrived home on Saturday afternoon to find bedlam reigning in my own room. Shamey and Bridie were there, as were their three boy cousins, Malachy, Thomas and James, and they were leaping over my furniture with feathers stuck in their hair.

"Jesus, Mary and Joseph! What's going on here!" I clapped my hands and the children froze.

"We're playing red Indians," Bridie said, giving me her most innocent smile. "Aunty Nuala plucked a chicken and there were feathers."

"If you want to run around like savages, you go outside and find the nearest park," I said, wagging a stern finger at them. "You know better than to play that kind of game indoors, and especially in my room."

"Sorry, Molly." Shameyboy tried an endearing smile.

As they shuffled out, I heard one of Nuala's boys mutter, "She's going to be a right old tartar, isn't she? Is she like that all the time?"

I smiled to myself as I straightened up my bedclothes and the pillows that had fallen to the floor. I had just taken off my new costume jacket and was hanging it on the peg when my door burst open and Nuala herself came in. "You've heard the terrible news then?" she demanded.

"I thought I told you to knock first," I said, glad that she hadn't come in two minutes later and thus caught me in my undergarments. "What terrible news? It's not Seamus, is it? He's not taken a turn for the worse?"

"Seamus is on the mend, thank the Blessed Mother and all the saints. He'll be up and walking again in a week or so. No, 'tis Finbar and myself that have suffered misfortune. With me not around to keep an eye on them, things went from bad to worse. The long and short of it is that Finbar lost his job at the saloon, lazy no-good bag of bones that he is, and the boys were up to such mischief that we've been thrown out of our apartment."

"Dear me. That's terrible. I hope you've found a new place."

She gave me a sly, sideways look. "What with looking after our poor cousin being such a full-time job, I'll not have a chance to go looking, and anyway, Seamus has graciously agreed that we can move in with him for the moment, until he's on his feet and Finbar finds himself new employment."

"All of you? In that one room?" I demanded. "Mrs. O'Hallaran would never agree."

"Oh, but she has agreed. I spoke to her myself. We're fellow Irishwomen. We understand each other. She told me I was a saint, giving up my own thoughts of happiness to nurse my sick cousin. And she knows it will only be for a while. Just until things straighten themselves out again."

What could I say? It was, after all, not my house, even though I had rented the top floor and invited Seamus and the little ones to join me. I could hardly go down to Mrs. O'Hallaran and demand that she not let Nuala, Finbar and the three horrors move in without seeming unfeeling and hard-hearted.

"So I'll be keeping Young Seamus and Bridie with me a while longer then?"

"And I thought I'd move in here too," she said, giving me what passed for a friendly smile. "Then we can have one room for girls and one for boys. It's up to young Seamus which one he chooses. Maybe he'd rather stay with his sister and you."

"I'll try to make you as welcome as you made me," I replied smoothly and she got my meaning.

"It won't be for long," she said. "With the good food you've been buying, we'll have Seamus back on his feet and working again in no time at all."

The smile she gave me was one of triumph as she closed the door behind her. I stood in my own room wanting to hit somebody, so frustrated was I feeling. I had little doubt that she had been working up to this the moment she set eyes on the place. And I knew it wasn't going to be easy getting rid of her again. I just had to pray that her boys would drive Mrs. O'Hallaran crazy within the week.

So Sunday was not the day of rest I had contemplated, nor could I look forward to my usual Sunday outing with the children. Nuala announced that she and Finbar would be taking the children to mass and I could come along if I'd a mind to. I hadn't a mind to go anywhere with Nuala. I made myself a sandwich and took the train all the way out to Coney Island. So, it seemed, did the rest of New York City. The car was packed with screaming children, laughing young couples and shouting Italians. By the time I got there, any hope of solitude was dashed. The beach was so full it was hard to see the sand between the people. I wandered around, listening to the screams from the Steeplechase Amusement Park on the boardwalk, where riders on mechanical horses were whisked around a racetrack high in the air, and then beaten with paddles by waiting clowns when they descended again. What strange things people will pay money for.

In the end the temptation of the ocean was too much for me. I knew I shouldn't be spending Paddy's money on things for myself, but it was only ten cents to rent a bathing suit and use the changing facilities. The suit was heavy serge with so many frills that I looked like a giant chicken, but the first feel of the cold Atlantic on my toes made it all worth it. There were ropes extending out into the waves. I held on, just as a precaution. I'd never needed ropes to swim out through the waves at home, but then I hadn't been wearing a hundred-pound monstrosity of a garment. Then I was out at the end of the rope, farther than anyone but the strong male swimmers. I struck out and started to swim. Waves broke over my face and I felt the joy of being propelled forward with strong kicks. I turned on my back and floated, shutting out the whole world but the blue sky and white clouds above me.

"Are you all right, miss?" An arm grabbed me and I turned to see a young man in lifeguard's red and white stripes beside me.

"I'm just fine. Thank you. Floating and looking at the sky."

"Only you're awfully far out, for a woman."

"Thank you for your concern, but I can swim as well as you can. I'll race you into shore if you want." I gave him a challenging smile.

"All right. Ready. Go."

We both struck out for the shore with powerful strokes. He beat me, but not by much. "You're a grand swimmer," he said, helping me to my feet among the waves. "If you hadn't been hampered by the swimsuit, it would have been level pegging. Too bad you're not a man. We could use more lifeguards on the beach."

"As you say, too bad I'm not a man."

He smiled, looked at me, went to say something, then shrugged his shoulders. "Nice meeting you, then," he muttered and walked away.

Had he been about to ask me for a date? At any rate, the encounter had made me feel good. There were plenty of young men in the world just waiting to meet me. The swim had felt good too, although the looks of horror I got from the other young ladies when they saw my wet, bedraggled hair almost made me laugh.

I returned home rejuvenated, refreshed and ready to tackle Monday's problems and a houseful of children. I wasn't so confident about tackling Nuala.

❧ Fifteen ❧

On Monday morning I dressed with care in my new business suit and added my boater with its new brown ribbon. This would be an important day for me. By the end of it I might be one step closer to solving Paddy Riley's murder. I would also have to tread very carefully. One of the people I was going to interview today might be desperate enough to kill again.

There was no point in visiting either Angus MacDonald or his wife Elizabeth before ten o'clock. The upper classes were notoriously late risers. So my first call was to Berger and DeBose, importers and exporters of fine foods and wines. Their office was in a tall brick warehouse building along the Hudson River. It was an overcast morning, with the promise of rain later and I had walked instead of taking the elevated. I needed a clear head for my encounters today. I knew I must convey no hint of suspicion in any of my conversations. I must be the innocent newcomer, trying to clear up the odds and ends left by my former partner. I need not even give away that Paddy was dead, if they didn't already know.

I presented my card to a skinny youth who returned to escort me to an inner sanctum where a large, bewiskered man rose to his feet and introduced himself as Mr. DeBose. "Miss Murphy?" The tone was not friendly.

"Mr. DeBose. I am the new junior partner in the firm of

P. Riley Associates. My senior partner being indisposed, I am trying to tie up the loose ends in his current cases. I saw your name in our files and came to see if I could be of any assistance."

"You're too damned late, aren't you?" Mr. DeBose's flabby cheeks puffed out like red balloons. "Tell your confounded senior partner that if he'd been doing his job when I asked him to, he might have caught young Hofmeister before he skipped off to South America with my money."

"When was this?"

"When was it? Friday a week ago, that's when it was. He went to put the weekly takings in the bank and never came back. We found out from the police that he had passage booked on a liner sailing to Montevideo on Friday night. Of course we only found out he was missing on Monday morning, and by then it was too late, damn him."

"So he was the one who had been cheating you?"

"Cheating us? I should say cheating was an understatement. Robbing us blind, madam. That's what young Hofmeister was doing. We had no idea of the scope of it when we called in your Mr. Riley. Now it turns out the young scoundrel was billing us for fictitious clients, creating fictitious inventories, and all of it going into Hofmeister's pocket. So what has your man got to say for himself, eh? Why did he take on the commission if he was going to sit on his fat behind and do nothing, eh?"

"I'm sorry to tell you that Mr. Riley is dead," I said quietly.

"Well, I'll be—" he muttered. "My condolences, of course. Had he been ailing for a while or was he taken sudden?"

"He was killed, Mr. DeBose. Brutally murdered."

He turned white now. Truly he had a most expressive face. "Well, that is another kettle of fish, isn't it? I hope they've caught the scoundrel."

"They will, Mr. DeBose. I'm confident of that. So I'll bid you good day. Since no work was apparently done on your case, there will, of course, be no bill."

He nodded. "Much obliged."

130

"My condolences on your dishonest employee. It must be a hard loss to bear."

"You can say that again, Miss Murphy. A hard loss indeed. And not just financial. It's a question of trust, isn't it? Now we won't be so anxious to trust our employees again, I can tell you that."

He held out a meaty hand. "Thank you for stopping by."

Another suspect to cross off my list. The wicked Mr. Hofmeister was already on his way to South America when Paddy was still alive and well.

Which left me with the MacDonalds. Angus was the only son of a very rich man who was also a puritan. If Paddy had uncovered some kind of wayward behavior that would incur his father's wrath, maybe even lead to disinheritance, then he might have resorted to murder. My first true motive. And he had the funds to pay for a hired killer too. I must be careful not to expose myself to danger.

I decided to start with Mrs. MacDonald, the client who had hired Paddy Riley. It would be only natural that I should pay a call on her, to apprise her of the situation. So I took the Broadway streetcar to Central Park and then walked beside the park, trying to concentrate on my mission and not be reminded of happier times spent among those shady boulevards. I had been surprised to discover that the MacDonalds—millionaires or at least future millionaires—lived in an apartment house. Surprised, that is, until I saw the Dakota Building for myself. The street was lined with impressive turreted buildings, rivaling European castles in their grandeur, and the Dakota, taking up a whole block at Seventy-second Street, was the grandest of them all.

I was admitted to a lavish foyer by a doorman dripping in gold braid, looking like a European prince. "I will inquire whether Mrs. MacDonald is at home," he said, taking my card. "Please take a seat." He motioned to an armchair among the potted palms and disappeared into a small office room.

I sat there admiring the scenery until he returned. "Mrs. Mac-

Donald will see you. Ask the elevator operator for the eighth floor. You will see the front door straight ahead of you."

The elevator glided effortlessly upward. The operator opened the door and I stepped out into a thickly carpeted hallway. Before me were grand double doors. Looking up and down the hall, I realized that this was the only apartment on the eighth floor. Before I could knock, the door was opened by a maid and I was admitted to a magnificent living room with windows overlooking Central Park. The furnishings were ivory and gilt and the whole effect was one of lightness and space. A slim and fragile-looking woman was reclining on a day bed, a half-finished breakfast tray beside her, reminding me that the upper classes began their days much later than the rest of us.

She looked up, her face alight with anticipation. "You come from Mr. Riley? He has news for me?"

"I'm afraid I have bad news, Mrs. MacDonald. Mr. Riley died last week. I wanted to inform his current clients as quickly as possible, so that they could take appropriate measures."

Her face fell. "I am sorry to hear about Mr. Riley," she said. "Really, his death is most inconvenient. Do you know if he had almost completed his work for me?"

"I'm afraid I have no idea."

"He had procured no evidence then?"

"I'm afraid I have no way of knowing that, Mr. Riley did not discuss his cases with anyone. He observed a strict code of confidentiality with his clients."

"This is most annoying," she said again. "I had hoped to nip this in the bud. I've put up with Angus and his unsuitable relationships for long enough. But this one has gone too far. I'm doing this for his sake as well as my own, you know. There is the family name to think of. His father would be appalled."

I said nothing. She looked up at me sharply. "It is strange that Mr. Riley didn't keep his partner informed. Wait a minute. You're not working for one of those muck-raking newspapers, are you?

This wouldn't be the first time I've had newspaper reporters trying to worm their way in here under various guises."

"I assure you, Mrs. MacDonald, that I am not a newspaper reporter. I am merely trying to do what Mr. Riley would have wanted of me."

Her face had become a mask. "Well, thank you for calling. My condolences about Mr. Riley."

She waved me away with a languid hand.

I wasn't as good at this as I had hoped, I thought as I rode down in the elevator. If only I could have thought of the right things to say, asked the right questions; she had been on the verge of telling me everything. She may even have known the name of Angus's unsuitable relationship. But at least I still had the motive—she had been planning to tell Angus's father. I would have to tread cautiously when I went to see Angus.

I had learned from the file that Mr. Angus MacDonald had an office in the financial district on Wall Street, in a building owned by his father. I traveled south again on the El and spent some moments brushing off the dust of travel, making myself presentable before I approached that marble edifice, the MacDonald Building. I was told by his secretary that Mr. MacDonald was in a meeting and couldn't see me. I asked when a good time might be and the answer implied never. At that I decided I had been humble and polite long enough. I asked for a piece of paper, wrote a note and asked the secretary to take it to Mr. MacDonald right away.

This he did, and it wasn't long before I was shown into Angus's office. He was an attractive young man, slim, dark-haired with the same languid grace as his wife. He rose to his feet as I came in.

"Miss Murphy? I understand that you have something of a most confidential nature to discuss with me—concerning the well-being of my family?"

I nodded. "It is of a most delicate nature, Mr. MacDonald. I should prefer it if . . ." I glanced at the secretary. Angus waved at him. "Thank you, Biggs, that will be all."

Angus indicated a leather chair and I sat. "Please proceed. I am most intrigued."

"I'm not sure if you know this, Mr. MacDonald, but your wife is gathering evidence to divorce you."

The reaction was not what I expected. He looked, if anything, rather amused. "Elizabeth is planning to divorce me? And how do you happen to know this, Miss Murphy?"

"Your wife had hired a private investigator—a Mr. Riley. He unfortunately died last week. I was brought in to go through the contents of his office and to box everything up so that it could be let to a new tenant." I had decided on the journey to Wall Street that it might be wise, for the purposes of this interview and my own safety, not to appear too closely linked to Paddy. "Your wife appears to be one of his current clients."

"So why, exactly, did you come to see me?"

"To warn you, of course."

"Very charitable of you." The smile indicated otherwise. "Not hoping to make a little on the side? You haven't found some delicious scrap of incriminating evidence that you'd like me to have, for a price?"

"I found no evidence," I said coldly. "And I have no personal interest in the matter, sir. I'm just trying to tie up loose ends. I understand that your father is a man of the highest principles and I thought you might want to take steps so that no hint of scandal reached him."

"Then I suppose I am in your debt," he said. "There are, indeed, aspects of my lifestyle of which my father wouldn't approve. But why Elizabeth had to go to the trouble of hiring a private investigator I have no idea. If she had asked me for a divorce, I would willingly have given her one. It wasn't as if we were ever very compatible. We were chosen for each other as a suitable match before either of us was old enough to know better. I'd be quite happy to set us both free."

"But your father," I blurted out. "Surely he wouldn't approve of a divorce?'

Angus smiled. "Oh, the old man would rant and rave for a bit, but he'd get over it. To tell you the truth, he never really took to Elizabeth. He didn't approve of her spending habits, and she has failed so far to produce an heir." He got up and extended his hand to me. "Thank you for taking the time to come here, Miss Murphy. Now, if you will excuse me, I'm supposed to be working. My father is constantly badgering me to improve my work habits and I suppose I should be seen to be making progress in one area of my miserable life."

He leaped ahead of me to the door and opened it. "Goodbye," he said.

I stepped out onto the street to find that the promised rain had begun. A solid downpour, with the rumble of thunder in the distance. I had no umbrella with me and did not wish to ruin my new business suit by getting drenched. So I moved to a pillared overhang of the next-door bank and waited, hopefully, for the storm to pass. I hadn't been standing there long when a figure sprinted out of the MacDonald Building, climbed into a waiting automobile and drove away. Even with an overcoat on and the collar turned up, I recognized Angus MacDonald. And as he drove away, I considered something else. Angus MacDonald was dark-haired, lithe, and moved with considerable grace.

❧ Sixteen ❧

The downpour continued unabated, giving me considerable time to ponder what I had just seen. Could Angus Mac-Donald really have been the young man who leaped from Riley's window? It was hard to believe—he was the son of a millionaire. Why would he need to do his own dirty work when a hired killer would be well within his means and readily available in a city as large as New York? Then a second question arose: Why would Angus MacDonald need to kill? The news of the impending divorce suit did not seem to cause him any alarm. Indeed he had expressed surprise at the trouble his wife was going to when he would have willingly granted her wish for a divorce. He didn't even seem alarmed at the thought of his father finding out.

As I stood, watching the rain get heavier by the minute, I had to admit that my efforts in the field of detective work so far had been far from stellar. I had followed up on the only three cases that Paddy appeared to have been working on, and I had met three dead ends. Lord Edgemont was about to go home to his wife in England, the embezzler at the import company had already absconded with the kitty before Paddy was killed, and Angus MacDonald seemed rather relieved that his wife wanted to break up their marriage. Either these cases had nothing to do with Paddy's death, or I was not skilled enough to have asked the right questions. I was frustrated at my own lack of skill. If only Paddy had stayed alive a little longer, I could have learned so much from him. Now I wasn't sure that I had the potential to be an investigator. If I couldn't solve this case, then I had better think about a rapid change of profession.

A hansom cab pulled up to let out a passenger. I decided to be reckless for once and sprinted to seize it.

"Where to, lady?" The cabbie asked.

I wasn't sure anymore. I had exhausted all my leads. It seemed likely that Paddy's death had nothing at all to do with any of these cases. I hated to admit it, but Sergeant Wolski was probably right. Paddy had betrayed one of the violent city gangs and had paid the price. I decided to go back to Paddy's office and see if there was anything I had overlooked, but then I'd just have to give up and leave any detecting to the police.

As we splashed northward along Broadway I felt guilty at this wanton extravagance with Paddy's money, especially since he had been so frugal in his own lifestyle. So when the downpour eased when we were level with Bleecker Street, I signaled to the cabbie that I wanted to stop and hopped out. This was a mistake as I stepped straight into a deep brown puddle and emerged dripping to the ankles, the hem of my new suit sodden. I seemed to be doomed to make a mess of anything I undertook these days.

With these gloomy thoughts hovering over me, I reached Washington Square. Just as I entered the square, a torrent of students swept out of the main entrance of the university building and they flooded into the square, talking, laughing. I remembered that I was still in possession of the little black book and needed to find a language professor to translate it. I fought against the tide of students until I realized that they were vacating the building for their lunch hour. Their professors would also have gone to lunch, and I too was remarkably hungry. So I put off my task and followed the mob until I found a café with an empty seat in it. It was one of the little French cafés that cluster in the backstreets around the square. It had speckled-mirrored walls and a high counter around the perimeter. I climbed onto a stool at the counter and ordered the plat du jour for eight cents. While I waited for it to arrive, I observed with interest the animated conversations going on around me. There were heated arguments about politics and literature and even the prospect of votes for women. How passionate they were about everything. How I envied them. The conversation broke off briefly as a fire engine galloped past. I hadn't heard the bell tolling this time, but maybe the noise of the students had drowned it out.

"It's all right, Freddy, you didn't succeed in blowing up the chemistry lab—it's going right past," one of the young fellows shouted. There was noisy laughter and conversation resumed again just as my plat du jour arrived. It was a thick beef stew with vegetables, more suited to the cold of winter than a muggy summer day, but it was tasty enough and I managed to clean my plate as effectively as the students around me. Then, feeling daring, I ordered a cup of café au lait, wanting to be part of this lively scene for as long as possible. As I fished for my coin purse, I spied the little black book and brought it out. I cast a hopeful glance around the room, wondering if one of these educated young people might provide the answer for me.

It fell open at the last written page. "Was OR htiw CL ta SC'O."

Still as incomprehensible as ever. What foreign tongue might use the English word WAS? After this the script became hurried and agitated. This last page was what Paddy had been writing when I had come in on him. "Was OR htiw CL ta SC'O." This last word intrigued me. I muttered it out loud to myself a few times. I knew Italian and Spanish had words that ended in *o*, but surely not an apostrophe then *o*.

I put the book down on the counter as the waitress leaned across to deliver my coffee. I took a sip, enjoying the rich frothy taste. As I stared at myself in the mirrored wall, my gaze wandered down to the black book on the counter. In the mirror I could read one of the words. HTIW had become WITH.

Suddenly it hit me. This wasn't written in a foreign language at all. Paddy himself had given me the clue when he had spoken about Cockneys speaking entirely in slang. He had been raised on the streets of London, where the delivery boys and apprentices hid their conversations from their masters by speaking what was known as backslang. I had heard of it and read about it in books, but I had never encountered it in my own life until now. I understood that backslang consisted of ordinary words pronounced backward. So the word "saw" became "was." It had been simple but effective as a secret language of the Cockneys in London and was equally effective here. If the book was lost or stolen, most New Yorkers would be as stumped as I had been. The first sentence on the page now read, "Saw KL with LE at DELS.:" Kitty and Lord Edgemont at Delmonico's. Of course. Then I went on. The next page was scribbled hastily but there was a bold black doodle in the left margin. It looked as if Mr. Riley had attempted to draw a bull. "Saw RO with LC at O'CS." This one made no sense to me. I hadn't come across an RO or LC in his cases, but if I guessed correctly about O'CS, then Paddy had indeed stopped off at O'Connor's on his return home that night, and had overheard something that disturbed him. I worked out the words, one by one, and came up with the following: "Can't believe what I heard. Just talk? Wouldn't go through with it? Not the type. Should check, tell someone."

Suddenly I felt quite exposed, sitting reading this at the counter. Paddy had wanted me to summon Daniel Sullivan. He had muttered as he lay dying in my arms that it was too big for him. I closed the book, shoved it into my purse and hastily finished my coffee. The first thing now was to take another look at Paddy's office, to see if any of his cases contained mention of RO or LC.

The sky had cleared while I had been eating, and steam was rising from wet sidewalks. I crossed the square, entered Fifth Avenue and turned into the alleyway. A group of young boys was playing on the cobblestones. As I started up the steps to Paddy's office, their playing ceased and they became unnaturally quiet. I turned to look at them and found they were staring at me.

"You can't go up there, miss," one of them called to me.

"Why not?"

"It ain't safe. You might fall through the floor."

"The firemen said no one was to go in," another boy chimed in.

"The building was on fire?"

Delighted, excited faces looked up at me and they all started yelling at once . . . "There was flames coming out of the window and everything. You shoulda seen it. And then the engine come and the hoses went *whoosh* and there was a whole lotta smoke."

"When was this?" I asked with a sinking heart.

"Why, they only left half an hour ago. If you'd been here earlier you'd a seen it all."

Half an hour ago—the fire engine I had seen galloping past. I ignored the boys' warning and pushed open the door. The place stank of smoke, but the back window was wide open, so there was plenty of fresh air coming in. The front office wasn't too badly affected, although walls were singed and blackened and the piles of papers were now reduced to charred scraps. I went through to the back office, treading very cautiously, as the firemen's warning had been valid. The floorboards here were blackened and scorched. They might indeed easily give way. It was here that the fire had raged. Where the file cabinet had been there was a blackened, sodden pile of ash.

I stood staring at all that was left of Paddy's world. My first thought was annoyance that I hadn't come straight here from the cab, and thus maybe averted this disaster. Then reason took over and I reminded myself that I had been fortunate. I could easily have walked in on a man who had killed once and who would not hesitate to kill for a second time. For it had to have been Paddy's killer who had done this. He had tipped over Paddy's file cabinet on the first occasion, in a frustrated attempt to get inside. And now he must have returned, just to make sure that no evidence remained.

But evidence of what? I had taken the three folders on his only active cases and they had all proved to be relatively harmless. A closed case would be of no interest to anyone, as Paddy would already have turned over the information to his clients. None of it made sense, and yet I wished I could have had that second look. Maybe I had overlooked something—a secret file hidden among the rest? Anyway, there was no point in moping about it. It was too late now. Paddy's records were effectively destroyed.

"What do you think you're doing here?" a voice behind me demanded.

I jumped a mile, realizing I hadn't heard footsteps on the stairs. Surely a good detective is always on guard—clearly I was lacking in many ways. Sergeant Wolski was standing in the doorway, eyeing me coldly. Come to think of it, I don't think he had any other expression, but it was definitely chilling.

"I heard about the fire and came to see for myself," I said. "How about you?"

"It should be quite obvious that this place is no longer safe," he said. "I want you out of here right now. Until the building owner is notified and decides what he wants to do with this wreck, nobody is to enter. Do you still have your key?"

I nodded.

"Then hand it over immediately, please. I'm going to have the front door boarded up, just in case you get any more silly ideas."

I handed him the key. "How is the investigation coming along?" I asked. "Have you got any leads?"

"The investigation is none of your business," he said, pointing me to the doorway. "But so far the results have not been encouraging."

"Wait." I shook myself free from his grasp on my arm. "If the place is to be condemned, then I'll remove what can be salvaged of Mr. Riley's things." I went back into the burned room and took down the clothes hanging on the wall: a big cloak, a raincoat, an umbrella, a top hat and a fancy waistcoat. They were all the worse for their recent experience—singed, wet, smoke-damaged. I couldn't think how they might be useful to me—I just didn't want anyone else to get his hands on them. "You've no reason why I shouldn't take these with me?" I asked. "Since they belonged to Mr. Riley's business."

Wolski looked at me with distaste. "Take them by all means, although I can't imagine you'd get anything for them if you tried to sell them."

It was my turn to look at him with scorn. "I wouldn't be thinking of selling them. They belonged to Mr. Riley's business. I might even decide to keep that business going on my own."

A supercilious smile. "Then I wish you good luck." This time he gripped my arm and led me to the steps. "Just don't think of trying to come back here again."

"I don't need to," I said over my shoulder. "There's nothing here anymore."

I walked down the steps and out of the alley, trying to keep the cloak and raincoat from trailing in the mud as I carried them home.

There was blissful peace as I came into the O'Hallarans' front hall. No Mrs. O'Hallaran to leap out at me, wanting to know my business or tell me gossip, no sound of monster children leaping and screaming upstairs. I tiptoed up the stairs and let myself into my room. My arms felt as if they were about to fall off with the heavy garments in them and I dropped them onto the nearest chair. I was about to sink into the other chair myself when a loud snore from my bed almost had me jumping out of my skin. My bed was occupied by Nuala and Finbar, both out like lights, on their backs and snoring. First my apartment, then my room and now my own bed—this had gone too far.

I strode across the room and shook them awake. Nuala sat up, arms flailing and demanding, "What? What is it?" in the panicked voice of one woken from deep sleep.

"What in heaven's name do you think you are doing, sleeping in my bed?" I demanded.

"You weren't here to use it yourself," she said in an aggrieved voice. "The little 'uns went out to play, so Finbar and me thought we'd catch forty winks of peace and quiet. I've been missing out on my sleep, up at all hours ministering to my sick cousin in there."

"Catch up on your sleep by all means, but not in my bed," I said. "Come on, out. I want you both out of there right now."

Nuala prodded Finbar, who still seemed to be in total oblivion. At last he jerked awake, spluttering and snorting. "Wassamatter?" he growled.

"We're being thrown out, Finbar. Miss Ungrateful here, who shared our own bed and board without paying a cent, has decided that she can't spare the use of her bed for a half hour."

I said nothing but stood there with arms folded, watching as they got up—Finbar an alarming sight in long grayish combinations—and slunk to my door.

"And if you had any decency you'd offer to wash the sheets," I called after them.

"Wash the sheets!" Nuala retorted. "Anyone would think we had fleas. Come on, Finbar. We know when we're not wanted."

She slammed the door behind them. I was so angry and frustrated I felt I could burst. There was no place I could call my own anymore. I was sure she had snooped through my things before now, but knowing that she could be sleeping in my own bed every time I went out was something different again. I wasn't sure what to do—I could complain to the O'Hallarans and have the lot of them thrown out, of course, but that might risk having Seamus and his two out on the streets. And however much I told myself that I wasn't responsible for what happened to them, I still felt responsible.

I crossed to the window and opened it wide, wanting to blow away the stale smell of their bodies. I'd have to do something with my life to get me out of here—find a paying, respectable job and earn enough money for my own place. Which was essentially back to square one. I did have Paddy's money in the bank, but I still couldn't justify using it outside of business purposes.

I stripped the bedclothes off the bed and then sank down on the mattress. What a fiasco. What a hopeless failure. Now all the potential evidence was gone, the killer had gotten away scot-free and I was proving to be a rather mediocre investigator. I had learned nothing from the fire, had I? Shouldn't I have looked for fingerprints on the windowsill or worked out what had been used to start the blaze? Useless, I said to myself. You useless bag of wind—I stopped because I was sounding just like my mother again.

As I got up from the bed, I realized that I had learned one thing from the fire. Sergeant Wolski couldn't have been right after all. If it had been a gangland revenge killing, then the killer would not have needed to come back. He had wanted very badly to make sure that some kind of evidence was destroyed. I knelt down and pulled out Riley's briefcase from under my bed, then I spread out the three folders on the floor. Lord Edgemont and Kitty— what could Paddy possibly have uncovered about that case to put himself in danger? I worked backward through the little black book. Several mentions of LE and KL—times that he came and went from her house, when they were seen together in a box at the theater. All harmless stuff.

Paddy had hardly started on the embezzlement case, so the file was almost empty. Besides, if the embezzler really had taken a ship to South America a full four days before Paddy was killed, then he could hardly have slipped back to be the killer. I could double-check with the shipping company, just to make sure—but I rather thought that Mr. DeBose would have been thorough in his own attempt to retrieve his money.

Which left us with the MacDonald case. Elizabeth MacDonald had become hostile when she thought I might have been from a newspaper—could she have something to hide? But then she was the one pressing for the divorce. I sat and thought about this . . . It was possible that she wanted incriminating evidence against Angus so that he was taken by surprise and didn't have time to dig up any dirt against her. Now that was a thought worth looking into.

Then I remembered something else—I had observed Angus leaving his office building in a big hurry right after he thought I had gone. And not too long after that, Paddy's office had been burned down. This was the case worth digging into then. There had been some piece of very important evidence hidden in Paddy's office—evidence so vital that it was worth killing for and then burning the place down.

I went through the MacDonald file again. It contained details of Paddy's original conversation with Elizabeth, a documentation of Angus's movements, including visits to certain clubs and a weekend out at Newport, Rhode Island. Again all seemingly harmless stuff. Nothing. I closed the files and went to put them back in the briefcase when I noticed that something had fallen out. There was a small snapshot caught in the leather fold of the briefcase. I took it out and looked at it with interest. It looked like the sort of snapshot someone would take on holiday—a beach scene with two young men in bathing suits standing in the waves laughing, their arms around each other's shoulders.

Completely harmless, except that I recognized the two men. One of them was Angus MacDonald and the other was the beautiful Irish playwright, Ryan O'Hare.

❧ Seventeen ❧

I shoved the briefcase back under my bed, but I slipped the snapshot inside Riley's little black book and put that back in my purse. Ryan O'Hare was friends with Angus MacDonald. Ryan O'Hare frequented O'Connor's Saloon. And the last cryptic message in Riley's black book had read, "Saw RO with LC at O'CS." Clearly I would have to investigate the dashing Mr. O'Hare.

I spent the afternoon at the public library, reading back issues of *The New York Times*. Ryan O'Hare was proving to be an interesting—and very flamboyant—man. From the snippets I read, I could gather that he had been the darling of the English stage, and of English society, too, until he blotted his copybook by writing a satirical comedy about the Queen and her beloved dead Prince Albert. He hadn't called them by their names, of course. He had made them archduke and archduchess of a fictitious Central European country, but they were still easily identifiable. I mean, when you have a Central European archduchess who insists on sleeping between plaid sheets and says, "We are not amused," even the slowest brain among theatergoers could put two and two together. The fact that the play was hysterically funny made it even worse. Ryan had had to flee from England in a hurry and was no longer welcome there.

Since then he had made quite a name for himself in New York. His experience in England hadn't taught him to play it safe.

His new plays were bitingly witty and he was learning just enough about his new country to hit hard with his satire.

Frankly I couldn't wait to meet him. I wasn't sure how I was going to accomplish that, but I did have a place to start from. I knew he frequented O'Connor's; I would just have to start frequenting the saloon for myself. I felt hot all over at the daring nature of my thought. In the eyes of society, women who went into saloons alone were no better than they should be, and asking for trouble. And yet I had sensed that somehow in the neighborhood of Greenwich Village the rules were different. I had seen respectable-looking women drinking there. I'd just have to make sure I looked like a bluestocking, so that nobody got the wrong idea about me.

There was no point in waiting. I would go to O'Connor's that very evening. However, I was in a dilemma about what to wear. If I was to turn the head of Mr. O'Hare, then presumably I should look my prettiest and most feminine. And yet if I wanted to blend in with the women who I had seen at the saloon, I should have to resemble a *frump*. I decided to steer a middle course between the two. Unfortunately I owned no black garment. I had no wish to own a black garment since I had had to wear black for a year following my mother's funeral. And yet those women were all dressed mannishly in somber colors. The most mannish and somber I could look would be in my new business suit—already a little the worse for wear after its encounter with a puddle—and the white shirt I had appropriated from the pile of cast-offs meant for Shameyboy. I also sneaked a tie from the same pile. I couldn't see young Seamus needing a tie for a while yet, and the shirt was far too big for him. If I left either of them lying around, no doubt Nuala would help herself to them for her own sons.

When it came to my hair, I decided that the severe bun did me no justice, and left it curling around my shoulders, tied back with a green ribbon. There was, after all, a difference between looking serious and frumpish.

I set off for O'Connor's around seven, still a little apprehensive about what might befall me there. At least the landlord knew me and I could presumably seek his protection if needed. With this reassuring thought I strode out along Fourth Street, then got lost yet again in the bewildering maze of backstreets before I came out to the broad thoroughfare of Greenwich Street and located O'Connor's. The place was still half empty and quiet. I realized that the hour might be too early for the artistic set, but I wasn't going to risk walking home across Broadway too late at night. This was merely a foray, to spy out the lay of the land.

The landlord greeted me with a nod of recognition and brought a glass of ginger beer to my table. I wasn't brazen enough yet to order myself a real beer or a glass of wine. I sat in the corner, trying to make the glass of ginger beer last for a long time, and looked around the room. Even at this hour it was quite smoky and my eyes started to smart. Two women were sitting at the table beside me, and as I turned to glance at them I was horrified to see that one of them was smoking a cigar! It was all I could do not to stare rudely. I wished I had positioned myself across the room, where I could have observed them without having to swivel around. My second brief glance revealed that the lady cigar smoker also had her black hair cropped short to her cheeks and was wearing what looked like a man's embroidered silk smoking jacket.

I was just digesting these interesting facts when there was a minor commotion in the kitchen and a pale young man wearing an apron was pushed out into the middle of the floor. He stood there looking sheepish and embarrassed. I wondered what sin he could have committed when the landlord came up behind him, clamped a big hand on his shoulder and said, "Here he is then. Come to say good-bye. Young Johnny Masefield's last night here before he goes home to England. Have a drink on the house, then, Johnny lad."

The young man gave a hesitant smile and requested a half-pint of bitter.

"Bitter be damned, boy. Bitter's no good for a send-off. Here. A tot of Irish whiskey for you—the best money can buy! You'll need it, going back to that heathen country where it rains all the bloody time."

The young man grinned, took a swallow, choked, then drained the rest of the glass to the applause of all the customers.

"What are you going to be doing with yourself in England then, Johnny?" a voice demanded from across the room.

"I'll tell you what he's going to be doing with himself," the landlord exclaimed before Johnny could speak. "Thinks he's going to try his hand at poetry. 'Nobody ever got rich writing poems, boy,' I told him, but no, he still wants to try it."

"I've seen some of his poems and they're quite good," a male voice added. "Good luck to you, Johnny. You make old George here eat his words!" The speaker emerged from the darkness of the corner and draped an arm around the young man's shoulders. He was a large, pudgy young man, made even larger by the artist's smock he was wearing. "A toast to young Johnny," he said.

Glasses were raised.

"Pray be upstanding, ladies and gentlemen, and let's give the boy a rousing send-off."

Everyone in the saloon rose to their feet, so I did too. Arms were being linked as we were drawn into a circle. A hand came around my waist from one side, and then from the other. I returned the favor, cautiously, as voices started to sing, in several keys, "Should old acquaintance be forgot, and never brought to mind . . ."

"For Au'd Lang Syne, my dears," we sang, swaying. How exciting and new it felt to be part of this intimate, uninhibited crowd. I was almost sorry when it was over. I was about to return to my seat when the person beside me spoke.

"You're not wearing a corset, I notice," she said. "Does that mean you're one of us?"

It was the lady cigar smoker and I realized that hers had been one of the hands around my waist. "I'm not sure what one of you means," I said, "but I've never worn a corset in my life and never intend to either."

150

"Splendid," she said, nodding encouragingly. "You are rebelling against the restrictions of society then."

"I just don't think it's anybody's business but mine what I wear."

She clapped her hands, laughing. "Then you *are* one of us. Come and join us at our table, unless of course you are awaiting an assignation."

"No assignation, I assure you," I said firmly.

"So you're a man-hater too—excellent."

"I wouldn't say I'm a hater of all men," I ventured cautiously. "It's just that the men I've met recently haven't given me cause to either like or trust them."

"Words of wisdom. I can see we're going to get along famously. Do come and meet Gus."

I let her slip her arm through mine and drag me across to the neighboring table.

"I've just snared us a delightful new companion, Gus, dear," my captor said. "Do sit down and tell us your name."

"Molly," I said. "Molly Murphy."

"Molly. How delightfully quaint," the person named Gus said. I found myself staring again. Gus was a slight, pretty woman, with fine bones and her face framed with wild curls. She was wearing a severe black dress, but had topped it off with an exotic lace shawl flung carelessly over one shoulder.

"Am I so repulsive that you stare like that, Miss Murphy?" the woman asked, her voice severe but her eyes sparkling with merriment.

"I'm so sorry," I stammered. "It's just that when she said Gus, I naturally expected—"

"I was baptized Augusta Mary Walcott, of the Boston Walcotts," she said, still laughing. "It was Sid here who renamed me Gus."

"Sid?" I looked at the dark, interesting young woman in the smoking jacket.

"Sid the Yid," she said with an impish smile at my startled reaction. "Sid the Yid was a character in a racial cartoon a few years back. I decided to adopt the name as my own, thus preventing anyone else from being embarrassed by it. Being Jewish by birth, I was never baptized anything, but my given names are Elena Miriam Hepsibah, so you can see that Sid was a big improvement." She spread her hands out wide. "So Sid and Gus we have become and are content."

I looked from one face to the next. They were both smiling at me, pleasant open smiles, as take place between friends. For once in my life, I was tongue-tied. I had grown up, in our remote cottage on the west coast of Ireland, unused to the close companionship of women, or of men outside of the louts in my family, for that matter. I now found my social skills sadly lacking.

"You'll have to forgive me, I'm brand-new here," I said. "I've just come from Ireland where—"

"Where the non-wearing of corsets is no doubt a sin," Sid chuckled. "That's why we've all gravitated to this delightful place where there are no rules. So let me tell you about us. I write scathingly brilliant articles championing women's rights and Gus here is a painter."

"Trying to be a painter," Gus corrected.

"Don't be so modest. Your stuff is damned good and you know it."

"You're biased," Gus said and a quick smile passed between them.

"And what brings you to the Village?" Sid asked.

It was neither the time nor the place to tell them my true motive. "I'm—I'm thinking of becoming a writer." This seemed the safest route to take. If I said I was a painter, I might be called upon to produce an example of my work.

"What kind of writer?" They both leaned forward in their seats.

More rapid thinking. "Poetry, mainly," I said. "But I think I'd like to try a play someday." It couldn't hurt to create this possible link to Ryan O'Hare.

"Poetry. I just adore poetry," Gus said. "You must read us some."

"It's not really good enough for public performance yet," I said hastily. "It still needs a lot of polishing."

"Rubbish. Poetry needs to be fresh and unpolished. Raw words—that's what I like," Sid said. She snapped her fingers as the bartender passed our table. "Another round please, George. What were you drinking, Molly?"

I didn't like to say ginger beer. "What were you having?"

"What else in O'Connor's but Guinness," Sid retorted. "When in Rome, drink Marsala. When in O'Connor's, drink Guinness."

I had tried Guinness once or twice in my youth and didn't like it, but I wasn't stupid enough to refuse. "A Guinness for me too, please."

"So where are you living, Molly? Are you settled in yet?" Gus asked.

"I'm actually sharing a top-floor flat way over on East Fourth Street," I said, "but it's not working out too well. The noisiest, nosiest Irish family in the world is gradually taking over my life. I found two of them in my bed this afternoon."

"How interesting—male or female?" Gus crossed her legs and I saw she was wearing men's trousers.

"One of each," I said, laughing with embarrassment. "A married couple, actually, and they weren't doing anything except sleeping. It was the use of my bed that I objected to."

"I should think so," Sid said, turning to Gus. "How are you expected to write if you can't have privacy?"

I saw another look pass between them that I couldn't interpret.

"Look, Molly," Gus said. "Why don't you come round to visit us tomorrow? We've a dinky little house on Patchin Place, close to the Jefferson Market—do you know it?"

"I know the market," I said.

"Then you can't miss it. It's the alleyway, right behind the market buildings," Gus said. "Come round anytime you like. We're always home in the mornings. Sid isn't the earliest riser in the world."

"I was born a night owl, what can I say. I was almost sent down from Vassar because I could never make any nine-o'clock classes."

"Until she met me and I made it my life's quest to drag her out of bed," Gus chimed in. "Thus she is deeply indebted to me for getting out of Vassar with a good degree."

I hadn't heard of Vassar, but was not about to betray my ignorance. "So you met while you were students at Vassar," I said.

They nodded. "Do you know Vassar well?" Sid asked. "We had a wonderful time. Truly a heaven on earth, apart from lectures at ungodly hours. Imagine living among women who actually expect to use their God-given intellect, with female professors who expect them to do more than learn how to sew and have the vapors."

"My parents had the shock of their lives," Gus added. "They thought that Vassar would be some kind of glorified finishing school—just a way for me to pass the time out of harm's way until a suitable husband was found for me."

"And instead, she fell among rogues like me," Sid chuckled, "and never went home again."

"And never found the suitable husband, either," Gus said.

"But surely there's still time for that," I said and didn't quite understand the look that passed between them.

"So where did you get your education, Molly?" Gus asked.

"My education was unfortunately cut short by the death of my mother," I said.

"Then you must make up for lost time." Gus looked at Sid for approval. "But you've come to the right place. Loaf around here and you'll meet every intellectual in the land, not to mention the best painters and writers. They all pass through the Village at some time or another."

"I'd really love to meet Ryan O'Hare," I ventured. "I understand he comes in here quite often. Do you know him?"

"Everyone knows Ryan," Sid said, "and conversely, Ryan knows everyone."

"What's he like?"

Another amused glance between them that was hard to interpret. "Ryan is the most entertaining man in the world, and the most infuriating," Sid said. "Great fun but completely untrustworthy."

"He's like an overgrown child," Gus added. "Playing with one toy, then dropping it because he's found a better one. But as Sid says, very entertaining. Nobody can make you laugh like Ryan can."

"I understand he comes in here a lot," I went on. "Is he likely to be here tonight?"

"Who knows, with Ryan," Sid said. "He is the last person in the world to have any kind of schedule."

"Does he live in the Village?"

"He has a room at the Hotel Lafayette, over on University Place," Gus began but Sid cut in, "For the few times he sleeps in his own bed."

I wasn't sure how to progress with this topic, not being used to discussing subjects so obviously taboo. I wished I could develop the worldly ease of Sid and Gus. They seemed to be comfortable talking about absolutely anything and nothing made them blush. But if I was to be an investigator, I had to throw off these stupid fetters of modesty and learn the ways of the world.

"Does he have a particular attachment at the moment?"

They both laughed. "Who can tell with Ryan? They never last long," Gus said. "As I told you—a little boy constantly in search of new toys."

"But I heard he is actually getting down to serious work on his new play. He told Lenny and Hodder that he was not to be disturbed yesterday." Sid got out a new cigar and clipped the end professionally.

"Well, the play is scheduled to open in a month." Gus chuckled. "And it can hardly open without a last act."

"Ryan claims he does his best work under pressure, but I'll

wager that he can't stay disciplined for more than a day or so. By Wednesday at the latest he'll be back in here, cadging drinks and cigarettes."

"That reminds me—where are my manners," Gus said, bringing out a slim silver case. "Do you smoke, Molly? Try one of these. They are Turkish and absolutely divine."

I took the thin brown cigarette from her and put it in my mouth as she lit a match for me. Then I sucked in, felt the hot, acrid taste of smoke and fought against coughing. "Marvelous," I said. "Absolutely topping."

They beamed, like proud parents who have selected the perfect present for their adored child.

By the end of the evening I had smoked two cigarettes, drank a whole pint of Guinness and met several of Sid and Gus's friends, including the large chubby man in the smock who was a painter called Lennie, a Russian with a thick accent called Vlad and an earnest writer whose name I never learned. As I walked home I felt very wicked, and very excited. It was as if someone had opened a door to a new world I had not known even existed. The world with no rules, as Sid had said. And yet, as I went through the events of the evening, they had all seemed so harmless and benign. It was hard to believe that it was at this same O'Connor's Saloon that Paddy had heard something that alarmed him and possibly led him to his death.

✦ Eighteen ✦

T he next morning I presented myself, at what I hoped was a suitable hour, at 9 Patchin Place. Having had it described as an alleyway, I was unprepared for the charming backwater, removed from the bustle of the city. It was a gracious little street, quiet and empty at this hour. There were even trees, growing behind railings and casting delightful pools of shade, outside each brick house. Some of the houses had shutters at their windows, giving an exotic and European effect. Number 9 had sculptured bay trees in pots on either side of the front door and a window box spilling over with petunias. I rang the doorbell and it was opened by Sid, wearing a Chinese silk robe and slippers.

"I'm so sorry," I exclaimed. "I hope I haven't woken you."

"Not at all. I've been awake almost since sunup—or at least since nine o'clock."

"Oh, I see. I thought, when I saw the robe . . ."

At which Sid laughed. "This is my usual form of attire around the house. I find clothes a perfect nuisance, if you want to know. I wish we could all run around naked like the animals do. It would solve so many problems."

"Only in the summer," I suggested.

"I grant you New York in winter would not be so pleasant. But all one would need would be a giant fur coat and boots. That's all the Indians used and they were very healthy."

I smiled. "It would certainly solve my problem, having a very meager wardrobe with no clothes suitable for the city."

"You must let Gus give you some of hers," Sid said over her shoulder as she led me down a bright hallway and pushed open a door at the end. The room was intended to be the kitchen, I suppose, as there was a cooker and sink against one wall, but the outside wall had been knocked out and a glass conservatory now extended the house into a pretty back garden full of flowers and ferns. Gus was lounging out there on a wicker chaise, reading *The New York Times*. She, too, was attired in a robe, only hers was bright purple satin.

"Here she is, as promised." Sid motioned me to a wicker chair. "I'll go and make some more coffee. The poor child was just lamenting that she has no clothes, so I told her you'd have to give her some of yours."

I felt myself blushing furiously. "Oh, but I couldn't possibly," I said.

Gus laughed. "My dear Molly. I have upstairs a whole closet-full of clothes that I never wear. My parents outfitted me for life in society. When I came here I realized I didn't have to conform to their vision of the sweet and innocent young girl, so I started dressing to please myself. But the dreaded garments still lurk in an upstairs closet. You are welcome to help yourself, as I swear I won't be seen dead in them again. Although some of them may be even too adorable and civilized for you."

Again I wasn't quite sure what to say. I lowered myself to the wicker chair. "What a lovely spot you have here," I said. "I had no idea that gardens existed in the middle of the city."

"One of the reasons we fell in love with the house," Gus said. "I had grown up with a large backyard."

"And she simply couldn't exist without her flowers and shrubs," Sid added, coming back out with a coffee tray. "So I absolutely insisted she buy the house instantly."

"You own this house?" I was horrified at my own rudeness but it just slipped out.

Gus didn't seem to be in the least offended. "Fortunately for me, I had a wonderful godmother," she said. "When my parents cut me off without a penny, she came up trumps and left me a large settlement in her will."

"Why did your parents cut you off?"

She looked amused. "They didn't approve of my lifestyle, of course."

"I don't see what is so wrong with wanting to be a painter, and independent," I said.

"Nor I, but there is only one path open to young women in their kind of society—you make a good match and link the family fortune to that of another family."

"And disapproving of me probably had something to do with it," Sid added as she poured thick black coffee into tiny cups. "I hope you like Turkish coffee. Gus and I went through a Turkish fad last year. We were even wearing baggy pants and smoking a hookah for a while, but we've become positively addicted to the coffee and cigarettes."

I took the tiny cup she gave me. The coffee was almost as thick as milk pudding, and so very strong. I didn't think that I'd ever become addicted to it as they were, but I managed a brave smile as I sipped.

"Have you had breakfast?" Gus asked and indicated the basket on the table. "Luckily the most divine baker in the world delivers to us each morning."

I took a crispy roll and spread it liberally with butter and apricot jam. The first bite took away the lingering bitterness of the coffee.

"And now we must give you the tour of the house," Sid said. She grabbed at Gus's arm. "To your feet, lazybones. As mistress of the establishment it is your duty to lead the expedition."

"Co-owner of the establishment," Gus said as she got to her feet. "When will you get it through your thick skull that this is your house as much as mine?"

"It was your money that bought it. Get on with the tour."

Gus shook her head, smiling. "So damned stubborn," she muttered as she went ahead of us back into the house.

During my time in New York I had been exposed to the worst of tenements, a refined home of the middle class, a palacial home of the very rich, even a gentleman's bachelor apartment, but I had seen nothing like this. All of these had been furnished in conventional style. There was nothing conventional about 9 Patchin Place. The living room was furnished with Turkish rugs, a lot of huge velvet pillows and low tables. There was a sofa at one end, but it looked rather forlorn and out of place.

"This room is a remnant of our Turkish phase," Gus said, "but we got into the habit of lounging around on the floor and decided to keep it as it was."

The dining room was more conventional, except for a huge bronze statue of a Chinese goddess in the corner and some very modern paintings on the walls.

"That's one of Gus's recent efforts. Isn't it heavenly?" Sid asked.

It seemed to be a painting of a woman and a dog, but it was hard to tell. I nodded politely. "Interesting," I said.

Up a flight of stairs and I was shown into a bedroom dominated by a huge canopied bed piled high with an assortment of pillows. The walls were draped with purple velvet and flying cupids. It was the most outlandish room I had ever seen and I only just stopped myself from blurting out, "Holy Mother of God!"

In contrast the other rooms on that floor were a study lined with books, another, more conventional, bedroom and a bathroom with the biggest tub I had ever seen.

"I do a lot of my best writing in the bath," Sid said, as if this were a normal thing to do.

Then I was led up another flight of stairs. Up here there were just two rooms. The room at the front of the house was an artist's studio, bare-floored, with easel and a half-finished painting. The room behind, with a view out over the gardens, was full of old furniture and boxes.

"What a pity you're not using this room," I said. "It has the best view."

"We always intended to do something with it but we've been too lazy," Gus said. "And as you can see, we've dumped our unwanted clutter in here."

"What we needed was an impetus to make us clear it out," Sid said, looking at me. "If you'd like to help us, Molly dear . . ."

"I'd be happy to," I said.

She held up her hand. "You didn't let me finish the sentence. What I was going to say was, if you'd like to help us clear it out, you'd be welcome to use it."

"To use it?"

Gus laughed at my surprised face. "Come and live with us."

"Oh, but I couldn't think of imposing . . ."

"Who said anything about imposing?" Sid said. "We talked it over last night. We like you. You need a place to live. We have a spare room that needs cleaning. What better use for it?"

"But—but I'm afraid I don't have a regular source of income at the moment. It might be hard for me to pay the kind of rent you could expect for this lovely room."

"Who said anything about rent?" Gus demanded. "Bring us a bottle of Chianti from time to time and we shall ask for nothing more."

"Oh, but I couldn't possibly," I said but I was weakening.

"Look at it this way," Gus said. "We need the impetus to clean out our room, and what better impetus than to help a fellow free spirit get her start in the Village?"

"Why don't you give it a try?" Sid added. "If things don't work out, then you can always look for another place."

"You are too kind," I said, blushing furiously, "and I would love to live in such a delightful place. I can't tell you what a relief it will be to have a room of my own, with no interference."

Sid and Gus were giving their benevolent parent smiles again.

"Good, then it's all settled. We'll start cleaning today and you can move your chattels in as soon as it's done."

Thus, by the end of the week, I had bid farewell to Seamus, Nuala and the O'Hallarans and moved into my own little patch of heaven. Nuala hadn't been able to conceal her delight at seeing me go. "Off to live with your fancy man, I've no doubt," she exclaimed.

"On the contrary, I'm moving in with two highly respectable women friends who would never dream of entering a room without knocking and where my possessions will be safe from pilfering," I replied, staring her straight in the eye.

My only concern was leaving Bridie and Shameyboy in the hands of those terrible relatives. I promised to bring them to see my new place as soon as I was settled in and told Seamus he could always send Shameyboy or one of his cousins to fetch me if he needed me. Having thus appeased my conscience and discharged my obligations, I set off into the unknown. And, after all, I reminded myself again, I wasn't family.

I set myself up comfortably in the top-floor room, augmenting my meager possessions with some of Sid and Gus's cast-offs—a fringed lamp with the base in the shape of a nude woman, some luxurious-looking velvet draperies, and a curled-wood hat stand. Gus insisted that I help myself to the despised clothes that hung in the wardrobe in the back bedroom. I didn't like to express too much joy when Gus and Sid so obviously hated them, but there were some lovely garments there. If ever I met Miss Arabella Norton again, we could be on equal terms!

I was sitting in the back garden resting after carrying the final load of my belongings up the stairs, when I was reminded with a jolt that I had done no work on Paddy's case for several days now. It was true that I was waiting for a chance to be introduced to Ryan O'Hare, but surely there were other things I should have been doing. Falling into paradise like this had dulled my senses. Living here was like being on a sweet and powerful drug. One had no wish to venture past the front door into the real world outside.

"Next week," I said firmly to myself, "I will be all business again."

I had just said the words when the doorbell rang. I waited,

then realized that Sid and Gus were not back from the market. They made a pilgrimage there every morning, returning with exotic fruits and armfuls of flowers. I jumped up and ran to answer the door.

I found myself staring up at the beautiful face of Ryan O'Hare.

He looked as surprised as I was. "You're not Sid or Gus. Don't tell me I've come to the wrong address." He looked around him. "No. I recognize the bay trees. And you can't be the maid. You look most unmaidlike. So what have you done with them?"

"They're—out at the market," I stammered. "I'm Molly, their house guest."

"Confound it," he said, his face falling. "And here am I, about to die for lack of nourishment, desperate for a cup of their Turkish coffee."

"I don't expect they'll be long," I said. "Won't you come in and wait?"

"Why not—especially when there is the opportunity to be entertained by such a delightful fresh face. I'm Ryan, by the way, and I've seen you before."

"In O'Connor's saloon," I said. "You winked at me."

"And you blushed. It was quite charming. Lead the way then, Molly."

I opened the front door wider and he stepped inside.

"I don't suppose you know how to make Turkish coffee?" he asked expectantly as I led him through to the conservatory.

"I'm afraid not."

"But you could possibly find me a morsel of something to eat before I pass out." He smiled endearingly. He had the most enchanting smile. His whole face lit up and his dark eyes flashed.

"There are some rolls left from breakfast," I said. "And I can furnish butter and jam. Will that do?"

I went into the kitchen and came out with a tray for him. As I set it in front of him he took my hand, brought it to his lips and kissed it. "You are an absolute angel," he said. "I am your devoted servant for life."

163

I was annoyed at myself for blushing. How did one learn to become worldly?

"I knew I'd be fed and nurtured here," he said. "I haven't been out all week, you know, trying to finish the blasted play. I've barely stopped to eat or drink. In fact, if good old Lennie hadn't brought me a pastrami sandwich last night, it might have been too late. My whitened bones would have been discovered on the floor of my hotel room."

I laughed, making his attempted woeful expression dissolve into a smile.

"So tell me about yourself, Molly. To be sure but you're from old sod itself, begorra and all that sort of thing?"

Still smiling, I told him I was newly arrived from county Mayo.

"And were sensible enough to come straight to the only part of the city worth living in," he finished for me. "The rest of America is full of boors and philistines who don't know a good play from a piece of trash. Show a few legs, make a few suggestive jokes and they'll call your play a hit. But anything subtle, anything that delves into the true depths of human nature the American public will pronounce boring and suggest it needs a buffalo stampede in Act Two to liven it up." He leaned back in his wicker chair, studying me. "Lovely hair," he said. He reached over and lifted a strand. "The color of fire. Dangerous hair. Are you dangerous, Miss Molly?"

"Only to those who betray me."

"Ah, then I had better profess my lifelong devotion right now. So tell me, Miss Molly, what do you do with yourself, or are you a creature of leisure?"

"I'm hoping to establish myself as a writer," I said. I was tempted to add that I was currently involved in solving the murder of a dear friend, but lost my nerve at the last minute. Besides, I found it hard to imagine this delightful man leaping out with a knife and delivering one efficient and fatal blow.

"I knew the moment I set eyes on you that we had much in common," he said, still gazing at me. "A fellow Irishwoman and a fellow writer too. Our paths were truly destined to cross. It was fated in the stars." He took another bite of roll, wiped the crumbs from his black velvet jacket, then asked, "So is there a great love in your life at the moment, Molly, my darling?"

"None at all, sir," I said, then, emboldened by his familiarity, I asked, "How about you?"

"Alas not. I am between affaires, as the French say. Unfortunately they never last long with me. I am destined to fall madly in love only to become bored to tears a week later. Of course, if I ever meet my true soul mate, it will be different."

"I'm beginning to wonder whether soul mates exist," I said.

"Such cynicism in one so young and lovely. I've been out in the world longer than you have and still entertain the forlorn hope that one day I will find true and lasting bliss."

I was disappointed to hear the sound of voices in the front hall and Sid and Gus swept down on us.

"What did I tell you?" Sid demanded. "I said he'd only last a couple of days before he was round here cadging food again!"

Ryan turned wounded eyes on her. "I'll have you know that I have written all of twenty-five pages this week, day and night, not stopping for food or water, until I was on the brink of collapse."

"You and your Irish blarney." Sid chuckled. "I just met Lennie and he told me he had been supplying you with brandy and sandwiches."

"I didn't say anything about going without brandy," Ryan went on. "There are some things without which existence is meaningless."

"I see you've met our new friend, Molly," Gus said. "I hope you haven't already corrupted her with your wicked ways."

"Not at all. I have been most well-behaved and gentlemanly, haven't I, Molly?"

"Most," I said. "And very charming."

"I'm always charming." Ryan gave us a beneficent smile. "Even stone-hearted women like Sid and Gus here can't resist me."

This was true. They pretended to grumble, but they fussed over him as much as I had done. And by the time he left, later that day, I was already a little in love with him myself.

❧ Nineteen ❧

On Sunday morning Gus and Sid informed me that it was their custom to go for coffee and pastries to Fleishman's Bakery on Broadway. It was the only thing to do on Sunday mornings. I think the priest back home in Ballykillin might have disagreed with them, but I was not about to argue. Now that I no longer had the responsibility to see that Bridie and her brother attended mass, I was free as a bird and had no great desire to attend mass myself—even if it was supposed to be a mortal sin.

We set off arm in arm across Washington Square, past the silent university buildings and on to Broadway. Fleishman's was buzzing with activity, full of fashionably dressed people as well as the more eccentrically dressed inhabitants of the Village. There was even a crowd waiting to be served.

"Why aren't all these people in church, where they should be?" Gus demanded. "We can't have New Yorkers getting lax about their religion, or we'll never get a table at Fleishman's again."

Sid was scanning the depths of the large room. "Wait—there's Lennie in the corner. Let's see if we can squeeze ourselves around their table."

She forced our way through the crowd. There were three other young men at Lennie's table. One of them was Ryan.

"I'm sure you've got space for three slender females," Sid said, "especially females who are dying of starvation and might faint if they have to wait in that long line."

The young men had risen to their feet. "You've never fainted in your life, Sid darling," Ryan said and kissed her on the cheek.

I felt a great surge of jealousy.

"True, but Gus and Molly have been raised more delicately than I and are capable of a swoon when necessary." Sid sat on the chair that Lennie had brought across for her.

The other young men were finding seats for Gus and me. "I don't think we've met." A pale, shy-looking boy dusted off the chair before he offered it to me.

"You haven't met our sweet Molly yet?" Ryan asked. "Then let me do the honors. Molly, these disreputable gentlemen are Lennie, whom I think you already know, Hodder, who professes to be a poet, although none of us has ever been allowed to see his poetry, and Dante, who has just returned from Paris and is making us all wild with jealousy at his descriptions of the salons there. He actually dined with Monet. Imagine that."

The pale young man gave me a shy smile. "And with a new man called Matissé," he said. "His paintings are so daring—all those primary colors and distorted shapes. I'm having a go at it myself."

"Does this mean you've finished the last act of your play, Ryan?" Gus asked, putting her arm around his shoulders as she perched on a chair beside him. "I seem to remember you swore you would not leave your self-imposed exile until it was done."

"One has to eat occasionally—even geniuses like myself need nourishment," Ryan said. "But the end is truly in sight. You'll be the first to know when I write those magnificent words, 'The curtain falls to tumultuous applause.'"

"You hope," Lennie said.

"I'll invite all my friends to the premiere," Ryan said. "I know enough people to create tumultuous applause."

How wonderful it felt to be part of this noisy, laughing group.

168

I was half-tempted to abandon my plans to be an investigator and really try my hand at poetry or playwriting so that I could truly count as one of them. I noticed heads turned in our direction as we made our exit from the café around midday. There were still people milling around, waiting for tables. As I was about to pass through the front door, someone grabbed my arm. I started in alarm and looked up into Daniel's face.

"Molly, thank heavens you're all right." He was still holding my arm, gripping it fiercely. "I've been trying to locate you."

"Of course I'm all right. Why shouldn't I be?"

"I heard there was a fire at Paddy Riley's place. Then I went to your old address and Mrs. O'Hallaran said you'd moved out and she'd no idea where you'd gone. I thought something might have happened to you."

"I'm very well, as you can see, thank you, Captain Sullivan," I said. "I have a new life and a new group of friends and I'm very happy."

"So you've given up this crazy notion of being a detective," he said. "I'm so glad. I can't tell you how worried I was that you might try and get involved in Paddy's murder yourself."

"Have the police solved the case, then?"

"It's possible they never will," Daniel said, "and it's also possible that there's a dangerous element involved. Unfortunately, I don't think we'll ever find any proof now. But it's definitely not the kind of thing I'd want you mixed up in."

Ryan poked his head around the door. "Come on, Molly. What's keeping you? If you delay me from my garret any longer, it will be all your fault if the play's not finished."

"Coming, Ryan," I said.

I could feel Daniel looking at me. "I have to go," I said. "So nice to meet you again, Captain Sullivan."

Ryan put an arm around my shoulders and escorted me from the café. I didn't look back to see Daniel's reaction, but I permitted myself a broad smile. The fact that my heart wasn't aching must mean that I was truly getting over him.

As we walked back toward Washington Square, Ryan kept his arm draped over my shoulders, and I did nothing to dissuade him. But my talk with Daniel had reminded me that I had been neglecting the task I had set myself. What better moment to glean some facts from Ryan than during an unguarded moment when we were strolling in the company of others.

"Tell me, Ryan," I began casually, "someone said that you might know Angus MacDonald, the millionaire's son. Is that true?"

A brief spasm of annoyance crossed his face. "Used to know," he said.

"So you're no longer friends?"

"We parted amicably enough," he said. "He a little less amicably than I, but that's usually the way it goes. I told you how I am, I fall in and out of love so quickly, and leave behind me a trail of broken hearts."

I think the world stopped turning for a second as I tried to digest what I had just heard. Ryan was still chatting away easily. "Poor old Angus took it rather hard, but I always shy away when it's getting too serious. To tell you the truth, I can't stand the thought of having another human being dependent on me— besides, there was a rumor that his wife might be divorcing him and you know how I abhor scandal. Think what harm it would do to the new play. It would have been an absolute disaster. You know how positively puritanical New Yorkers are."

The blood was pounding through my brain. With my sheltered upbringing in Ireland, it had never crossed my mind that Angus MacDonald and Ryan O'Hare had been more than friends. I think I had heard whispers and insinuations that this kind of thing happened, and my parish priest had once preached an incomprehensible sermon about the destruction of Sodom and Gomorrah, but it had never been part of my world. So it was really true that a man could fall in love with another man! I took this idea one stage further and felt the flood of embarrassment turning my face crimson. It came to me with a shock of realization that Gus and Sid might also be more than friends. I remembered their amused glances when I suggested that Gus still had plenty of time to find a suitable husband, and my bewilderment that there was only one luxuriously decadent bedroom in the house. Now I considered it, they were, to all intents and purposes, a married couple.

I managed to attempt a normal conversation until we left Ryan outside his hotel. And when Gus asked me, "Molly, darling, is something wrong?" I replied that I must have drunk too much coffee and it had given me a headache. Then they were both most solicitous and insisted that I lie down in a darkened room with an ice pack on my forehead.

I lay there, hearing their conversation and laughter coming up from the garden below. My thoughts were still in turmoil. How stupidly mortified I felt that I had believed Ryan might be attracted to me. Now I examined his behavior in the cold light of reason, I saw that he was equally friendly to everyone. To flirt, to put an arm around a shoulder, to kiss on the cheek were part of his nature. I had deceived myself in hoping for too much.

Then I sat bold upright, the ice pack tumbling to the floor, as something else occurred to me. If Ryan and Angus MacDonald had been more than friends, if he had been the person that Elizabeth MacDonald was going to cite as the co-respondent in the divorce case, then there was a powerful motive for stopping Paddy Riley from presenting evidence. J.P. MacDonald, the puritanical patriarch, might forgive his son a dalliance with a young woman, but he would never forgive what he perceived to be a terrible sin. He could easily have cut Angus off without a penny.

I took this further: all three of them then had a motive. Angus, to prevent his disinheritance; old J.P. to prevent the shame and scandal from tarnishing the family name; and Ryan himself, who had just stated to me that a scandal like this could ruin his new play.

I went to my purse and got out the little black book. There

was no mention of Angus, nor, it seemed, of J.P. But there was that cryptic message about RO and LC at O'Connor's. I had no idea who LC might be, or how he was concerned with the case, but I now had a clear line of inquiry ahead of me. I must take every opportunity to probe into the movements of Ryan O'Hare and to uncover what might have happened that night at O'Connor's saloon.

And so I attempted to turn myself into a social butterfly. I urged Sid and Gus to come with me to O'Connor's every evening. How could I hope to become a writer, I said, if I didn't have a chance to observe life? My upbringing in Ireland had been so sheltered that I knew nothing about human relationships at all. They were amused and, like all good parents, indulged me. So we became regulars at the saloon. Sid and Gus chatted with friends while I sat listening in to conversations, observing people around me. Ryan didn't show up for four infuriating days in a row. I hoped he'd complete his play quickly and come back into society. If not, I wasn't sure how I was going to get in touch with him. I could hardly go to call on him in his hotel room—that would be too forward, even for Greenwich Village.

In the meantime, I made it my business to chat to his friends. This was not easy, given the noise level at O'Connor's most evenings and the fact that people were always coming and going. Every time I asked about Ryan, the reaction was the same—"Oh, well, you know, Ryan is Ryan. One of a kind."

Ryan was fun, Ryan was unreliable and Ryan thought of nobody but himself. Nobody suggested that Ryan might be dangerous.

Then, one night, Lennie came in, beaming broadly. "Drinks all around," he called to the bartender. "I've just sold a damned great painting. I'm fifty bucks richer!

Everyone clustered around him, congratulating, slapping him on the back and making sure they were included in the free drinks. Only Sid and Gus didn't rise from their table. "Fifty dollars for a genuine Lennie Coleman! Cheap at the price," Sid said, with sweet sarcasm, "What did you do, Lennie, put a gun to the poor soul's head and force him to buy it?"

"It wasn't a he, it was a she, if you want to know. Her husband is making a fortune in steamships and she wants to set herself up as a patroness of the arts."

This produced an instant reaction, with ten other starving artists wanting to know her name and address. Myself, I sat lost in thought. I had just heard his surname for the first time. It had never crossed my mind before that this regular at O'Connor's was an L.C.

Luck was in my corner that night. Lennie, tired of having to buy drinks for an ever-increasing circle of admirers, came to sit with Sid, Gus and me.

"Gee, but it's tiring being famous," he said. "I don't know how Ryan handles it."

"He laps it up," Gus said. "Loves every second of it. Haven't you ever noticed—if he's not the center of attention, he sulks?"

Lennie chuckled. "I hope to God this play he's working on is good. You know how he hates failure. He's unbearable when things go wrong."

"He's working hard, which is a good sign," Sid said. "Earlier in the summer he was making flippant remarks about getting the cast to ad-lib the last act and create their own ending."

"So what are you going to do with the fifty dollars, Lennie?" I asked.

"Live a little longer, I hope," he said, laughing. "Buy more paints. Pay the rent on my studio for a couple more months. Paint another damned painting to sell." He seemed to notice me for the first time. "How would you like to be painted, Molly?"

"Me?" I was thrown off-guard.

"Sure." Lennie was smiling at me. "I've got a yen to do more life studies. You'd make a perfect model with all that red hair."

I realized this was my opportunity, the chance to chat, one-on-one, with Lennie Coleman in his studio. If I couldn't unearth any useful facts during long painting sessions, then I wasn't much of an investigator.

I gave him my most charming smile. "I'd love to, Lennie. When do you want to start?"

It wasn't until I let myself in to the building on Tenth Street the next morning that I began to have misgivings. It was a long warehouselike structure, housing many artists' studios, and the inside hallway felt damp and cold after the muggy heat outside. My feet echoed up stone stairs. Not a sound in the whole building. No hint that it was occupied. "Saw RO with LC." Paddy's words flashed through my mind. Lennie might look pudgy and benevolent, but I would have to watch every word I said. As I tapped on Lennie's front door, I reminded myself to watch my tongue. If he was the L.C. in Paddy's book, then he mustn't know that I was in any way connected to Paddy.

In contrast to the cold, dark hallway, the studio itself was bathed in light from tall windows. It was a big room, half living area, half studio by the looks of it. On my left were a bare wood table holding the remains of a breakfast, a gas ring and sink and an unmade bed. On my right it was uncarpeted and unfurnished except for an easel with a new canvas on it, a table containing paints and a palette, a stool and another stool backed by cloth drapery.

"Hi, Molly. Ready to get started then?" Lennie greeted me as I came in.

"Indeed I am." I looked around for a place to put my purse.

"I hope it's warm enough in here," he said. "You can go behind the screen to take off your clothes."

"Pardon me?"

He pointed casually to the far corner, behind the bed, where there was a wooden screen. "You can go over there to get undressed."

"Now just a minute." I heard my voice rising. "What kind of girl do you think I am? You lure me here on the pretext of wanting to paint me and then you start making indecent suggestions the moment I step in the door. I'm not staying another second."

He came across and grabbed my arm. "But I do want to paint you, you silly goose," he said. "I want to paint you in the nude."

"In the nude? With no clothes on, you mean?"

"Of course. I told you I wanted to practice life studies. That's what life study means—painting nudes."

"I couldn't possibly . . ." I began, but he started laughing. "You'll be perfectly safe, you know. I'm not at all interested in young women like yourself, except as models. And I'm a very trustworthy kind of guy. Ask anyone around the Village. Good old reliable Lennie. Come on, Molly, what do you say? How is an artist supposed to improve if he can't work with live models? And everyone else has posed for me—Sid, Gus, even Ryan."

"All right," I said. I had forced myself to take a good many chances recently. One more could hardly matter. I went behind the screen and unbuttoned my blouse with trembling fingers. Was it my imagination or was it very cold in that studio? My eye fell on my straw hat, lying on the chair. Swiftly I pulled out the hat pin that held the silk rose in place and wrapped my fingers around it. If he had been spinning me a yarn and he tried anything indecent, then I was going to be ready.

I came out feeling horribly self-conscious. Lennie was standing at the little table mixing colors. "Go and sit on the stool, please. Watch out how you step on the velvet, won't you. It was horribly expensive."

I perched on the stool, wishing myself anywhere else but here. Lennie picked up his palette and stood behind the easel, eyeing me critically. "Swing to your left a little. Good. And let your hair fall over that shoulder, and maybe put your hand on your thigh. And don't look as if you're a Christian about to be fed to the lions. I don't see you as a woman, I see you as a design. You can chat away quite normally, only don't move."

I can't tell you how strange it felt to be sitting in the nude on a cold hard stool talking about the weather and how seasonable it was for the time of year. I almost wanted to laugh at the absurdity of it all. But gradually I did relax, and remembered the point of my mission.

"So tell me about Ryan O'Hare," I said. "I find him fascinating."

"You and half the population of New York," Lennie said.

"You two are good friends, aren't you?"

"I'm not sure Ryan has good friends. I don't think anyone knows the real Ryan," he said. "Ryan plays the part that is expected of him wherever he goes. But I suppose I am as close to him as he lets anyone get."

"And you spend a lot of time together, don't you? You go to theaters and bars together?"

"Sometimes," Lennie said. "When he doesn't have anyone better to take him out. What Ryan really likes is to be whisked into the whirl of high society by the rich and the beautiful. Since I am neither rich nor beautiful, I am usually the last resort."

"Is Ryan often with the rich and the beautiful then?"

"Whenever he finds a suitable love interest." Lennie jabbed at his canvas.

"Ryan told me he never stays in love for long," I said. "Do you think he'll ever find his soul mate and settle down?"

Lennie chuckled. "His soul mate would have to be very rich. Ryan has expensive tastes."

"So he doesn't have money of his own? I'd have thought, being a famous playwright, he'd be rich."

"He spends it as fast as it comes in," Lennie said. "He needs another Angus MacDonald with an inexhaustible supply of cash. Actually"—he looked up with the hint of a grin—"I told him what he needs is a rich elderly widow. He could marry her, then feed her a steady supply of arsenic."

He started laughing. "We had a long, earnest talk along those lines, one night when we were both in our cups. We sat there discussing painless and undetectable ways to bump off old ladies."

"At O'Connor's, was this?" I asked.

"Where else? Now hold still. You moved your head." And he went on painting.

I tried to hold still, but I couldn't wait to get off that stool. Maybe this was what Paddy had overheard at O'Connor's that night. Ryan and Lennie had been joking, but Paddy had taken their plans seriously. In which case the overheard conversation had nothing to do with his death after all. In which case I was wasting my time sitting on a cold hard stool!

❧ **Twenty** ❧

I was stiff and numb by the time Lennie announced that he had painted all he could for one day. He was pleased with the result, though. "Another session and I think we'll have something marketable here," he said, but he wouldn't show me the canvas. "I never show anyone until it's finished. It's bad luck."

So I agreed to come back the next morning and walked home briskly, trying to restore the circulation to my legs. In a way I was relieved to have solved the mystery of the overheard conversation and to know that Ryan and Lennie were not involved in Paddy's death. It would appear, then, that his death had nothing to do with Ryan, for which I was glad. But that meant that I didn't know where to go from here. If either Angus MacDonald or his father had hired a killer, then I couldn't go delving into the New York underworld to unmask him. This made me realize how useless I was as an investigator. Paddy would have known where to go and whom to question. He had contacts in all the gangs. He moved on both sides of the fence, as Sergeant Wolski had said. He was lucky to have that facility. On the other hand, it might have been the cause of his death.

So it looked as though I would have to leave the investigation of Paddy Riley's murder to the police. From my brief conversation with Daniel a week ago, he had hinted that he had been looking into the case himself, and that a dangerous element might be involved. I told myself I was well out of it. If I started probing around, asking questions about gangs and hired killers, I might well wind up dead myself.

I stopped at the post office on my way home, to see if any letters had come for Paddy. I had asked the post office to hold any mail, but until now nothing had shown up. So I was surprised to find two letters. One contained a check for a hundred dollars, along with a note in slanted green ink apologizing for the delay in paying the fee. The other was from a Mrs. Edna Purvis of White Plains, asking him to call on her at his earliest convenience to discuss a matter of extreme delicacy. A new divorce case, obviously. I was tempted to call on Mrs. Purvis myself and take on the case as the junior partner in the firm. Then I reminded myself that I hadn't been at all successful in solving Paddy's murder. I had better stop these foolish aspirations right away and find myself a sensible job I could do well. At least I now had contacts in the Village. Sid and Gus knew everybody. And if everything else failed, I could always make my living as an artist's model.

That night I woke from a deep sleep with a jolt. I had been dreaming again about Paddy's coat. "It's too big for me. You take it," he was saying. I lay there, shaken, and unable to sleep. Was there something I had missed? Had I been too quick to dismiss Ryan and Lennie's little joke? Now that I analyzed it calmly, I had to admit that the scenario did not ring true. Paddy was an experienced, streetwise detective. He had lived on both sides of the law. Overhearing two men discussing how to poison an old woman would not have upset him to that degree, and it wouldn't have been a case he couldn't handle either. All he had to do was see Daniel and pass on his suspicions to him. Whatever Paddy had overheard that night at O'Connor's, it was something quite different.

The next day, after my session with Lennie, I went to see Paddy's former landlady.

"I'm glad you turned up again," she said. "I want to get that room cleaned out and the first of the month is coming up."

"I'll help you," I said. "I'll see what things I'll need to carry on the business and you can have the rest."

"Carry on the business?" She looked alarmed. "You're never thinking of carrying on Paddy's work, surely? That's no job for a woman—dirty, dangerous. I can't tell you how many times he told me about narrow escapes he'd had. What's more, I can't tell you how many times I had to patch up cuts and bruises when he got himself into a fight. You find yourself a nice husband, dearie, and leave that kind of work to the men."

"All the same, I'll take his disguises, in case someone else wants to take over the business," I said. I didn't let on that his office building had burned. I took down the box of wigs and makeup, some items from his desk, including the roll of film and the negatives, and the long flowing cape. It might come in handy if I ever needed to disguise myself as a man. I helped Mrs. O'Shaunessey put the rest of his stuff into boxes and watched the gleam in her eye as she worked out how much she could get from the used-clothing merchants.

Then I carried my bounty home. As I passed O'Connor's I saw Dante and Hodder crossing the street toward the saloon.

"Hey, Molly. Drinks all around tonight. Ryan's finished the play," Hodder called.

"He appeared, pale and wraithlike, but still alive, saying that it's the best thing he's ever written—a work of utter genius," Dante added with a grin, "and he expects all his friends to be at O'Connor's to tell him how clever he is. Typical Ryan. Never get the medal for modesty."

"So tell the girls, will you?" Hodder said. "Ryan will want them there, I know."

I hurried on home and was exhausted by the time I dropped the packages on my bed. Why had I bothered to bring all this stuff? Fake beards and noses and eyeglasses—when would I ever need them? The cape, though, might be very welcome this winter. I remembered how cold I had been last winter and the cape was of good wool, with only a few moth holes in it. I put it on, looked at myself in the mirror and twirled around, watching it fly out. Then something bumped against my leg. I felt for pockets, reached in, and my hand closed around something hard and square. It was Paddy's camera.

I stood turning it over in my hands. I knew I should hand it over to the police, but I didn't want to. If there was a vital clue in one of those pictures, then I wanted to know about it first. I'd have the film developed, then I'd hand over the pictures when I'd looked at them. After all, the police had searched Paddy's room. If they hadn't been clever enough to find the camera, that was their hard luck.

I ran out again and asked around until I located a photographer's studio. Its proprietor agreed to develop and print the film for me. I should come back in a week. Never having been the most patient of souls in my life, I begged, pleaded and urged for him to do the developing on the spot, but he refused. He was booked solid with important clients for the next few days—clients who paid good money. My little job would just have to wait.

I thought of looking for another photographer, but came away resigned to patience. A week, after all, was not the end of the world, was it?

Meanwhile I had other things to keep me busy. My conscience had been bothering me about my desertion of Seamus and the children, considering my current good fortune. However much I reasoned with myself that they were not my responsibility, Bridie's little elfin face kept appearing before my eyes. And I had not even given a thought to how Seamus was faring either. If he didn't make a full recovery, there would be no job for him. So I bought a basket of good, nourishing food, then added a wooden top and a hair ribbon as extras and set off for my old abode.

Nuala was sitting on the stoop, fanning her vast body.

"So yer fancy man has thrown you out then, has he?" she asked triumphantly.

"I just stopped by to see if your cooking had managed to poison the children yet," I said, brushing past her. "And to pay my respects to Seamus. I hope he's still making a good recovery."

"As good as can be expected," she said cautiously. "Seeing as how there is precious little money to buy him the good food he needs to build up his strength."

"I've brought a chicken and some grapes," I said. "That should help."

"Well, that's might decent of you, I have to say," she said, following me into the house. It was the first word of praise for me that had ever passed her lips. Seamus was sitting up by the window, but still looked the shadow of his former self. I put the chicken on to boil so that he could have broth as well as meat and handed him the grapes. He was pathetically grateful.

"So good of you, Molly," he said. "The doctor says I'll be able to go back to work, but I seem to be weaker than a kitten."

"You need fresh air and exercise," I said.

"Not with weather like this. It's all I can do to drag myself across the room. It feels like the whole world is melting," he said.

"You're right about that, but it's September tomorrow. This kind of weather can't last forever, can it?" I looked around. The place was awfully quiet. "Where are the children?"

"Out with my boys, swimming in the East River, I expect," Nuala said, standing, hands on her hips, in the doorway behind him. "That's what they do when it's too hot to stay indoors."

"I hope Bridie's not thinking of swimming in that filthy river," I said. "You should forbid her, Seamus."

"Oh let the little body have her fun," Nuala said. "All the children do it."

Seamus half nodded agreement, so there was nothing for me to say. I left them, tempted to go and check on Bridie myself, but returned to Patchin Place feeling strangely discontented. I had been glad to hand over my responsibility for the children, but now I was finding that it wasn't easy to let them go.

Then that night, all worries about Seamus's little family were put from my mind. I had delivered Ryan's summons to witness his triumphal return to society at O'Connor's saloon. By eight o'clock all his friends were dutifully assembled when the door of the tavern was flung open. Ryan's style of dress was always more flamboyant than was usually seen on the streets of New York, but tonight he had surpassed himself. He wore a black opera cape lined with scarlet satin, top hat, purple silk cravat at his neck with a large diamond in a stick pin, and he carried a silver-tipped cane. He stood in the doorway waiting for the full effect to be realized upon his admirers.

"My children, I have arisen," he said, holding out his arms. "I am here to report a great victory. The task is ended. The play is finished. The battle is won. Ryan O'Hare has triumphed."

He beamed at the expected applause.

"And now, George, my good man, a bottle or two of your best French champagne, if you please. I wish to celebrate with my friends."

"Not wishing to be rude, Mr. O'Hare," George said, "but you will be paying cash for this tonight, won't you? Champagne's an awful big item to add to your bar tab."

"My dear, sweet George." Ryan went over and put an arm around the bartender's shoulders. "How long have I been coming here? And have I ever failed to make good on my debts?"

"Well, I suppose, in the end, after a few proddings . . ." George had to admit.

"Then trust me, my dear man. Next week I take the new play out of town for some preview performances before it returns in triumph to open in New York. It is, without doubt, the most brilliant thing I have ever written. So in a few weeks I shall be able to buy not only French champagne, but a large ocean liner equipped to go over to France to replenish supplies."

George laughed uneasily, but went to the cellar to produce the champagne. Ryan came to sit at our table.

"Ah, the divine Molly." He took my hand and brought it to his lips. "You may be the first to give me the congratulatory kiss."

"I haven't seen the play yet," I replied, "so how am I to know what it's worth?"

That produced chuckles and comments.

Ryan put his hand to his breast. "My dear Molly, I am mortally wounded. You mean to say you believe me capable of writing anything other than sheer brilliance?"

I didn't want to admit that I hadn't seen any of his plays. "Of course not," I said, and kissed his cheek. "And I congratulate you on your fortitude at working so hard to finish it."

"If you need convincing," he said, "then come to a rehearsal tomorrow. Daley Theater—my grandfather's name. I hope that's not a bad omen. I couldn't stand my grandfather—we'll be rehearsing all afternoon and evening. My long-suffering cast has been furnished with the pages of the last act as I wrote them and they have had to wait with baited breath to see if Cameron goes to jail or Fifi dies."

The champagne arrived. George opened the first bottle with a satisfying pop and started pouring the bubbly liquid into tall, thin glasses. I had never tasted champagne before, although I'd read about it enough. It was as good as I'd imagined it would be. The bubbles tingled and went up my nose, but the wine slipped down easily enough. After my second glass I was feeling relaxed and pleased with myself. Ryan was still sitting beside me. I was at the center of the bright, witty group. This is how I had always pictured life should be.

More people arrived. The party became noisier as more champagne was ordered and produced. Then the solemn Russian, Vlad, came to stand behind us.

"By the way, Ryan, Emma has been asking after you," he said.

Ryan spun around. "Emma? She's in town? Why didn't somebody tell me?"

"You had locked yourself away in your room with strict instructions not to be disturbed, remember?" Lennie said.

"Yes, but Emma—that's different. You know I'd even forgo finishing my play to see her."

I had no idea who Emma was, but already I was feeling jealous. Supposedly Ryan wasn't interested in women, so I'd given up all hopes of falling in love with him. But this one woman's name had such a powerful effect on him that I saw her instantly as a rival.

"So where is she? How long will she be here?" Ryan had put down his glass and was perched at the edge of his seat.

"She's only passing through on her way back from Europe," Vlad said. "She said she'll be at Schwab's tonight, if any of her friends want to find her."

"Then I must go to Schwab's this instant," Ryan said. "I can't let her go without seeing her again. How did she look, Vlad? Is she well?"

"She looked fine, Ryan. In the best of health."

Ryan had risen to his feet. "I am sorry to desert the party, but I must answer to a higher call."

He put a hand on my shoulder. "I fear I must leave you, dearest Molly."

The champagne had made me bold. "Who's Emma?" I asked.

"Only the most fascinating woman in the world," he said. "There's no one like her." Without warning, he grabbed my hand. "Come with me. You have to meet Emma. She loves the Irish."

Before I could think rationally, he had whisked me out of the saloon and into the crisp night air.

❧ Twenty-one ❧

I t felt like September. The night air had a chill to it, which made walking delightful. I was still bubbling with the champagne, and floated along easily, tethered to earth by Ryan's hand. We flew across Washington Square, with the marble arch looming ghostly in the lamplight to one side of us. Late-night student revelers came out of cafés and taverns, laughing and singing. Couples drifted like spirits along leafy paths, pausing to kiss in the shadows. Sharp painful memories stabbed at me, dragging me down to reality for a moment.

Then we passed on into quiet backstreets where we only encountered a policeman on his beat. How far were we going? The wine had dulled my brain, but not enough to stop me from wondering what the fascinating Emma would think about Ryan's bringing another woman to meet her.

At first glance, Schwab's Tavern, tucked away in the more seedy section of the Village, was not particularly inviting—a drab sort of place and lacking the noisy gaiety of O'Connor's. It was dimly lit and full of smoke. The front tables were empty but there was a large group clustered around a table in a far back corner. They huddled like black shadows around a single candle on the table. The barman gave Ryan and me a curious look, but Ryan released my hand and rushed to the back table. "Emma, darling, you have returned to me," he announced with great drama.

A figure rose from among those at the back table. She turned, saw Ryan, then let out a little gasp of delight as she held out her arms in an embrace. "Ryan—my dear boy. It's been too long. I'm so glad they found you and passed along my message. How could I possibly visit New York without seeing you? I would have been devastated." Their arms came around each other and they stood there, embracing.

I was completely dumbfounded. I had expected a gorgeous young creature, exotic enough to sweep even Ryan off his feet. Instead Emma was a dowdy, almost middle-aged lady. She had a severe round face, unadorned with any powder or rouge, and her dark hair escaped in untidy wisps from her bun. Her dress was black, high-necked and unadorned. In fact, she resembled a governess I had once known.

As they embraced, her eye fell upon me. "And who is this, Ryan?" she asked, breaking away from him.

Ryan took me by the hand again and led me to her. "This is Molly. You'll like her. She's Irish and opinionated."

"Excellent," Emma said. "We're always glad to meet new recruits, aren't we, Sasha?" She turned to the man beside her. In the light of the candle flame he looked gaunt but rather good-looking in a poetic sort of way. He was dressed in worker's garb with a black cap on his head. "Sit down. Sit down," She clapped her hands. "Come, make room for them." I noticed there was some kind of foreign accent to her speech. "We're drinking tea, but I expect they can find you something stronger."

"We're already floating on champagne, Emma dearest. In celebration of my new play, you know."

"You have a new play coming out?"

"Opening shortly in New York, after we've taken it on the road to iron out the creases. You'll love it, Emma. It may seem funny on the surface, but it's very deep. It deals with the whole question of nationality and loyalty—do I owe loyalty to a country, a clan, a family, just because I was born into it?"

"Interesting," Emma said. "And do you?"

Chairs were produced for us. A few inches of space was made at the table for Ryan to sit beside Emma. I was squished in between two young men in black, both of whom smelled unwashed. Now I had a chance to look around the table, I noticed that the company was composed entirely of young, earnest-faced men in black, with the exception of Emma and one equally dark and severe-looking young woman. This latter was staring at me now, so intensely that I felt uncomfortable.

"Who are these people?" I heard her ask the man beside her. "Look at them. They're not one of us. What are they doing here?"

"Ryan's a friend of Emma's. He used to come to meetings," I heard the man reply in a low voice, also glancing my way. "I don't know who she is."

"So I hear you've just come from Europe, Emma darling," Ryan said. "What news?"

"A very successful year, so I'm told," Emma said. "Our Italian and Baltic comrades have been very busy."

"They have dealt more stunning blows for democracy over there following last year's successful coup," the rather good-looking man beside her added.

"Death to all tyrants," one of the unwashed young men beside me muttered.

"So what have these blows for democracy achieved, do you think?" Ryan asked. "Are the Italian peasants now living like Medicis?" He reached across, grabbed himself a tall glass mug in a raffia case and poured himself tea from a curiously shaped teapot in the middle of the table. I was still doing splendidly on the effects of champagne and had no wish to follow suit.

Emma didn't even smile at the quip. In fact, none of these people looked as if they smiled at all. "To tell you the truth, I'm not sure what we've achieved," Emma said. "Frankly, I question whether the masses are ready to take control in many of these countries. As long as they go on breeding like rabbits, I don't see much hope." She paused to sip tea. "I met one young woman who had just had her tenth child, and she was younger than me. When I questioned her about it, she said it was God's will. 'Rubbish,' I replied, 'it was the will of some man who can't keep his pants buttoned up.'" She looked around at us with intensity in those dark eyes. "This is our next big crusade, comrades. How do we make people take control over their own bodies? How can women ever achieve equality if they can't stop having children all the time?"

"Is that what you think we should be doing over here?" the young woman asked. "Not try to bring down the rich until the poor can stop having children? I fear we have a long task ahead of us. I know. I come from an Italian family. Tell the Italians not to have bambinos and they'd rather die."

"She's right, Emma," one of the unwashed males chimed in. "The average laborer doesn't see children as a liability, but an asset—making sure someone is there to take care of them in their old age."

"I didn't say no children at all," Emma replied. "Of course there must be children if the human race is to continue. My point is that there do not have to be ten or twelve children anymore. As medicine advances, more children will live to grow up. If a woman has three or four children in her life, and those by choice, when she wants them, think how productive she could be to the cause. She could be a full member of society, protesting, voting, making sure laws are carried out fairly. That is my aim."

"And wonderful it is too, Emma," Ryan said, taking her hand and kissing it.

"But what of the cause?" the young woman demanded. "You're not going to abandon the cause, are you?"

"I'm not abandoning any causes," Emma replied sharply. "In fact I aim to stir up as much trouble as possible for the rest of my life. It's just that I have started to question whether our aim should continue to be to bring down without the means to build up again. Trade unions, birth control, equal rights for women—those should be our aims here in America."

"And what about tyrants?" the girl asked. "Surely it is our sworn duty to bring equality to the people, and to make filthy millionaires pay for their greed."

"Ryan would be happy to join you in that cause, wouldn't you, Ryan?" The speaker was yet another haunted-looking young man in the darkness at the far end of the table. He was wearing the same uniform black worker's cap and a large black jumper, even though the heat in the saloon was uncomfortable.

"Oh, Leon. I didn't notice you. What are you doing here?" Ryan asked.

"Just passing through, like Emma," Leon said. "I didn't expect to see you here."

"Nor I you. Exactly what cause should I be happy to join?"

"Making millionaires pay for their sins—or at least a certain millionaire."

Ryan looked amused. "Why do you say that?"

"One hears rumors, Ryan. I understand that he bolted."

"I must correct you there, Leon dearest. If there was any bolting done, it was I who was bolter and Angus was boltee. In either case, it is over, done, finito, schluss."

"So you've moved on to a new lover?" I was looking straight in front of me, but I got the feeling that I was being scrutinized.

"My new lover has to be the theater at the moment. I have no time for outside dalliances until my play opens."

"Tell me more about this play, Ryan." Emma leaned forward between the two men and latched on to Ryan's arm, drawing him toward her. A private conversation began at their end of the table. I looked back to find the young woman in black watching me again.

"You're from Ireland," she said. "Tell me, how goes the cause over there? Is there hope of expelling the tyrants anytime soon?"

"Driving out the English, you mean?"

"What else?"

"I'm afraid I don't know."

"You were not involved with the cause over there?"

"I lived on the remote west coast," I said. "Far from Dublin and politics."

"The struggle must be carried on everywhere if success is to be achieved," she said coldly. "I could tell you weren't one of us. What are you doing here?"

"I came with Ryan," I said.

"With Ryan? But I thought that Ryan . . ." One of the young men beside me looked confused. I guessed his meaning.

"I'm a cousin, visiting from Ireland," I said hastily, hoping this would stop the questions. "He wanted me to come and meet Emma."

"And now you've met her, what do you think?" the same young man asked. "Isn't she wonderful? Doesn't your heart leap in your breast when she speaks?"

Personally my heart hadn't stirred an inch, at least not in the way it leaped when Ryan kissed my hand or caressed my shoulder, but I nodded politely. "She seems a very interesting woman."

"And powerful, too. They listen to her over in Europe as well, you know. And they fear her over here. She's been in jail more than once."

"So you do intend to join our little group?" The young woman wasn't going to let up. "You are remaining in New York for a while, aren't you? You could be instructed in how to pursue the fight when you go back to Ireland. More soldiers are needed on that battlefield, you know."

"Are women now supposed to fight?" I asked. "Frankly, I find the petticoats too hampering."

The young woman glared at me. "Emma fights," she said. "And not all fights involve weapons. Words can be weapons too. Instructing the masses how to rise up against their oppressors— opening the eyes of the blind to the corruption and greed around us—those are ways we women can fight. Are you with us or not?"

I glanced across at Ryan, hoping to catch his eye. Now that I had met Emma, I had no wish to stay longer. I found these people rather alarming and pathetic. I certainly had no wish to be one of them. And I was beginning to feel very uneasy. Maybe I was just sensing the girl's hostility, but I started feeling as if I couldn't breathe. I couldn't wait to get out into the fresh air again. Just when I couldn't stand it any longer and was thinking up a way to excuse myself, Ryan seemed to tire of them also. He drained his glass of tea and got to his feet. "Well, I must be going, Emma darling," he said. "I must make sure this adorable creature gets home safely before midnight, or she will turn into a pumpkin." He leaned to give her a kiss on the cheek. "Do let me know where you will be and I promise to write. Will you be going home to Rochester? I'll be heading to the wilds of upstate New York myself in a week."

He scribbled down her address on the back of an envelope, then put an arm around my shoulders and steered me out of the building. As we left, I could feel eyes on my back.

"So what did you think?" he asked as we set off back toward Washington Square. "Isn't she a hoot?"

"Why didn't you warn me?" I said. "Those people are anarchists, aren't they?"

"Oh, very much so. They meet at Schwab's and talk about taking over the world. Death to all tyrants."

"How on earth did you get involved with them? Surely you were never an anarchist yourself?"

We paused to let a hansom cab clatter past on the cobbles. "I was introduced to Emma when I first got here. For a while I was rather entranced—she has that effect, you know. It seemed like rather a noble cause to blow up that fat old tyrant Victoria, especially after what she did to me. But the enthusiasm soon wore off. Victoria died and nobody could feel violent about poor old Edward. Anyone who has to do what his mummy tells him until he turns sixty should at least be allowed a few years of fun, ruling the British Empire, don't you think?"

"So you're no longer part of that group?"

"I never really was, but don't tell them that. But I do find them rather amusing, don't you? Good for a giggle, wouldn't you say?" He looked at me, eyes sparkling. "They are all so bloody earnest. They publish their little left-wing newspapers, they organize strikes and protests, they go to jail and come out feeling like martyrs—"

"But are they actually dangerous, do you think? They're not planning to start a revolution in this country, are they?"

Ryan laughed. "America's already had one revolution. I can't see the inhabitants wanting another, can you? And we are supposed to have government for the people and by the people already. No, I think the comrades over here are more concerned with wealth. Too many rich people. Too much inequality."

"Your friendship with Angus can't have gone down well, then."

We exchanged grins.

"Luckily I am a law unto myself. Nobody knows what to make of me, so they keep quiet and leave well enough alone."

We turned onto Sixth Avenue.

"You really don't have to see me all the way home," I said. "I'm sure I'm perfectly safe from here."

"Nonsense. I wasn't raised a gentleman for nothing. And besides, Sid and Gus might still be up and could be persuaded to make me a cup of coffee. I still have the taste of that disgusting tea in my mouth."

Ryan's mention of Sid and Gus had me thinking—Ryan had said that those people we had just met were involved in extremist newspapers and women's rights. Sid had told me she wrote articles on women's rights for certain journals. Was it possible that she was somehow involved with them? And as we picked our way through the debris around Jefferson Market, yet another thought came into my head. Until now I had not been able to suspect

Ryan of any involvement in Paddy's Riley's death, because he had seemed so lovable and harmless. Now I saw that he also had a dark side. That cryptic remark, "Saw RO with LC at O'Cs" and the words that followed it showed that Paddy thought he was dangerous. And Paddy had lived only a day after writing those words.

❧ Twenty-two ❧

I didn't sleep well that night. As I lay staring at the ceiling, listening to the muted noises of the city, I still couldn't believe that Ryan was involved in anything dangerous and subversive. I wasn't even sure that he was the RO mentioned in Paddy's notes. He obviously wasn't closely connected to the group we had met tonight. Some of them didn't even know who he was. So why was I lying awake and worrying?

I got up and paced the floor. Ryan couldn't be involved in anything dangerous. It just wasn't like him. Sid and Gus had described him as a little boy who played with one toy, then dropped it for a new one. Even if he had had a fleeting interest in anarchism and had toyed with the idea of blowing up Queen Victoria, it would have been just a passing fantasy.

"Is something wrong, Molly dearest?" Sid asked me as I sat at breakfast next morning. "You look as if you carry a burden on your shoulders."

"I didn't sleep well last night," I admitted.

She nodded wisely. "An evening with Ryan can do that to a person." She leaned across and rested her hand on my sleeve. "Look, Molly, I know it's none of my business, but you're not thinking of falling for him, are you? Because if you are, I'd like to save you from possible heartbreak. For one thing, Ryan isn't exactly—" She broke off, considering how to phrase it.

"Interested in girls?" I finished for her. "Yes, I know that."

"That doesn't mean that he isn't a terrible flirt with anything that walks on two legs," Sid went on. "He knows how to flatter and make a person feel wonderful. I just don't want you entertaining false hopes."

"Thank you, Sid, but I don't," I said. "I find Ryan quite delightful company, but I know him to be quite fickle."

"Fickle is a good word for it." She nodded again, seriously, and leaned forward to pour herself a thimble-sized cup of coffee.

"Do you think I run a risk by being associated with him, then?" I phrased the question as cautiously as possible.

"Only that Ryan uses people as playthings. If you are this week's favorite, you will surely be discarded by next week."

"So you don't think that Ryan might have . . . a dangerous side?"

She looked amused. "Jack the Ripper in disguise? Whatever made you ask that?"

I attempted a laugh. "He seems too good to be true."

"As long as you don't trust him any further than you could throw him, you'll be just fine. And as I said, by next week he'll have forgotten all about you, unless he wants something."

The conversation left me feeling a little better. Sid and Gus, after all, knew Ryan well. If he was involved in any shady activities, surely he'd have dropped hints to them. Ryan didn't seem the type who would hold his tongue too successfully. But I decided it couldn't do any harm to ask a few more questions. So after breakfast I presented myself again at Lennie's studio. Lennie was delighted to see me.

"My lovely model has returned to me," he said. "I finished the first sketch of you last night. As soon as the paint dries, it's off to a gallery to make me rich."

"I don't know if I like the thought of myself hanging in someone's gallery without any clothes on," I said.

He laughed. "You'll be the toast of New York. You'll have suitors battering your door down."

"Hardly a comforting thought," I said, and removed my clothes behind the screen.

"So how was your adventure with Ryan last night?" Lennie asked, as I perched on the stool and he draped fabric around me. "He took you with him to visit Emma, didn't he?"

"It was interesting," I said.

He chuckled. "They are a rum bunch, aren't they? That Emma creature and her followers. I have no idea what he sees in her. He usually goes more for glamour and status. And yet, if she snaps her fingers, he comes running."

"Have you ever been to one of her meetings?" I hadn't forgotten that his initials were L.C.

"Me? You wouldn't catch me wasting my time with a group like that. I have no wish to overthrow society. I like things the way they are. Give me enough money to buy paint and beer and a good pastrami sandwich at the delicatessen and I am content."

"So you really think that Ryan is under her influence, do you?" I asked, staring past him out of the window, so that I wouldn't appear too interested. Pigeons were settling on the coping opposite. I watched their fluttering and strutting. "It was hard to tell from one brief visit last night. He wouldn't really do something stupid if she commanded him to?"

"What sort of stupid thing did you have in mind? Hurling a bomb like the anarchists do in Europe?"

I attempted an unconcerned laugh. "No, I can't see Ryan hurling a bomb."

"And what would he wish to blow up? America has welcomed him with open arms and he displays no interest in going home to take up the Irish cause. What made you ask that question?"

"Nothing. Forget that I asked it."

Lennie daubed on paint in silence.

"Although he did consider blowing up Buckingham Palace once," Lennie went on. "But I think he only toyed with the idea for the drama it caused. You know Ryan. He lives for the dramatic."

I left the studio two hours later. If Lennie was really the LC mentioned in the black book, then he was a superb actor. I could swear, from talking to him, that neither he nor Ryan could possibly be involved in anything violent or dangerous.

I was about to head home when, on a whim, I turned left instead of right and made for the house on West Eighth Street where Emma was staying. I had noted the address when Ryan wrote it down the night before. I knew I was taking a risk going to see her, but I decided I would be safe if I seemed to be naive enough.

An elderly foreign-looking woman with a plain round face and vacant blue eyes opened the front door. "Ya?" she said.

"I understand that Emma Goldman might be staying here?" I said cautiously.

She ushered me inside without saying a word, leaving me unsure whether she was a landlady or a friend, or whether she spoke any English. I was shown through to a sitting room where Emma was reading correspondence. She looked up with interest. "The little Irish miss. I didn't expect to see you again. Don't tell me you have had a change of heart and wish to join our little group?"

"Not exactly," I said. "I'm not sure how to put this, but I'm interested in Ryan's relationship with you and your group."

"Ryan's relationship with me? By that, I presume you are implying intimate relationship." A rather wicked smile spread across her face. "You are jealous! I never believed for a second that tale about being a cousin from Ireland. You want him for yourself."

"I may be naive, but I'm not thick enough to believe that I could have Ryan for myself," I said. "It was mere curiosity that brought me here. I was so surprised when he took me to meet you last night. I just couldn't believe that Ryan had ever been connected to a group like yours."

"You're right," she said. "He might have played at being a member of our little set for a while, but the novelty soon wore off—as it always does with Ryan."

"But you still exert a very strong influence over him. I saw his reaction when he heard you were in town."

"Yes," she said calmly, "I have that effect over quite a number of people, so I am given to understand. You are obviously not affected by my magnetic personality."

"But Ryan is such a strong personality himself," I said. "It seems hard to believe . . ."

"Nonsense," she said. "Ryan is a very weak personality. Why else would he constantly need to play a part and never let his true self show through? If he stops playing at being Ryan O'Hare, world-famous playwright and man-about-town, for one second, the whole world will collapse around him."

"So he could be influenced by someone like you."

"Not for long. He has the attention span of a two-year-old, as you must have noticed. And if by your statement you insinuate that he would rush off to London and assassinate King Edward at my behest, then you are sadly mistaken. Ryan likes to be comfortable. Prisons are notoriously uncomfortable. I know. I have been inside quite a number of jail cells in my life. And hanging is even more uncomfortable, so I'm told." She looked at my worried face and laughed. "Is that what you concern yourself about? That your precious Ryan will risk his life for me? No. It will never happen. Why would he need to strike such a blow? He has his words. They are more effective as weapons than any bomb. See what happened when he wrote the play about the British royal family? The whole country was in an uproar, just over a few silly words."

She leaned back in her chair and cradled her head in her hands. "This is what I try to get through the heads of those earnest young people who surround me wherever I go. If you want to change the world, use words—they are powerful. Blow up one tyrant and another will step forward to take his place. But write a clever piece that is published in a newspaper and the masses will read it." She paused, almost as if she was waiting for applause. "Ryan unfortunately is completely taken up with his new play. He is choosing to waste his talent on fame and fortune."

"Thank you," I said. "You are quite right. I'm sorry. I should never have troubled you."

"You still haven't asked me if I had an intimate relationship with Ryan." Again the wicked smile. "I didn't, but it might have been very nice."

I came away from Emma Goldman feeling quite reassured. She was right. Ryan's new love was his play. He wouldn't do anything that might jeopardize its success. If Paddy thought he had heard Ryan and someone called LC discussing something dangerous, then he had been mistaken. I had nothing to worry about at all.

It was with a lighter heart that I took the streetcar up Broadway to the Daley Theater where Ryan's play was being rehearsed. I hadn't been through this part of the city before and found it very exciting, with billboards advertising new plays and electric lights winking from theater marquees. *The Belle of New York.* "A Doll's House, by Mr. Ibsen." So many plays I hadn't seen, so many exciting things still waiting to be done. The city was like a giant banquet spread before me, and I had only yet had a chance to nibble at the first course.

The Daley Theater looked spendid from outside, with ornate pillars and an impressive set of glass front doors, but its marquee was dark and its front doors firmly locked. I went through an alley and discovered a side entrance. I opened it and found myself in a dark, narrow passageway. I could hear voices on my left and followed the sound until I could see light. I was standing in a backstage area and could just get a glimpse of the backs of several actors on the stage. No sign of Ryan, though. As I stood there, unsure what to do next, a girl came past me, wearing a paint-daubed smock and carrying a large paint pot in her hand.

"Hey, what are you doing? You shouldn't be here," she hissed at me.

"I'm a friend of Mr. O'Hare's. He invited me to watch a rehearsal."

"Did he? Well, he's in a foul mood today—the cast aren't word-perfect on Act Three and they open on the road in a couple of days—so I'd stay out of his way, if I were you. If you want to watch, go down there and through the pass door. That will take you to the house."

I hadn't any idea what house she was talking about, but I followed her directions, pushed open a heavy door and found myself in the darkened theater. The only light came from the stage. In the gloom I could make out gilt-trimmed balconies and the huge chandelier in the ceiling. I felt my way back along an aisle and found myself a seat at the back of the stalls, beside an ornately decorated pillar. I had never been in a theater before and was rather overawed at the magnificence around me. The seats were soft plush, and there was a Greek mural over the stage. It would have been an entertaining place to visit even if there had been no play to watch.

The play also proved to be entertaining. Having come in halfway through the Second Act, I couldn't catch up with the whole story, but it seemed to be a satire about a small fictitious country that had locked its doors to the rest of the world and refused to admit that any world existed outside of its borders. In the behavior of the despotic emperor I noticed several references to Queen Victoria, and in the behavior of the citizens of Nowheria a wicked caricature of American isolationism. "We're all right, so damn the rest," as one character said.

The Second Act finished, and we moved into the troubled Third Act, which Ryan had only just completed. I could see the poor actors struggling with their lines and heard Ryan's voice, offstage, "Get it right, for God's sake, Ethel. Is it too much to ask that an actress learn her lines?"

"I was prepared to learn lines back in April, Ryan," she replied coldly, "only the lines weren't there to be learned."

The act continued. Not quite as funny as its predecessor, but deeper. I was sitting lost in the entrancement of watching a real play for the first time, when I felt suddenly cold, as if a door behind me had been opened and let a draft come in. I turned around. The doors to the foyer were all closed, but I still felt chilled. As I turned back, I thought I saw a movement, as if some-one had ducked behind another pillar. My skin prickled. Some-body was in the darkened theater with me.

"Don't be stupid," I told myself. Any one of the cast could have popped through to take a look at the play from the audi-ence's side. Maybe one of the set builders was taking a break. I peered into the darkness, but there was no sign of the other per-son. Nobody sitting in another seat. And yet I could still feel a presence. Call it my Celtic gift of second sight, if you will, but I have always had the ability to sense when danger was near. I was sensing it now.

Instantly I realized my complete isolation. The actors onstage were absorbed with their play. I was alone and far from help. What a perfect situation for anyone who wanted to silence me. He would only have to crawl along the row behind me, grab me from behind and finish me off. Nobody would find my body for days. I fought to remain calm. I could jump up and scream. Ryan and his cast would be angry, of course, but I'd have scared away my potential attacker.

Seconds passed and nothing happened. I just couldn't bring myself to run screaming to the stage. How very absurd I'd look if I had been frightened by some trick of the lighting. But with the knowledge that I could scream if necessary, I got to my feet and started to walk determinedly to that pass door. It was hidden from here, behind a half-drawn curtain and up a little flight of steps. I had a great desire to break into a run. I reached the door, tugged on it and found that it wouldn't open from this side. The actors went on with the scene, unaware that I was down here in the dark. There was a large orchestra pit between me and the stage. No way of leaping up to light and safety.

As I turned back, again I caught sight of a fleeting movement. He was closer to the exit door now, cutting off my escape. Two could play that game, I decided. I dropped to the floor and moved at a crouch through one of the front rows of seats. I came out on the far side of the theater. Then, still at a crouch, I made my way up toward the exit doors on that side. If my potential attacker was waiting to intercept me on the other side, then it would give me a few seconds to make my escape. I reached the last row of chairs, then, praying that one of the doors was unlocked and led somewhere, I rushed to the nearest door and pushed. It swung open easily and I was in a carpeted hallway. The hallway was almost as dark as the theater had been. I could make out ghostly shapes of Greek and Roman busts in alcoves as I hurried past. When I came out into the foyer, I was surprised to find it was also dark. I had been in the theater longer than I had intended and night had fallen outside.

As my feet tapped across the marble foyer, I heard the sound of a door swinging shut on the far side. I didn't hesitate a moment longer. I ran for the front doors. The first one I tried wouldn't budge. I tried the others in turn, fighting back the rising panic, until the door on the end swung open for me and I was out into the bustle of a Broadway night. But not safe yet. It would be easy to follow me through the darkness and wait for a moment when I would be alone. He could even follow me all the way home if he wanted. Patchin Place was always deserted. I considered running a block to the Sixth Avenue El, but the thought of standing, waiting, on an El platform was too alarming.

I stepped out onto the crowded sidewalk and attempted to blend into the crowd. As I glanced back, I thought I saw a dark figure emerge from the theater and scan the crowd, looking for me. A streetcar came down Broadway, its bell clanging to warn pedestrians out of its way. As it was slowed by the human tide. I made a desperate sprint to catch it. I grabbed at the handrail just as it picked up speed again and heard the conductor shout at me as it sped off, abandoning me on Broadway.

No other streetcars were in sight. I ran back to the sidewalk and weaved through the crowd as fast as was possible. An occasional glance behind me convinced me that a man was also dodging through the crowd, keeping me within sight. One block passed, then another, still no streetcar in sight and still the sense of that presence behind me. Somehow I had to lose him. I reached Madison Square Park and stood on the corner where Broadway parts from Fifth Avenue. Ahead of me the skeleton of a new skyscraper was lit by kerosene lamps and the sound of hammering announced that construction work was still proceeding in the dark. I looked up at the skinny, oddly shaped building, and a memory resurfaced. Someone had described this very building to me. I even remembered its name—the Flatiron Building. The building on which my friend Michael Larkin worked as a foreman. I sprinted across the street, dodging a motorcar which honked imperiously, and plunged into the dark skeleton half-encased in wood scaffolding. Two men were emerging, swinging their lunch pails as they headed home. I grabbed one of them by the sleeve. "Excuse me, but would you know where I might find Michael Larkin?"

The man started at the sight of a strange female on his own territory.

"You'll be in trouble if they catch you in here, miss," he said in an Irish accent thicker than my own. "Michael Larkin you're wanting, are you? Is it urgent?"

"Very," I said. "If he's here, I have to speak to him. I've got important news for him."

The larger of the two men looked around him. "I don't think he's knocked off for the night yet, has he, Denny?"

"Last time I saw him, he was up on the eighteenth floor, waiting his turn to ride down," the other man replied. "If you wait on the street outside, he'll surely be passing this way in a while."

"Is there no way you could go and fetch him for me?" I had no wish to wait alone in the dark for a Michael who might or might not materialize, making myself a sitting duck in the meantime.

The men laughed. "You'll not get me riding up there again in the dark, even if you paid me," one of them said with a nod of agreement from the other. "I'm done for the day, off home to my supper and my bed."

They moved forward, ready to drive me out of the building before them. I didn't know what to do or what to say to keep them with me. It sounded so dramatic to say that I feared I was being followed by an unknown assailant. I wished now that I had taken my chances and tried to outrun him through the crowd, or even found a policeman to help me.

Then there came a shout from above. One of the men grabbed my arm and dragged me aside. "Watch yourself," he warned.

With the squeaking and grinding of wheels, a contraption came flying down out of the darkness and landed on the concrete beside us. It was nothing more than a flimsy wooden basket on pulleys, but four men stepped out of it, nodded to my two companions and headed away. With a great flood of relief I realized that one of them was Michael Larkin. At the same time one of my companions called out, "Here's the boy himself then. The Lothario of the scaffolds. One of your lady loves come looking for you, Michael me boy."

Michael spun around, a shocked look on his face, stared blankly for a second, then his boyish face broke into a big smile. "Well, if it isn't Molly. What in God's name are you doing here?"

"Paying you a little visit, like you said," I replied, conscious of the smiling men around us. "Actually I have something important I need to tell you. News that couldn't wait, from the Old Country." I took his arm and led him away.

"It's not bad news, is it?" he asked. "You've not heard something bad from home?"

We were out in the street again. I looked around, but could not pick out my assailant in the crowd. "No, no bad news," I said. "In fact, no news at all. I'm sorry. I had to tell a little untruth to get you on my own."

"You? An untruth? I'm shocked." He was laughing at me, having been told the full details of my flight from Ireland and the subterfuges needed to bring me this far. I laughed with him, feeling the tension dissolving. I tried to think how best to phrase my request.

"The truth is, Michael, that I'm being followed by an unwanted suitor. I can't seem to get rid of the man, so I wondered if you'd do me the favor . . ."

"And pretend I'm your beau?" He was still smiling. I knew he was years too young for me, being no more than eighteen, but for a moment I wished that this wasn't such an outlandish proposition. A steady, reliable man to protect me seemed like a rather desirable thing.

"If you possibly had time to escort me safely home?" I suggested. "Or at least see me safely onto a streetcar."

"I'll do one better than that," he said. "It was payday today. I'll take you out for a bite of supper if you like."

"You don't have to do that."

"It's the least I can do," he said. "Do you not think I owe you a favor, Molly? Thanks to you I'm living the life of Riley." He took my hand in his.

"You don't think your lady love will object?" I asked.

He laughed merrily. "I've told her about you and she knows you're nothing more than a big sister to me. In fact, she's dying to meet you sometime. Come on, I know a good place where they serve the best boiled beef and cabbage you can imagine. Just like home."

The food was hot and filling, I'll say that for it, but my own tastes had broadened a little, now that I knew there was more than boiled beef and cabbage in the world. We had a grand old talk, though, and I found I could relax enough to stop glancing out of the window every few seconds. And when Michael delivered me home, there was no dark shadow in sight lurking behind us.

❧ Twenty-three ❧

B y the time I reached Patchin Place safely, I had decided
not to tell Gus or Sid about the incident in the theater.
They pounced on me the moment I came in through the
front door, peppering me with questions about the play. I was in
the middle of telling them when Ryan himself arrived, still in a
bad mood and demanding a whole pot of Turkish coffee to calm
his nerves.

"Coffee is a stimulant, my sweet," Gus told him as Sid went to
make it.

"Then your divine presence will calm me down," Ryan said,
smiling from her face to mine. "Who could fail to feel serene
among such beauty?"

"Irish blarney," Gus muttered to me. "He's full of it, isn't he.
Tell him how bad his play was—that will shut him up."

Ryan's gaze swung to me. "You came to the theater today? You
saw the play?"

I nodded.

"Where were you? Why didn't you come to find me?"

"You were otherwise occupied, yelling at an actress named
Ethel for not knowing her lines."

"Stupid cow," Ryan exclaimed. "She has precisely five lines in
that scene. Is it too much to ask that she learn them? Does she
expect to walk out in front of an audience in a few days and ad-

lib?" He sank onto the wicker chaise longue. It was a warm night and we were still sitting out in the garden. "So was the play really terrible? Tell me the truth—I'm man enough to bear it."

"It was brilliant, Ryan. Funny, yet moving at the same time. And very wicked—all those gibes at the American upper-class society women."

A smile lit up his face. "Yes, it was rather naughty of me, wasn't it. But somehow I couldn't help myself. The words just spilled out and there they were on the page. But you give me hope, dearest Molly. I just pray that the first-night critics are equally perceptive and kind."

When Ryan left, well after midnight, I went to bed in a much calmer mood. How could I have reacted so hysterically in the theater? Anyone would think I was turning into the kind of frail and sensitive young thing who got the vapors at the slightest provocation. Thank heavens I hadn't told Gus and Sid about my encounter with the shadowy stranger. They would have told Ryan and all had a good laugh at my expense. I was almost tempted to laugh at myself.

And yet my sixth sense hadn't let me down before. I had sensed a presence in that theater and felt myself to be in danger. I sat on the edge of my bed and tried to analyze it calmly. Who could have known that I would be alone in a darkened theater? Apart from Sid and Gus, nobody knew I had planned to watch the rehearsal. Even Ryan hadn't known I was there. But any one of the cast or crew could have known—the girl with the paint pot could have told them. But why would any of them have wished me harm? They didn't know me from Adam. So who could possibly wish me harm? The only person I could come up with was the man who killed Paddy. But why wait until now? Why risk going into a theater? I had walked alone through the Village on several occasions. I had ridden the El. I had slept with my bedroom window open.

I got up from my bed and hastily closed it. The annoying

thing was that I should no longer feel safe when I went out alone. It would only be a matter of time before my stalker found out where I lived, if he didn't know already. I should pluck up courage to go back to that theater again, and this time get a good look at the cast and crew. Only this time I'd make sure I stayed close to Ryan.

I fell into a dreamless sleep and woke next morning feeling refreshed. The whole thing seemed like nothing more than a bad dream. I found it hard to believe that I had let myself get so alarmed over nothing. The product of an overstimulated imagination, I concluded. My mother had always insisted that my imagination would bring me to a bad end, if my sharp tongue and my airs and graces didn't do it first.

In the afternoon I went back to the theater, only to find the doors locked and no apparent way in. I walked around a little up and down Broadway, examining the crowd, in case my assailant habitually lurked outside the theater—although for what reason I couldn't imagine—then, reluctantly, took the Sixth Avenue El home again.

"I expect Ryan was in a temperamental mood and wanted no interruptions," Sid said about the locked doors. "They take the play on the road at the end of the week, don't they?"

That was reassuring. If my shadowy figure was part of the company, he'd be safely far away by the end of the week. But I'd dearly have loved to have been allowed a quick look at the company, although I wasn't sure I would recognize Paddy's killer again if I met him. When I tried to picture his face, all I remembered was dark intense eyes, a black hat or cap of some sort, and lithe movements as he leaped to safety. Not a lot to go on—it was an apt description of half the young men around the Village. I felt as if I was fishing around in the dark. I still wanted to solve Paddy Riley's murder. I also wanted to make sure I stayed alive, but I wasn't sure what to do next. Paddy would have known, of course. He had the experience to know how to follow a case through to its conclusion. Daniel would also have known, but I wasn't going to Daniel unless I really had to—at least not until I had some concrete facts to present to him.

The next day a late-summer hot spell arrived, making us all too languid to embark on anything more than pouring iced tea and fanning ourselves. I knew I should be pursuing my investigation, but I hadn't the energy. I did manage to stroll across town to see Shamey and Bridie and take them out for an ice cream. My worries about their catching diseases from swimming in the East River seemed to be unfounded. They both looked revoltingly healthy and Bridie's little face had filled out. I returned home feeling relieved.

That evening, Sid and Gus were invited to a showing at a friend's studio. They invited me to go with them, but I declined, not being wildly enthusiastic about the kind of modern art that Gus and her friends painted. I sat out in the garden until the temperature dropped pleasantly, then decided to go to O'Connor's. Maybe Ryan would be there and I could ask him about the members of his theater company. I found that I was looking around cautiously as I walked out of Patchin Place, then down Sheridan Street, but I reached O'Connor's without mishap.

The place was deader than a doornail. It soon became obvious that the clientele of the tavern were all at the showing to which Sid and Gus had gone. I waited half an hour while I sipped a ginger beer, then left again. Ryan certainly wasn't going to come tonight—he'd never appear anywhere where there wasn't a guaranteed audience. I was tempted to join the others at the showing, but decided against it. It was still too muggy for walking. So I went home. I'd indulge in a long cool bath before Gus and Sid came back. I crossed Greenwich Avenue and stood at the entrance to Patchin Place peering into the darkness. Only one gas lamp illuminated the far reaches of the street. A breeze had sprung up, causing the trees to move in grotesque shadow dances and sending the first leaves fluttering. I suddenly regretted my foolishness at going out alone. I had only taken a few steps when a black cat leaped from behind a tree and streaked across my path, causing my heart almost to leap out of my mouth.

"Nonsense!" I said out loud. Just because of one alarming incident in a theater, I was not going to be intimidated for the rest of my life. I walked forward with brisk, firm steps and head held high. The street was deserted. I reached my front door without incident, turned the key and let myself in. I stood in the hallway and heaved a sigh of relief. I was turning into an alarmist—this would never do. I put down my purse on the hall stand and felt around for the matches that we kept on the little shelf below the gas bracket. The shelf was empty. I felt my way down the hall to the kitchen. There were always matches beside the stove. As I pushed open the kitchen door, I heard a crash. At that moment I felt a breeze in my face and noticed, with horror, the outline of the French doors leading from the conservatory to the garden. I had gone out leaving them open. From what I could make out, the breeze had blown over the small vase on the conservatory table.

I was about to reach for the matches when I heard another sound. This one didn't come from the direction of the garden. It was soft enough to be barely audible, but my senses were already fine-tuned. I stood frozen with fear. The sound I had heard was the unmistakable creak of a floorboard. Someone was in the house with me.

I wasn't sure what to do next. I had no idea where the sound had come from. I didn't think the floorboards on the ground floor creaked. I knew there was a squeaky board on the stairs, and one on the upstairs landing. If the intruder was upstairs, I might have a chance to escape through the front door. But if he was on the stairs, he'd see me trying to open the front door. On the other hand, he could already have come down the stairs and be waiting for me in the hallway. Not a comforting thought. There was no point in going out to the garden. It was surrounded by high, ivy-covered fences on two sides and the bare wall of another building at the back. Encumbered as I was with skirts and petticoats, I knew I wouldn't be able to scale either of those fences.

I decided against lighting the lamp, on the off chance that he didn't already know I was here. Holding my breath and moving as silently as I could, I pulled open the dresser drawer that contained the cutlery. I would definitely feel more secure with a large carving knife in my hand. My fingers closed around a knife handle and I lifted it from the drawer. There was a gentle swish of metal against metal that made me hold my breath again. Then, knife at the ready, I walked down the hallway.

He wasn't on the stairs. Enough light came through the glass pane at the top of the front door to highlight the shape of the hallstand and to shine on the middle of the staircase. He could, of course, be standing at the top of the staircase, waiting for me to come past. In which case, maybe the glint of a long blade in my hand might dissuade him. My breath sounded as noisy as a puffing steam engine and I pressed my lips together to stop the sound from escaping. I drew level with the hallstand. I had reached the front door and still nothing moved. My hand reached for the door handle. One turn, one tug, and I'd be free.

At that moment I heard an intake of breath behind me. I spun around as a dark shape leaped from the drawing room doorway.

"Stay away from me, I'm armed!" I shouted loudly, waving the knife. I lashed out as he came at me and I saw the glint of metal in his hand. He also had a knife, though not as big as mine. He went to stab and I parried with my knife. There was a satisfying clash of metal and for a wild second I felt as if I was playing the part of D'Artagnon. As soon as this vision flashed through my head the knife came again and I was reminded forcefully that this wasn't playacting, it was real. He made another jab and as I reached to parry, he grabbed my wrist.

"I should have killed you then," he hissed in a voice little louder than a whisper. His face was close to mine. It was then that I saw his eyes. I had seen those eyes before, in the second before he leaped at me in Paddy's office—that intense, desperate, burning gaze of hate or panic, or both. I struggled violently, trying to free my hand from his grasp.

"How much . . . did he tell you . . . The old guy?" he demanded. The words came out between jerks of my arm, trying to get me to drop my knife. I responded with a hefty kick at his shins and a stomp on what I hoped were his feet. I heard another intake of breath, which indicated I might have struck my mark. I fought to get my wrist free but his grip was like steel. At least while I was flailing around with my own knife only inches from his face he wouldn't find me an easy target. His knife flashed toward me. I put up my free arm and the blade sailed harmlessly through the fabric of my leg-of-mutton sleeve. I mouthed a silent thank-you to Gus for providing me with such out-of-fashion garments. There was the sound of cloth ripping as he wrenched the knife free from the fabric. It caught for a moment and I decided to try his own tactic. I made a grab for the wrist that held the knife. My fingers closed around it—a slim wrist, slim as a woman's—and I held on. He let out a growl and hurled me back against the front door. My head crashed against the solid oak and sparks shot across my vision.

"Who did you tell?" he growled and braced to slam me against the door again. It occurred to me, as ridiculous thoughts often do at moments of crisis, that I should try to lead him on and find out what he thought I knew. But I didn't answer him for the simple reason that every ounce of my strength was needed that moment to stay alive. Obviously I couldn't keep going like this much longer. I could annoy and delay him for a minute or two, maybe, but he would have to triumph in the end.

But I certainly wasn't going to give in without a good fight. I had sparred and wrestled with my brothers in the past, but this was very different. They had been younger than me, and they hadn't been trying to kill me either. I cursed my stupid skirts that encumbered my attempts to deliver a kick where it might do the most damage, but I did manage to connect with his shins again. Then he used all his weight to slam me back against the door once more. As I braced to connect with the solid wood, the door miraculously opened. I felt myself falling backward into blackness, with my attacker pitching on top of me. I struck the ground. The wind was knocked from me. The knife clattered from my hand.

Then I was aware of my name being called, of shouts and screams. Figures were flailing and grabbing at my attacker. "Grab him round the throat, Gus!"

"Watch out, he's got a knife."

I summoned my own strength to bring up my knee as hard as I could and heard a satisfying yelp of pain. At that moment Sid snatched up my own knife, yanked back the stranger's head and held the knife to his throat. "Drop the knife this instant, or I'll cut your throat," she commanded.

The knife fell to the ground beside me. Gus snatched it up.

"Get up," Sid said, my knife still at his throat.

She half-dragged him to his feet by his hair. I scrambled to my feet.

"Did you think because we were women we were easy pickings?" Sid demanded. "Go into the kitchen and get string, Molly. We'll tie him up and then go for the police."

I ran through to the kitchen and found the ball of string in the drawer. As Gus and I attempted to bring his arms behind his back, he lashed out like a madman, sent Sid sprawling to the cobblestones and took off down Patchin Place.

"Are you all right, Sid dear?" Gus dropped to her knees beside her.

Sid sat up and put her hand to her mouth. "I think so, apart from a bloody lip and a nasty bang on the back of my head. But I'm furious that we let him get away."

"We didn't let him. He was just too strong for us," Gus said. "I'll go for the police. You and Molly get inside and take care of your wounds."

"No," I exclaimed. "Don't go for the police yet."

"Why ever not? They can catch him before he gets too far away."

"It's useless," I said. "A young man, dressed all in black? Half the inhabitants of the Village fit that description. Did you get a good look at his face?"

"Not really," Sid said. "It's too dark out here and it was all so sudden."

"I hardly had a chance to get a good look at him," Gus said.

"Then we will just look foolish if we call the police," I said. "Let us be thankful that we are all relatively unharmed."

"At least he had to flee without his loot," Gus said.

"Loot?" I asked.

Sid nodded. "He was most certainly a burglar, wasn't he? Why else would you have surprised him in our house?"

She led the way down the front hall, felt for the matches, then went on to the kitchen, where the gas bracket lit with a satisfying pop and warm, friendly light flooded the kitchen.

"I'm afraid it was my fault," I said. "I went out leaving the French doors ajar. He could have come in that way."

"Don't blame yourself, Molly," Sid said. "We often leave doors and windows open on hot evenings. It could have happened to any of us."

"I don't think so," I said. Shock was beginning to set in and I was shaking all over. I sank to the nearest chair.

"Some brandy, Sid. She looks as white as a sheet," Gus said. She came and put an arm around my shoulder. "Poor Molly. You've had a most terrible shock. How brave of you to fight him off, when he had a knife, too."

"I heard a floorboard creak and grabbed a knife from the kitchen drawer," I said. "That held him at bay for a little while. But if you hadn't come home when you did, I should surely have been dead by now."

Sid handed me the brandy. "Get that down you and you'll feel better," she said. "I'm going out to retrieve his knife. There will be fingerprints on it."

217

"No, there won't," I said. "He was wearing dark gloves."

"Damn," Sid muttered. "I'll retrieve it nonetheless. And our knife, too."

She went outside and as she came back, I heard her laughing.

"Molly, my sweet," she said as she came into the kitchen, "Next time you attempt to defend yourself against an armed intruder, I'd choose something other than this."

It was then that I realized the knife I had selected had been the large fish server, with broad, curved blade and rounded edges—not sharp enough to cut anything tougher than a poached salmon.

❧ Twenty-four ❧

I wonder what he was trying to steal?" Gus said as she attended to Sid's cut lip with warm water and iodine. I, amazingly, had come through my ordeal almost unscathed, apart from a bump on the back of my head and a nick on my upper arm where the intruder had succeeded in stabbing my sleeve. But I was just now beginning to face the reality of the attack and felt decidedly wobbly.

"As soon as I've done your lip, I'll scout around and see if anything has been moved," Gus went on, dabbing efficiently as she talked. "Of course, Molly could have surprised him too soon, when he'd just got here."

I sat in a turmoil of indecision. Should I let them go on thinking it was an attempted burglary, or should I tell them the truth? I decided they had a right to know. Their lives might have been at stake, might still be at stake if I didn't take action.

"It was no burglary attempt," I said, sitting up and removing the ice pack from my head. "I'm afraid I have been less than honest with you. You have just saved my life. I owe you the truth."

"You're really a gangster's moll," Sid exclaimed delightedly.

"No, I'm really a private investigator," I said. "Well, that's a slight exaggeration. I was working for a private investigator and I was there when he was murdered. My attacker tonight was the same man who killed my employer."

"Do you know who he was?"

"No and I've spent the past few weeks trying to figure out who might have wanted to kill Mr. Riley."

"And what conclusion have you come to?"

"I thought I was no nearer to solving the case. The police sergeant assigned to it decided that it might be a gang's retaliation. I didn't believe that, because I surprised the killer ransacking Paddy's office, and I know he returned on a later date, still looking for something."

"How dashed exciting." Sid perched on the table beside me. "So who do you think the killer might be, Molly?"

"I'm still not sure, but this isn't the first attack on me. Someone followed me into the theater the other night." Then something else struck me. "And this only started after I went with Ryan to visit the group run by that strange Emma person."

"Emma the anarchist?" Sid asked. "I met her once. She tried to recruit me to write articles for a radical journal she was editing. It was a little too radical, even for me."

"You think Emma could be behind this, do you, Molly?" Gus asked. "You think she might have sent someone to murder your employer?"

"I have no idea," I said. "All I know is that I wasn't personally threatened until I went to her meeting. It could easily have been one of the young men I met there who attacked me. They all looked very much like the man tonight." Again I remembered the uneasiness that had grown during that evening at Schwab's, the feeling that I was being watched as I left with Ryan.

"So why won't you go to the police?" Gus asked. "If someone is threatening your life, they should do something."

"Because I have no facts yet, just a lot of suppositions."

"Someone tried to kill you," Gus said. "I'd say that was a pretty conclusive fact."

"What will you do now?" Sid asked.

"I must move out of here in the morning," I said. "I have

already abused your hospitality by staying as long as this, and now I have put you in danger. I'm very sorry. It was selfish of me."

"Move away just when things are getting exciting?" Sid demanded. "You don't think we'll let you escape now, do you? Besides, you need two efficient bodyguards like us."

"You were wonderful," I said. "The way you held that knife to his throat."

"Thank God I didn't know I was wielding a fish slicer or I might not have sounded so confident." Sid broke into laughter again. "Will you try and find him and bring him to justice yourself?"

"I'm going to visit Emma in the morning," I said. "It's possible that she is involved in this and that she put one of her young men up to it, but it's a risk I've got to take. From what she said, she doesn't believe in violence, so I'm counting on her help."

In the morning I had to dissuade Gus and Sid from coming with me.

"Three of us might look a little intimidating," I said.

"Oh Molly, don't be such a spoilsport," Gus said. "You know we're dying to be sleuths and bring the criminal to justice."

"I think I have to visit Emma alone," I said, "but you could certainly help me by asking at the various neighborhood taverns if a young man in black came in last night, out of breath and distressed. He must have been distressed when he ran away, don't you think?"

"Good idea. We can certainly do that, can't we, Gus dear," Sid said. "I wish we'd managed to get a better look at him. I'd love to apprehend him and make him pay for my cut lip and your bruises, Molly."

"This isn't a game, you know," I said. "This man is a violent killer. I was lucky that I heard a floorboard creak last night or I would have suffered Paddy's fate." I touched Sid's arm. "Promise me you will be discreet and careful. And don't mention my name."

Having extracted promises from them, I set off for the house on West Eighth Street. When the door was opened by the old European woman, she stood there shaking her head.

"Not here no more," she said. "She gone."

"Gone—gone where?"

She shrugged. "Home. She gone home."

"Do you know where her home is?"

She shrugged again. "Chicago, maybe? Somewhere over there." She pointed vaguely in a direction that may have been west.

"Do you have an address for her?"

Yet another shrug.

Not much help. Now I would have to think of another way of identifying my attacker. The logical thing would be to ask Ryan. He must know at least some of the people in Emma's group, although . . . I stopped short, standing poised at the curb about to cross Eighth Street. What if Ryan himself was involved? RO with LC. I shook my head in disbelief. Ryan—dear, sweet Ryan some- how involved in planning my death? It was too absurd to think about. And yet the first incident had happened in the darkness at his theater. He had claimed he didn't know I was there, but he could have known. And he had arrived at our front door not long after I got home. Was that to check if I had made it home safely?

"Absurd," I said out loud. "Rubbish."

I had been alone with Ryan on several occasions, including the other night after we left Emma. If he had wanted to kill me, there would have been ample chances. A quick shove under the hooves of a passing carriage would have been enough. But instead he had insisted on escorting me home safely. Besides, I didn't want to believe he was involved.

I wasn't sure what to do now. Maybe Sid and Gus were right and there was no alternative but to go to the police. I should meet with Daniel. He would know what to do next. Of course, he'd be furious with me that I had continued to poke my nose into this case after he had specifically forbidden me to get involved. But a lecture from Daniel would be preferable to winding up stabbed in a dark alleyway. I knew I would never feel safe until my attacker was caught.

If only I had some kind of evidence to present to Daniel. Apart from Paddy's little black book which I had deciphered, all I had were hunches and suppositions. And the fact that I had recognized my attacker—that he thought I was spying on him. Not much to go on. Of course, when the photos were ready, I might indeed have something worth showing.

I decided to take the bull by the horns and went straight to the photographer's shop on Broadway. I knew a week had not yet passed, but if I stressed the urgency to him, maybe he'd be understanding and work on those photographs right away. He greeted me with an unfriendly "Oh, it's you" as I came into the shop.

"Sorry to trouble you, but I just wondered . . ." I began.

"If the photos were ready yet?" he finished for me. "Been ready for days. You made such a fuss that I thought you'd be back here pestering me long before this."

He pulled open a drawer below the counter and took out an envelope. "Here you are," he said. "That will be one dollar, on account of the rush job."

"One dollar?" I demanded, horrified at such extortion.

"Do you want them, or don't you?" The man pulled open the drawer again, ready to replace the photographs. Hurriedly I paid him and stepped outside. A gray morning had become progressively grayer, and now raindrops were spattering on the pavement. I stepped under the awning above the butcher's shop next door and carefully removed the prints from their folder. They weren't exactly photographic masterpieces—most of them dark, and blurred as well. I recognized Lord Edgemont leaving the house on Gramercy Park with a glamorous lady who had to be the famous Kitty. Then there was a snapshot of them entering what was presumably Delmonico's. There was also one taken in their private dining room, but it was too dark and blurred to identify either of the shadowy forms at the table apart from Kitty's outrageous hat.

Then I came to a picture that literally took my breath away. RO and LC at O'Connor's. It was dark again, of course, but I could just make out Ryan's handsome, smiling face as he leaned close to another man. And the other was a skinny young man wearing a black worker's cap. He had haunted, hollow eyes. He could easily have been my assailant. What is more, I recognized him. He had sat at the far end of the table at Schwab's Tavern that night.

A couple more pictures followed. Ryan and the same man, bent over a sheet of paper on a tabletop. And then the biggest surprise of all. I found myself staring at a picture of Sergeant Wolski talking with another man I didn't recognize. Had Wolski been involved in this? He had certainly responded quickly after Paddy's death. Did that mean he had been lurking in the neighborhood, even keeping watch while the dark fellow did the killing? He had done the most perfunctory of searches of Paddy's office, and made sure I was hustled out of the way. And he had seemed interested in Paddy's camera, too. Did he realize there might be incriminating evidence against him?

My heart was beating very fast now. I would turn the whole thing over to Daniel, and Daniel only. Now that I knew Sergeant Wolski might be somehow involved, I could no longer risk going to any other policeman. If Daniel wasn't there, I'd wait for another occasion. I started in the direction of Mulberry Street and police headquarters, then realized I was passing very close to Schwab's saloon. Maybe the barman could identify the man with Ryan in the photograph. I was about to cross the street to enter the saloon when a sudden downpour brought me to a halt under an awning and gave me time to reconsider. What if my assailant was in the saloon at this moment? Then my desire to present Daniel with a finished investigation won out. It was, after all, broad daylight. If my assailant was there, I could have the bartender and other customers hold him while I went for a constable.

But it was still with some trepidation that I pushed open the frosted glass door and plunged into the gloom. The fug was less at this early hour and there were only two customers, both sitting at the bar. I drew the bartender aside and showed him the photograph. He shook his head. Yes, he did recall seeing the man in there a couple of times but he wasn't a regular and he had no idea of his name.

"They'll know, though," he said, indicating the now-empty table at the back of the bar. "That lot you were sitting with. They'll know. Some of 'em are here most nights."

So I had to leave empty-handed again. The shower had passed over, leaving steaming sidewalks and a hot-house smell of rotting vegetation as I continued on to Mulberry Street.

I was some distance from the Mulberry Street police headquarters building when I froze. Sergeant Wolski was standing on the steps, talking with another officer. As I watched, they turned and went into the building, laughing together. That settled it. My interview with Daniel would have to wait for a safer occasion.

I had no alternative but to go home. I considered leaving a message at Daniel's apartment, but I really wanted the triumph of being able to name my assailant. It occurred to me that Sid and Gus, maybe even Lennie and some of his friends, could accompany me to Schwab's that evening. I would be perfectly safe with them. Then, of course, I saw the problem. I'd have to show them the photograph. Sid and Gus would want to know why we shouldn't go straight to Ryan and ask him to name the other man. This would be the obvious thing to do, except that I wasn't completely sure I could trust Ryan. If he was somehow involved in a plot, then who better at lying his way out?

When I got home, Sid and Gus had returned from playing detective, but they had not come up with any useful information. Nobody remembered seeing a fleeing man late last night. I told them of my plan to visit Schwab's that evening, and asked them to accompany me.

"Do you expect to find him there?" Sid asked, looking more excited than apprehensive. "I'd dearly love to pay him back for our bumps and bruises."

"The bartender says there will be people there who know his

name," I said and the photograph just slipped out without my meaning it to. Gus and Sid begged to see it, so I had to feign a call of nature and sprint up to my room. There were fortunately two photographs that clearly showed Ryan and my attacker. I took one of them and cut it in half. Then I ran down again. "This is the man," I said. "My former employer must have been tailing him and taken a photograph of him."

"That's him all right." Gus leaned over, "I'd know that face anywhere. Surly customer."

"But Molly dear, we've been talking it over," Sid said, "and we are not going to allow you to go to Schwab's this evening."

"I have to find someone to identify this man, don't you see?"

Sid was grinning. "That is why you must let us go in your stead."

"In my stead? Absolutely not. I've caused you enough danger as it is, and I—"

Gus held up her hand to silence me. "What if he's there, Molly? It would make more sense if we could get the information about him without arousing his suspicion."

"And I have been in there before," Sid added. "We are well-known around the Village. People expect to see us in taverns."

"Please be careful, then," I begged.

"We will," Gus said. "Let's think up a plausible reason for wanting to identify this man."

"He owes me money," Sid said, and laughed. "What could be more plausible in the Village."

That evening we walked together to Schwab's. I insisted on coming along and they agreed because they didn't want to risk leaving me in the house alone. So I established myself at the window of a little café across the street while Sid and Gus entered Schwab's. It seemed like an eternity. More people went into the tavern but nobody came out. I drank three cups of coffee and still they didn't come. I began to worry that something might have happened to them. What if the whole of Emma's group was somehow involved, and they had set upon Sid and Gus? What if the barman was also involved and had forewarned the group? I was almost ready to brave the tavern myself, wondering what I could use for a weapon, when I saw them emerge and cross the street.

"Sorry it took a while," Sid said. "We had to make it seem that we were being sociable."

"Sid was brilliant," Gus said. "She asked if Emma was still in New York because she had written the article she had promised for her journal. Of course then we were invited to join them and we were able to bring the photo into conversation most casually."

"You'd have been proud of us, Molly. First-class detectives, that's what we were."

"And you found out who he was?"

"We did, but it took a while. He doesn't live in New York City. He's shown up a couple of times before, but nobody really knows him. He's not one of their group, anyway. Not one of the comrades. In fact, they have been a little suspicious of him themselves. Nobody even knew his name, but finally someone thought that he was called Soulguts."

"Soulguts? What an extraordinary name. And do they know where we might find him?"

"Someone thought he might be staying at a boardinghouse down by the docks. On Barrow Street, they think."

"Barrow Street?" It had to be O'Shaunessey's. I almost laughed at the irony. He was rooming in Paddy's old boardinghouse. "I know the one," I said. "I've been there before."

"So will you go to the police now?" Gus asked. "They can go there and arrest him."

Darkness had fallen. Rain was threatening again. "In the morning," I said. "I'll go to the police in the morning."

"Molly—you're putting off the evil hour," Sid said, taking my arm. "What do you have against the police, apart from the fact that they are corrupt, violent and crooked?"

I laughed. "I have my reasons," I said. "A captain of police, a friend of mine—a former friend of mine—forbade me to get involved with this murder. He's not going to be pleased."

"He's not going to be pleased if your body turns up in the Hudson," Gus said.

"I promised I'd go in the morning. But I can only give my information to my friend Daniel. I have my reasons."

"This is damned exciting," Sid said. "I feel like Holmes and Watson, don't you, Gus dearest?"

I didn't feel in the least like Holmes or Watson. I felt sick. I just wanted this whole mixed-up business over and done with, so that I could get on with my life. The thought of passing my evidence over to Daniel became more appealing by the minute.

The next morning, again Sid and Gus were determined to escort me to police headquarters. I was equally determined that they shouldn't. I didn't want them to meet Daniel and have to explain to them the story of my relationship with him. And I didn't want them to see Daniel giving me a good scolding either. So in the end they gave in to my pleas, having made me promise faithfully that I would walk straight to police headquarters, taking no detours along the way.

To tell the truth, I was dreading the encounter with Daniel. He was going to be so angry with me, and I, of course, still felt rather angry with him. Some of that anger was bound to come spilling out. I've never been known for my gentle nature and lack of temper. But I did agree that anything would be better than being stabbed.

I asked at the front desk for Captain Sullivan. The young constable disappeared, then returned. "He's on leave, ma'am. Taken a few days' leave over the holiday. Is the matter urgent? I can take down the particulars for you."

"On leave?" I managed to sound calm. "Has he left town, do you know?"

He laughed. "I've no idea. I'm just a new constable here. I ain't privy to a captain's plans."

I had no alternative. I summoned a hansom cab and was taken

to Daniel's apartment in the area they call Chelsea, over on West Twenty-first Street. It was a quiet, respectable neighborhood after the noise and bustle of the Village. I rang Daniel's doorbell. There was no answer. I even rang the doorbell of the O'Sheas, with whom I had lodged briefly. No answer there, either. The whole street was silent, with blinds drawn, as if the entire population had vacated the city.

There was only one thing for me to do. I hopped on the Ninth Avenue El and rode back to Greenwich Street. I took a deep breath outside of Mrs. O'Shaunessey's boardinghouse. What if Soulguts was there and saw me? Would he be desperate enough to try something in broad daylight? Then I decided that I would be letting him know that I was on to him and wasn't afraid. Maybe that in itself would be a deterrent. I knocked on the door.

"I didn't expect to see you again." Mrs. O'Shaunessey looked as unkempt and slovenly as she had done previously, and she was not eyeing me with affection. "I hope you haven't changed your mind about any of Mr. Riley's belongings because it's all been disposed of, and I've rented to a new tenant."

"Nothing of the sort, Mrs. O'Shaunessey." I gave her an encouraging smile. "I'm trying to locate a young man who might also be a tenant of yours. I was told he stayed at a boardinghouse on Barrow. You'd be the only boardinghouse on the street, wouldn't you?"

"Apart from that stinking establishment on the corner over there," she said, nodding in the direction of the river while she crossed her arms across her large, sagging bosom. "Calls herself a boardinghouse, but it's no better than a den of vice, if you get my meaning."

"Then I hope I'll find that the young man is staying with you. I'm not sure of his name, but I think it's something like Soulguts, and he's sort of frail-looking and skinny and he wears a black cap."

"Oh, you mean Mr. Czolgosz." She spelled it for me. "A Polish name, so they tell me."

"Polish?" Now that was interesting. Wasn't Wolski also a Polish name?

"You're too late, deary. He was only here for a couple of days this time. He left yesterday."

"He left? Any idea where he went?"

"I thought he said he was going home. He comes from some heathen place out west—Ohio, if my memory serves me correctly."

My first reaction was relief. He was no longer in New York City. I was safe. Then I reminded myself that I was still a detective. I was still on a case.

"Have you cleaned out his room yet?" I asked. "I wondered if he left anything behind so that I could get in touch with him."

"I don't think he had much to leave," she said with a sniff. "Poor as a church mouse, if you ask me. But no, I haven't had time to get to his room yet. You're welcome to take a look. A friend of yours, was he?"

"Friend of a friend," I said. "I promised I'd try and track him down for her."

"It's back here," she said. "Opposite the kitchen."

She waddled down the hallway, puffing and panting, and opened a door at the end of a narrow, dark hallway. The room was equally dark and no bigger than a closet—even darker and gloomier than Paddy's old room had been. It contained a narrow bed, table, shelf and a couple of pegs for hanging. The window looked out onto a brick wall a few feet away. About the bleakest, sorriest room I had ever seen.

"He didn't want to pay much for the room this time," she said, as if reading my thoughts. "Seen better days, if you ask me. You can light the gas if you've a mind to."

I lit the bracket and the room became even more dreary. Cracking plaster, peeling wallpaper, pockmarked linoleum. I shuddered.

A brief glance confirmed that Mr. Czolgosz had not left anything of value behind. "Funny you should ask to see his room," Mrs. O'Shaunessey went on chattily. "It comes back to me now that poor Mr. Riley, God rest his soul, he took an interest in Mr. Czolgosz too. He asked to take a look at his room, on the quiet, like, although what he thought Mr. Czolgosz might have to hide I don't know. And Mr. Czolgosz got wind of the fact that I'd let him in. Proper tizzy he got in. Still, he was that kind of gentleman, wasn't he? Rather highly strung, if you ask me."

While she was talking, I found the wastebasket under the table and tipped out the contents. Sheets of angry black scribble, torn into little pieces. A postcard, also torn into several pieces. This was easier to put together, because I had a picture to go on. When complete it proclaimed itself to be a picture of gardens beside Niagara Falls, Buffalo, New York. A rather pretty subject for the violent Mr. Czolgosz, I decided, and carefully turned the postcard over to see to whom it was addressed.

Ryan O'Hare, Esquire. C/o Hotel Lafayette, New York.

The message said, "You didn't think I'd have the nerve to go through with it, did you? I promised I'd make you notice me." It was signed "Leon."

I gathered up the pieces of the postcard. "Thank you, Mrs. O'Shaunessey. You've been very helpful."

"Have you learned anything?"

"The postcard had a picture of Buffalo on it. I wonder if he was intending to stop off there on his way home?"

"Funny you should say that," she said. "He asked to borrow my railway timetable. I think he mentioned Buffalo."

I stuffed the pieces of postcard into my purse and hurried out onto the street. Then I walked as fast as I could, without actually picking up my skirts and running, to the Hotel Lafayette. Ryan had some explaining to do. I was going to get the truth out of him. Strangely enough, I wasn't afraid anymore. I was going to get to the bottom of this, if it was the last thing I did.

"Mr. O'Hare? I'm afraid you've missed him, miss." The young man at the front desk gave me an apologetic smile.

231

"Has he gone to the theater already?" Ryan was not known to be an early riser.

"No, miss. He's left New York. I understand that he's taking his new play on the road before it opens on Broadway."

"Oh." I felt like a deflated balloon. "Do you happen to know where he's gone?"

"I think I overheard that the play is due to open in Buffalo—makes sense, doesn't it, with all those crowds over the Labor Day weekend?"

"Crowds?"

"The big exposition," he said, looking at me as if I were soft in the head. "Been going on all summer. We've had guests here who've visited it and said it's like a dream—thousands of electric lights and towers and pavilions. They even have a Wild West show with a buffalo stampede."

My mouth went dry. That little doodle in Riley's black book. It hadn't been a bull at all. It had been a buffalo. RO and LC had now gone to Buffalo. They were planning somehow to disrupt the big exposition. I had to stop them.

❧ Twenty-five ❧

I was relieved to find that Sid and Gus were out when I returned to Patchin Place. My heart was racing with the crazy notion that was flying through my head. Someone had to go to Buffalo and intercept Ryan and Leon Czolgosz and, with Daniel gone, there was nobody I could trust at the police station—especially if Wolski was somehow involved. That meant I would have to go myself—an alarming proposition. I had never been out of New York before. I had no idea how far away Buffalo was, but I knew it was in New York State, so it couldn't be too far. Nevertheless, I might not be able to make it there and back in one day—I'd be required to spend a night there. I flung my nightdress and a hairbrush into Paddy's old briefcase and wrote a note to Sid and Gus to tell them where I was going. Then I wrote a longer, more detailed letter to Daniel, asking him to get in touch with the Buffalo police and laying out my suspicions. I included the photographs. I had no way of knowing when he would come back to his apartment to find the note. I just prayed it would be before I had to act on my own.

Throwing all financial considerations to the winds, I took another hansom cab to Daniel's apartment, hopefully rang the doorbell again, then put the letter through his mail slot. Then I withdrew some money from the bank and made for the Grand Central Depot.

I had never set foot inside that great smoky, bustling railway terminus before. I had passed through the station at Belfast once, but I had been on the run and too scared to notice much of my surroundings. Besides, it hadn't been anything compared to this vast, echoing place. Certainly nothing quite as daunting. I stood inside the doorway for a moment trying to get my breath. I fought my way through the crowds to the booking office and waited impatiently in the long line at the counter while shouts echoed through the building. "All aboard for Chicago, and all points west! Boston train on Platform Two!"

At last it was my turn to step up to the ticket window. A train for Buffalo was leaving at noon, I was told, but I'd be lucky if I got a seat. Half of New York was going to the exposition. I could wait and pay for a sleeper on the night train if I wanted.

"A sleeper?" I blurted out. "The trip can't take that long. It's in the same state, isn't it?"

"It's almost eight hours," the bewiskered man behind the bars said, looking at me with amused scorn. "I'll wager New York is a tad bigger than Ireland. Now, do you want the sleeper, or don't you? I have a whole line of people here waiting to snap it up."

"I'll take the noon train and risk not getting a seat," I said haughtily.

"A long time to stand," he said, smirking as he handed me my ticket.

I was on the platform in good time and of course I got a seat. I only had to walk through one carriage, looking suitably frail and helpless, before several courteous gentlemen leaped to offer me their seats.

I was still incredulous that the journey would take so long. Almost eight hours across one state? You could travel the length and breadth of Ireland in that time! The carriage was full of jolly, noisy families, off for an outing. I felt like an outsider, my stomach clenched into a tight knot. I stared out of the window as the railway ran beside the Hudson River and passed high cliffs, then pretty hamlets with white wooden houses. There were pleasure boats going up and down the river and picnics in meadows. On any other occasion I would have enjoyed the views, but not today. It seemed that the whole world was in a jolly festive mood except me.

Was I really doing the right thing? Had I not somehow misinterpreted the odd snippets of information and ended up with the wrong end of the stick? I had been known to do that before. So what did I really know? I asked myself, as I closed my eyes and listened to the rhythmic puffing of the engine. I knew that Leon Czolgosz had killed Paddy and then tried to kill me. Those facts were definite. I'd have recognized those eyes anywhere. So the next question had to be *why* Leon had tried to kill us both. He knew or suspected that Paddy had found out something about him and he also suspected that Paddy had told me. It had to be something pretty important to make him try to kill two people to silence them, and to burn down a place to destroy evidence. I wondered again what I might have overlooked among those papers. Then I decided that Paddy was such a secretive, cautious man that he'd never have spelled out suspicions in black and white. What he knew or suspected had gone to the grave with him.

And I could only guess what that could be. He had told me with his dying breath that it was too big for him. No normal crime then. He handled those with ease, all the time. And I had witnessed Leon at the anarchists' meeting. Anarchists did terrible, violent things. Their aim was to topple governments, kill kings, disrupt societies . . . And there was the exposition going on in Buffalo. Thousands of people would be there. It was too good an opportunity to miss for an anarchist. Somehow he was planning to disrupt the exposition.

The only question was whether Ryan was to be his partner in crime. Now that I had time to reflect, I still found it impossible to believe. Gay, debonair Ryan and violent, brooding Leon were chalk and cheese. How could they ever have decided to work together on anything? Unless, I thought, they were both under the spell of Emma Goldman and were doing her bidding. I remembered how Ryan had dropped everything and rushed to her summons that night. But she had told me that she no longer advocated violence. I shook my head in disbelief. I could not picture Ryan taking part in a violent plot or Paddy's killing or helping to orchestrate the attempt on my life. And yet Paddy had taken photos of the two of them together. RO with LC, equally dangerous in his mind. I shifted nervously in my seat. On this occasion I must not let my heart rule my head. Just because I thought of Ryan as my friend did not mean I would be safe when I reached Buffalo.

Now that I had eight hours to think, I realized that I had no idea what I was going to do when I got to Buffalo. In fact, as the miles rolled by, I became more and more convinced that I should have risked going to the police in New York, instead of trying to face Ryan—or worse still, Leon—alone. I could have gone over Sergeant Wolski's head But what could I have told the police? I had nothing to go on except that Leon Czolgosz had killed Paddy Riley and had tried to kill me. Only my word, however. No concrete proof except the photos, the words in Paddy's little book, and the drawing of a buffalo. Hardly enough evidence to make any policeman take my wild speculation seriously. And then there was Sergeant Wolski—if he, too, was involved somehow in this, he would make sure that I was not taken seriously. Or worse.

The journey seemed to go on forever. Farther down the car, a noisy group of young men were singing popular songs. "Daisy, Daisy, give me your answer, do," sung in several different keys, filled the smoky air. At another time I would have enjoyed it. On this occasion I wanted peace and quiet and time to collect my racing thoughts. I walked down the car and out onto the little platform at the end. Green fields and white farmhouses flashed past us, reminding me painfully of another rail journey I had taken earlier that year, when I had fled from Ireland. Such a lot had happened since then. My previously quiet life had been turned upside down.

Would I go back again if I had the chance? I wondered. It

wasn't hard to answer that one—there was no way I'd trade my present existence in New York for the dreary daily routine of Ballykillin. Even if my present life did have its risks, at least I knew I was living and breathing. And if only Daniel—I stopped that train of thought in a hurry. There was no point in thinking of Daniel that way ever again. A shifting wind gust covered me with smoke from the engine and drove me inside again.

Just before eight o'clock that evening, the train puffed its way into Buffalo station. Crowds streamed from the train, all seemingly with a purpose and direction in mind. I wasn't sure where to go next. I came out of the station into a street positively milling with people. The booking-office clerk hadn't been exaggerating. Half the world had gone to Buffalo today! Sidewalk cafés were full and the air resounded with competing strains of music—the string quartet at the fancy restaurant across the street being drowned out by the oompah band at a German biergarten. And to add to the cacophony, street vendors pushed their barrows through the crowd, shouting out their wares in a variety of accents: hot pretzels, only a nickel; ice cream, best Italian ice cream; lemonade, cotton candy, souvenirs . . . my head swam from the noise and bustle.

I stood beside a pillar and tried to get my thoughts in order. It was almost dark and it occurred to me that maybe I should find a place to sleep before I did anything else, but I decided that I shouldn't put off what I came to do any longer. This was something I shouldn't tackle alone, so I couldn't put off finding Ryan either. The logical thing to do would be to find a police station and tell them everything. Then it would be up to them. If Ryan was truly innocent he could go back to his play, and I could take the next train home with a clear conscience. I set off to find the nearest policeman, to ask for directions to police headquarters. Then I'd find the theater. Ryan would surely be there now, putting the final touches to his play.

I hadn't realized it until now, but Buffalo was a big city. Streets faded into darkness in all directions, trolley cars clanged past and tall buildings, just as imposing as those in New York, rose all around me. I wandered aimlessly until I came to the crossroads of two major thoroughfares. The sign on the corner said Main Street. At least I now knew I was in the center of town. As I stood waiting to cross, I saw a great glow in the sky, as if the sun had not set at all, but now resided just beyond those tall buildings. My first thought was that it was a huge fire, and waited for the sound of fire engines racing to the scene. Then, as I watched in awe, I saw a great beam, like a giant lighthouse, cut across the sky, lighting even the very clouds. Suddenly it dawned on me that this must be the famous exposition, illuminated with its thousands of electric lights. I had a longing to rush to see it for myself, and had to remind myself of my immediate and unpleasant duty.

I spotted a policeman on horseback coming down the boulevard toward me. I was about to cross the street when I spied the Pfeiffer Theater. A man was standing on a ladder, putting the sign on the marquee. "Opening tomorrow night: Special pre-New York showing. 'Friends and Neighbors,' by the Internationally Acclaimed Playwright, Mr. Ryan O'Hare."

I stood there staring at that theater, in one last turmoil of indecision. It would be so much easier to turn over my information to the police, but I just couldn't bring myself to betray Ryan before I had a chance to talk to him. Maybe this was foolhardy, but I still couldn't equate the Ryan I knew with a ruthless anarchist. It made even less sense that he would be planning a deadly attack on the very eve of the opening of his new play.

I made up my mind and picked up my skirts to cross the street. I was going to risk that encounter. And what better place to confront him than surrounded by his company? There would be safety in numbers. If my suspicions were in any way confirmed by his reactions, all I had to do was to ask one of his company to accompany me to the police station. I had nothing to worry about.

The front doors of the theater were shut but I went around to the side and found the stage door ajar. The doorman tried to stop me but I told him I'd come from New York with an important message for Mr. O'Hare.

"I wouldn't interrupt him now, miss," the little old man said. "They're in the middle of the final dress rehearsal."

"Don't worry, I'll wait for the right moment," I said and walked past him before he could come out of his cubbyhole and stop me. I made my way past dressing rooms and props closets to the stage. This time the stage was ablaze with light. The actors were in full costume and makeup and their words echoed down the hallway toward me. I could see shadowy figures standing behind the curtains, but there was no sign of Ryan, so I slipped through the stage door out into the theater. In the darkness I could make out several dim shapes sitting a few rows back from the orchestra pit. As my eyes accustomed themselves to the darkness I recognized Ryan's riot of curly hair among them. I heard the breath of relief escape from my lips. He was here and he wasn't alone. I wouldn't be in danger while other people were around. I hesitated in the shadows, my heart beating so loudly that I felt sure it could be heard over the actors' voices. A funny line was delivered onstage and the row of people in the audience laughed. I could see Ryan's white teeth as he too laughed at his own joke.

"Go on, get it over with," I told myself, but I couldn't make my feet move. I might have become fond of Ryan, but I was equally aware of how little I knew about the man behind that well-polished, amusing facade. Oh, well, there was no sense in standing here worrying. I had come to see him, and see him I was going to. I waited until a scene came to its end, then I moved out of the shadows and slid into the row of seats beside him. Ryan looked up, startled.

"Molly, what on earth—? Lovely surprise, but why didn't you tell me you were going to be in Buffalo?"

"I came to see you, Ryan," I whispered. "We have to talk. It's important."

He put his finger to his lips. "Only one more scene in Act One and they'll take a ten-minute break then," he whispered.

We sat. I was conscious of his presence close beside me. I tried to follow the play, I tried to laugh at the funny lines, as Ryan and the gentlemen around him were doing, but my mouth and throat were dry and my face felt frozen into a mask. Now I was here, I wished with all my heart that I hadn't come. I wished I could be anywhere else in the world than here about to confront Ryan.

"You'll be sorry for this," the actress onstage said. "By God, you'll be sorry!" and she stalked offstage as the curtain came down.

To my relief the house lights came up. Ryan turned to me and gave me a beaming smile. "I realize I am completely irresistible, my darling Molly, but surely chasing me to Buffalo is going just a teeny bit too far."

"Ryan, I'm afraid it's not funny," I whispered. "I must talk to you about something very important."

The man beside Ryan got up. "I'm just going to stretch my legs and have a puff at my pipe," he said. "Great stuff so far, O'Hare."

I hoped that the other men wouldn't follow suit.

Ryan was looking at me with amused interest. "Don't tell me that George at O'Connor's sent you after me because I haven't paid my bar bill?" The same old Ryan, flippant and amusing. I glanced across to see if those other men were listening, but they were talking together.

"I'm not sure where to start," I whispered. "I want to know about you and someone called Czolgosz."

"Leon?" He looked surprised but still amused. "My dear, that was all over ages ago."

"Over?"

He leaned closer to me. "We had a very brief fling last year. I got bored. I usually do. I met Angus. Leon went home to Cleveland. End of story."

"Not quite end of story," I said. "He came back here this summer, didn't he? You met him at O'Connor's."

"Have you been spying on me?" Ryan was still smiling. "Don't tell me you are jealous!" He glanced around and suddenly grabbed me by the arm. "I think that maybe you and I should carry on this conversation somewhere a little more private." He steered me out of the row of seats and up the steps toward the stage door. "The provinces tend to be—uh—rather narrow-minded, shall we say," he muttered in my ear. "Those men are reporters. Any hint of scandal and I shall be doomed, my dear."

Before I could do anything sensible to react, he hustled me before him through another door. It was a room with a couple of aged couches and a table littered with half-drunk cups of coffee. The door clanged shut behind us. I was alone with Ryan O'Hare, whether I wanted it or not.

"Now then," he said. "What is this very important thing you have to tell me about Leon? Is he back in town looking for me and pining again? He's not saying slanderous things about me, is he?"

I had no choice but to tell him the truth. "Leon is a very dangerous man," I said.

A smile crossed his face. "Leon dangerous? Deluded yes, but—"

"I work—used to work for a private detective. He was killed—I'm certain he was murdered by your friend Leon."

Before Ryan could say anything, I opened my purse and produced the postcard, now pasted together. "I went to the boardinghouse where he had been staying and I found this in his wastebasket. He was going to send it to you, but obviously changed his mind."

Ryan examined the postcard and the smile faded. "Oh, God," he said quietly.

"Do you know what he means?"

Ryan sighed. "He took it rather hard when I left him—they usually do. He told me he'd do something to make me notice him.

Then he launched into this grand plan to do something spectacular at the exposition. He tried to persuade me to be his partner in crime. I laughed, I'm afraid. Leon always had big ideas, but I thought he was all talk. He was melodramatic to the point of being boring."

"He's in Buffalo," I said. "He left his lodgings and asked the landlady for a railway timetable. He looked up trains to Buffalo."

"Jesus, Mary and Joseph." It was the first time I'd heard an Irish expression escape from his lips.

"What do you think he was planning to do?" I asked.

"I really don't know. He lived in a fantasy world, actually, and talked a lot of nonsense." He pushed back his hair in a gesture of futility. "Lucky he wasn't here today, wasn't it? The President toured the exposition and then went out to the new power plant at Niagara Falls. Leon was all for assassinating heads of state."

"We should go to the police," I said.

"It might be the wisest thing." He leaned back against the peeling paint of the wall. "This would happen when I have my opening night tomorrow."

A thought struck me. "You don't think he might try to disrupt your opening night?"

Ryan looked startled. "Now that's a thought. Punish me by bombing my theater? Yes, I suppose that could be why he's here."

"Then we must go to the police right away."

"The problem is, what can they do? Do you know how many people are in this town? Leon could be wearing a disguise, have registered in a hotel under a false name—there is no way they'll find him if he doesn't want to be found."

"But we must stop him, Ryan. He killed my employer. He tried to kill me."

"Tried to kill you? When?" Ryan gave me a startled look.

"A few nights ago. He broke into the house and came at me with a knife."

"Act Two, beginners on stage in two minutes," came the call down the hallway. Ryan moved toward the door. "I have to go

242

back. The second act is starting." He took my arm again. "Come on. We'll go looking for him tomorrow," he said as he led me back to our seats. "If he knows I'm in town, it's just possible that he will be tailing me. We'll lure him to us and make him see reason."

I watched the second act feeling an overwhelming sense of relief. Ryan was not involved in the plot himself. He was going to make everything all right.

"Where are you staying tonight?" he whispered as the curtain fell. I told him I hadn't found a hotel room yet. He shook his head. "There's no point in trying to find a bed in the city. Every hotel and boardinghouse is chockablock full. Half my crew are slumming in the green room. You'd better join them."

So I spent the night in the theater green room, lying on old cloths that smelled of paint. Again safety in numbers, I told myself, even though I had nothing to fear.

In the morning I waited impatiently while Ryan went through last-minute instructions in the theater, then talked to a bevy of news reporters waiting for him outside. It was past noon by the time we joined the human tide heading toward the main gates of the exposition. Then we had to wait in the hot sun as the line inched forward toward the turnstiles. Ryan paid for both of us, the turnstile swung and we were through.

I had been concentrating so hard on my task that I hadn't given much thought to the exposition itself. But as we passed through the entrance gates and crossed a beautiful lake by means of a triumphal causeway, I caught my first glimpse of that majestic tower rising at the end of a wide boulevard. It was like a tower from a fairy tale, and I let out a gasp.

"If you think it's impressive in the daytime, you should see it at night," Ryan said, smiling at my excited face. "That whole tower is one mass of electric lights. And a great beam at the top of it. You can see it shining out for miles away."

"I saw it last night," I said. "It lit up the whole sky. I've never imagined anything as magical as this in my entire life. This is how I pictured Rome and Florence and Paris all rolled into one."

We were swept by the human tide up the grand esplanade, lined with columns and dotted with fountains. Each fountain was grander than the one in Central Park. Elegant Spanish or Renaissance-style buildings stood on either side. Some of them had great domes, some of them were adorned with Greek pillars. I'd have loved to see inside each of them, but we were borne forward by the surge around us toward the tower, and by a sense of urgency. A brass band was playing on an outdoor stage. Flags of all nations fluttered in the morning breeze. Even the signs were intriguing. TO THE PLANTATION, TO THE AFRICAN VILLAGE, TO THE WILD WEST SHOW, TO THE TEMPLE OF SCIENCE. How wonderful it would have been to be a visitor here, with time to explore and no worries.

"Where do you think we should start?" I asked Ryan. We had reached the base of the tower and stood beside yet another pool with fountains playing. A breeze sprang up and the spray felt wonderful, as the day had become quite warm. Around us, men were mopping at foreheads with handkerchiefs and women were fanning themselves.

He shook his head. "I have no idea. This whole thing is futile, Molly. How can we possibly find him among these crowds? And I should be back at my theater. There are so many things to do before we open tonight."

"But we can't just give up and go home," I said. "What exactly did he tell you he was going to do? Do you remember his exact words?"

Ryan wrinkled his forehead. "He said he was going to make the damned capitalists sit up and take notice, pardon the language, and what better way than destroying that monument to capitalism, the Pan American Exposition. I asked him just how he planned to destroy a whole exhibition, single-handedly. I teased him that he'd need large pockets to carry in enough explosives to bring down even one of the buildings. And he said he'd find a way."

"Why didn't you tell someone?" I was shocked.

Ryan pushed back a lock of hair in a gesture of annoyance. "My dear girl, I've told you before, I didn't take him seriously. He was always making wild threats and wild promises. He was going to kill the King of England, he was going to blow up the Eiffel Tower in Paris. All talk, Molly. His family thinks he's crazy, you know. He is penniless and quite dependent on them. So why should this fantasy be any different from the others?"

"We have to assume that it is," I said quietly.

He nodded. "Yes, I suppose we do. Not a comforting thought."

"So he was planning to blow up one of the buildings," I said. "Then it would have to be the tower, wouldn't it?"

"That or the new electricity power plant they've built beside the Niagara Falls," Ryan said, thinking out loud, "Or my theater. Take your pick. All good targets."

We walked around the tower, then stood by the fountain, examining the crowd for any sign of Leon. As Ryan had said, it was hopeless. A hundred thousand people must have been at the exposition that day, and there was no reason that Leon would have picked this very day to carry out his plan.

"Let's at least go to the police and give them a description of him. Then we'll have done all we can do," I said.

Ryan nodded. "I don't see what other option there is. We can't station ourselves everywhere. I hate the idea of turning poor Leon over to the police, but what else can I do?"

"Why poor Leon? The man is a murderer, Ryan."

"Yes, but also a very troubled person, Molly. I told you his family thinks he is crazy. His father wanted to have him locked away."

"And do you think he's crazy?"

"Obsessed, I suppose, sums it up. He was obsessed with me for a while. Now he seems to be obsessed with anarchism."

"I imagine most anarchists must be crazy," I said.

"Leon isn't a true anarchist," Ryan said. "As I said, he is obsessed with anarchism at the moment, although he was very good at spending capitalist money when I was paying. He even developed a taste for Havana cigars." He gave a short, bitter laugh. "True anarchists are good at concealing their identity. They behave like you and me until the time comes." He jumped aside as he was almost mowed down by a group of children who rushed, screaming, toward a clown on stilts.

"Oh, this is ridiculous, Molly. Why on earth did I allow you to talk me into this? It's worse than looking for the proverbial needle in a haystack. I've got to get back to the theater. The opening-night curtain goes up in"—he consulted his pocket watch—"in four hours."

As we made our way back down the grand esplanade, we found that cordons were being set up. Men in uniforms were stationed along the cordons, channeling the crowds to either side. People were starting to line the route, many of them clutching American flags.

"What's this in aid of?" Ryan asked one of the soldiers. "More dignitaries coming today?"

"President McKinley's coming in a few minutes," the uniformed man said, not looking up.

"But I thought he toured the exposition yesterday," I blurted out.

"He did, but he liked it so well that he's decided to come back."

"He'll be driving around in his automobile, will he?" I asked.

"No, ma'am—he'll be in the Temple of Music over there, shaking hands," the man said. "Going to give the ordinary folks a chance to meet him. That's the kind of guy he is."

❊ Twenty-six ❊

I looked at Ryan to see if he was thinking the same thing I was. His face had also gone pale.

"Who would be in charge of the President's security?" I asked. "We need to speak to him."

The man laughed. "Don't worry yourselves about that. They've got enough National Guardsmen and Marines and Secret Service here to start a small war."

The crowd enveloped us and moved us on. It seemed that everyone else was heading in the same direction—to an ornate domed building halfway along the grand esplanade. It was the most magnificently decorated of all, with pillars rising to that great dome and the whole edifice adorned with statues and flags.

I grabbed Ryan's arm. "We have to tell someone," I said.

"Who?"

"We'll go up to the door and find out who is in charge. They can stop Leon from going in."

Ryan nodded.

But as we approached the temple, we saw that it was going to be impossible to get anywhere close. A long line had already formed, snaking its way between cordons and armed guards toward the entrance. Another line of guards stood around the perimeter to stop people from cutting into the line. Ryan took my hand and we forced our way through the crowd until we reached the nearest soldiers.

"We need to speak to someone in charge," Ryan said. "We have reason to believe that a dangerous anarchist is among this crowd."

"Anarchist, uh?" The soldier looked amused, if anything.

"He's of slight build, big dark eyes, probably dressed all in black," I said. "He likes to wear a black cap."

"Sounds like a regular good anarchist to me," the soldier said, still grinning.

"If you'd let us in, we could identify him for you," Ryan added.

"Oh, so that's your game, is it?" the soldier sneered. "Trying to cut the line? Go on, get to the end and wait your turn like everyone else."

"But we need to talk to someone in charge," I insisted. "Don't you realize the President could be in danger?"

"If that's what you're worrying about, little lady, then there's no need," the man said. "Anyone who goes into that theater has to pass a rigorous inspection. If we don't like the look of someone, he doesn't get in. The President will be safer than in Fort Knox."

He moved us away.

"I wish I could believe him," I said. "See if you can spot Leon in the line."

Ryan strained to peer through the crowd. "Too many people in the way."

"Hopeless," I said. "Maybe if we made a fuss, we'd get taken straight to the man in charge. He'd listen to us."

"We could also find ourselves thrown into jail," Ryan said. "Which would seriously disturb my opening tonight."

"Then what do you suggest?" I snapped. The heat and the enormity of the moment were getting to me.

"If we could find a way into the building"—Ryan was staring up at the dome above us— "then we could spot Leon the moment he entered, before he got anywhere close to the President."

"We'd have to make ourselves invisible." The temple was surrounded by a great throng, half of whom seemed to be armed guards.

"Let's see what happens round at the back of the building."

We forced our way back through the crowd still making for the end of the line. As we came around to the other side of the building, a great cheer went up, getting closer and closer. A band played a fanfare. We got a glimpse of the black roof of an automobile. The President had arrived. The far side of the temple was no better than the other. Here was the exit door where those who had shaken the President's hand would leave the building. It, too, was heavily guarded and there was a second perimeter of soldiers to stop anyone from getting too close.

"I wonder if they've locked the stage door," Ryan said. "It's a theater, isn't it? There has to be a performers' entrance." We went around to the back and, sure enough, there was a little door, half-hidden behind a pillar. We tried it and of course it was locked. Ryan glanced at the back of the armed guards who formed a circle around the pavilion. "Do you happen to have a hairpin, Molly, my dearest?"

"Yes, but . . ." I tugged one out of my hair. "You can't think of—"

"I have acquired some extremely useful skills during my long and checkered career, and picking a lock was one of them," Ryan said, kneeling down before the lock. "Keep guard for me."

I moved away from the door. The stage door was in deep shade and blocked from view by the pillar. If Ryan was quick, we might have a chance to get inside undetected.

Then I looked up to see one of the guards turning in my direction.

"Hey, you," he called. "What are you doing?"

I picked up my skirts, revealing a good expanse of ankle, and ran straight toward him, looking suitably distressed. "I'm sorry, sir, but it's my little sister." I gazed up at him and fluttered my eyelashes. "She's become separated from our party and my mother is fit to be tied. She sent me to look for her. You haven't seen her yourself, have you? She's the family beauty, you know. Only sixteen, but she has the biggest blue eyes and hair like spun gold, and she's so dainty, not like big, clodhopping me. You'd know her if you'd seen her. All the men swoon over our Eileen."

"I can't say that I have seen her, miss," the soldier said. "But I'd certainly like to if she's anything like you describe."

"Oh, she is. Even more so. All the boys are crazy for our Eileen," I said. "That's her name. Eileen Donovan. So if you'd be good enough to keep an eye out for her . . . Tell her that the family are waiting for her in line to see the President and if she doesn't hurry up, she'll miss her chance."

The soldier gave me a friendly wink as he tipped his cap. "Right you are, miss. I'll keep my eye out for her."

"I'd better get back to my poor mother in the line, then," I said. "I'm much obliged to you, officer. I'm so relieved to know you'll spot her if she comes this way." I fluttered my eyelashes yet again, then ran back, as if I were going around to the front of the building. Once the soldier had turned away, hoping no doubt to catch a glimpse of the ravishing Eileen, I dodged into the shadow of a pillar and crept back to Ryan. The door now swung open and Ryan was standing just inside it, looking very pleased with himself.

"What did I tell you? There is no end to the man's talents." He gave me an excited grin as we stepped inside to complete darkness.

I held my breath as we tiptoed along a dark passageway. At every step I expected to be confronted by an armed guard, but nothing stirred. At last we found ourselves behind the stage. The curtains were drawn, but through the gaps we could see the shapes of yet more men standing guard.

"We could alert one of them," I whispered.

"And if we took them by surprise they might shoot first and ask questions afterward," Ryan said. "This is America, land of the gun. No, we have to get to a position where we can see for ourselves."

He led on, following the back wall of the theater past the

stage and into another passage. We were now in almost total darkness again. Then we came to a stair in the wall. Ryan turned and gave me a thumbs-up sign.

"Watch your step, it's narrow," he said and started to climb. I picked up my skirts and followed. The door at the top opened onto an elegant hallway. Below us rose the echoing murmur of voices. We pulled back a red velvet curtain and stepped out onto a balcony. We stood in the shadow of the velvet curtains looking down on a vast auditorium. Around the walls were brightly painted pillars and archways, and above our heads the most amazing dome, decorated in the same brilliant red and gold. It was enough to take your breath away. To our right was the stage we had just passed and to our left, a pipe organ as big as a house, with pipes rising right up to the dome. What a noise that would make when it was played. Both the stage and the organ were still, however. The action was happening on the floor below us. Most of the seats in the auditorium had been moved to create a lane down which a solid line of humanity had begun to file. And there, almost directly below us, was an area draped with giant American flags and potted plants. A large gray-haired man in a dark suit was seated there, surrounded by dignitaries and flanked by an armed escort.

"Serious breach in security, wouldn't you say?" Ryan whispered. "He'd be a sitting duck from up here."

The first of the line of well-wishers was now approaching the President. Excited faces poked out of the crowd, craning to get their first view of the great man. My, but it was hot in that auditorium. Men were wiping their foreheads. I saw one woman dabbing eau de cologne on her forehead, another fanning herself with her program. I could feel the sweat trickling down my own neck, although whether that was from the heat or from fear, I couldn't tell.

We waited and watched. The line went on and on—an endless procession coiling across the auditorium like a giant snake, in one door and out the other. The President obviously had hand-shaking down to a fine art. While he shook hands with his right, his left was already motioning the person to move along.

Suddenly Ryan grabbed my arm. "There he is," he hissed.

"Where?"

"There. Behind the woman with the baby."

I stared at the person he was indicating and then looked up at Ryan in surprise. If this was Leon, I never would have recognized him. Gone were the black clothing and the cap. He was dressed conservatively in a brown jacket, shirt and tie. He looked like any other visitor—a serious young clerk or college student. And, more strangely still, I saw for the first time that his hair was light brown, parted in the middle and slicked down neatly. I had never noticed his hair, because he had always been wearing that black cap, so he had always given me the impression of being dark. Of course, I was too far away to see his eyes. I would have remembered them anywhere.

"What should we do now?" I whispered.

As I turned to Ryan, I saw him reach into his pocket. At that moment the world stood still. I saw how stupidly naive I had been. Ryan must have planned this whole charade. What had he just said about real anarchists not looking the part? Was he not a brilliant actor who had played his part perfectly? I realized how cleverly he had kept me in his sight and not let me go to the police, even to the point of making sure I slept in his theater. He had tricked me into thinking he wanted to prevent Leon from committing the crime, when he was the mastermind behind this plot, now poised in a perfect position in case Leon somehow missed his target. And I—I had become the accomplice, the hostage, trapped up here with someone who was a ruthless killer. I looked around wildly, but help was quite out of reach. Well, I wasn't going to let him carry out his deed if I could help it.

His hand came out of his pocket and I saw that the object he held was not a gun, but a white handkerchief. At that moment I noticed that Leon, like several other men, was holding a handkerchief in his hand. It had to be used for a signal.

As Ryan went to raise his arm I flung myself onto him. We staggered sideways together, and almost went over the railing.

"What the devil?" Ryan shouted, grabbing on to me to steady us both. "Have you gone mad?"

At that moment we heard the shot. It echoed back from that great dome, sounding just like the popping of a large firecracker. Then all hell broke loose. Women were screaming. Men were wrestling below us. Others had clustered around a fallen man.

"He's done it!" Ryan gasped. "He's really done it!" He spun around, grabbing my shoulders. "I could have stopped him! Who are you? Are you one of them? Did you wish the President dead?"

He was shaking me violently.

"I thought you did." I felt as if I was about to burst into tears and fought to master myself. "You got out that handkerchief. I thought it was a signal."

"The sweat was running into my eyes, you stupid girl!" We stood glaring at each other. "I was about to call out his name. He'd have panicked and they could have grabbed him. What on earth made you think I was in on it with him?"

"Paddy Riley, the detective that Leon killed—he snapped a photo of you and Leon the day before he was murdered. I've never truly known whether I could trust you or not."

He looked at me quite tenderly now. "Then you're a brave little colleen to come up here with me. I could easily have thrown you over."

"I know," I said. "I was well aware of that."

"It doesn't matter now," Ryan said. "We're too late. We failed." He gave a big sigh and turned to leave the balcony.

"Maybe he didn't hit his mark. Maybe the President is just wounded," I said.

At that moment there were shouts and the clatter of boots coming up the stairs. Before we could move, guns were trained on us.

"We've got them. More of the gang," a voice shouted.

Hands grabbed us and we were manhandled down the steps.

"Let go," I yelled in fright as my hands were wrenched behind my back. "We're not his accomplices. We were trying to stop him, you fools." But nobody listened to me as we were dragged out of the building.

"Do you know who I am? I'm Ryan O'Hare, the famous playwright," Ryan shouted. "We thought this man might do something and we tried to stop him."

"We tried to get into the building. We tried to talk to someone in charge, but nobody would listen to us!" I yelled. "You're making a big mistake. Get your hands off me!"

"Take them down to headquarters for questioning," a voice commanded. "Quick. Get them out of here before the crowd tears them to pieces."

The next moments passed in a blur. A crowd of angry faces surged toward us as I was dragged toward a waiting police wagon. The wagon door opened and Ryan was flung inside.

"She's the one. She shot the President! String her up, boys. Don't let them take her away," voices shouted in my ear. Hands grabbed at my skirt. I heard a ripping sound, someone fired a warning shot and I was thrown into the wagon after Ryan. Then whips were cracked and we were galloped away.

❧ Twenty-seven ❧

It seemed an eternity before we arrived at the Buffalo Police headquarters, then were yanked out of the wagon and dragged inside by armed guards. Once inside the building we were marched down a hallway and thrown into a holding cell. During the wild ride it had been impossible to speak. Now we gazed at each other in horrified disbelief.

"What do you think will happen to us?" I couldn't stop my voice from trembling. "They will listen to us, won't they?"

"The President's just been shot." Ryan sounded equally shaky. "I don't imagine they'll behave very rationally. They'll want to find scapegoats to satisfy the public outrage. My God, we were nearly torn limb from limb out there."

I hugged my knees to myself to stop myself from shaking. "If I hadn't been so stupid . . ."

"You did what you thought was right," Ryan said. "I'm sorry I got you into this."

"You didn't get me into it. I got myself into it. I should never have come to Buffalo."

"You wanted to go to the police. I was the stupid one who wanted to find Leon myself. I blame myself completely. I never thought he'd go through with it. I thought it was all fantasy. I should never have laughed at him. I drove him to it."

"It won't do any good blaming ourselves," I said. "We can't

255

undo what's done. I'm sure they'll realize they've made a mistake."
I tried to give Ryan a reassuring smile because he looked even
worse than I felt.

He shook his head. "It won't look good for me. They'll find out
that Leon was my ex-lover. But I'll make sure they know that you
had nothing to do with it." He reached out and patted my hand.

We sat together on the hard bench, both lost in our own
thoughts. Then, much later, the cell door opened and we were
led out.

We were taken down a white-tiled hallway, then thrust into a
brightly lit room. Several police officers were standing around. A
man was sitting slumped over a center table. He turned and lifted
his head as we came in. It was Leon, but I hardly recognized him,
he was such a sorry sight, so swollen, bleeding and battered was
he.

"Take a look at these people," a policeman shouted. "Do you
know them? Were you all in this together? You can make it easier
on yourself if you name your accomplices."

Leon turned the haunted eyes that I remembered so well
onto us.

"I never saw either of them before in my life," he said in a flat
voice.

"Come on. Own up. Someone must have put you up to this."

"I told you, I did it alone," Leon said in a flat voice. "Nobody
was in it with me."

"Someone must have given you the idea. You don't just wake
up one morning deciding you'll go and shoot the President. Come
on. Your silence isn't going to help you, you know."

"Nothing will help me now," Leon said. "If anyone made me
do it, it was . . ." He turned back to Ryan for a moment and his
gaze lingered on Ryan's face before he said in the same flat voice,
". . . it was Emma Goldman."

The interrogators looked at each other and nodded. "It figures," one growled. "What did I tell you. An anarchist plot. Have

256

this Emma Goldman found and brought in before she skips the country."

"Wait, I didn't say she put me up to it," Leon pleaded. "I said she inspired me. I told you I did it alone. Nobody helped me. It was all my idea."

The largest of the police detectives looked at Leon then at us with distaste. "Take them away," the policeman bellowed.

We were led farther along the hall into another room. Two of the officers followed us into the room.

"Look, officer," Ryan said as the door closed behind us, leaving us alone with two policemen, "what that man said wasn't true."

I gasped and gave Ryan a hasty glance.

"I do know Leon Czolgosz," Ryan said. "In case you don't know me—I'm Ryan O'Hare. I have a worldwide reputation in the theater. Leon was rather infatuated with me last year. He followed me around and he wanted me to join in one of his crazy schemes. Of course I refused. But when I learned that he was at the exposition today, I thought it was my duty to try to stop him. Miss Murphy and myself tried several times to be taken to someone in charge of security. Each time we were ignored and turned away. So we had to try and take matters into our own hands. I'm only sorry that we failed."

I could see the detective looking with distaste at Ryan's silk cravat and frilled shirt, trying to make up his mind as to whether he believed him.

"And may I ask what you are doing in Buffalo at the same time as Mr. Czolgosz?" he asked.

"My dear man, I can tell you are not a theatergoer. My new play opens tonight at the Pfeiffer Theater, in precisely one hour and forty minutes. So if you'd be good enough to let me get back to my company before the curtain goes up—"

"There won't be any play opening tonight," the policeman growled. "Have you no sensitivity, man? Our President has been shot. Nobody knows if he's going to live or die. The whole exposition is shut down. And we're not done with you yet, by a long way."

"But you can't seriously think that I am in any way involved." Ryan managed a light laugh. "My dear man, would I do anything to jeopardize a new play on which I have spent the last year working? My whole reputation is at stake."

"Take him away," the policeman motioned to a guard standing behind us. "Put him back in the cells. The feds will want to question him when they get here."

"I'm a citizen of the British Empire, as is this young lady," Ryan said. "It should be quite obvious that we have no interest in what happens to your President."

This wasn't the right thing to say at this moment either. The policeman aimed a kick at Ryan's backside. "Get him out of my sight!" he shouted.

He was taken from the room, leaving me alone with the two interrogators.

"Miss Molly Murphy?" One of them was staring at me with interest. I reminded myself that this was no time for smart remarks. I had to watch every word I said and not get riled. My only chance was to play the helpless and injured female.

"Yes, sir."

"How did you come to be mixed up in this?"

Over the past few months I had become adept at lying. What story should I tell them to get myself out of there? I fished around but my brain would not cooperate. "I was working for a private detective in New York," I said. "He was killed. I managed to find the identity of his killer—it was the man who shot the President. My employer had overheard a conversation in which Mr. Czolgosz tried to persuade Mr. O'Hare to join him in an act of anarchy. When I discovered he had gone to Buffalo, I feared the worst."

"Why didn't you go to the police?"

"Oh, but I did. I went to see Captain Daniel Sullivan of the New York Police Department, but he wasn't there, so I left him a letter detailing everything I had found out. He must have read it and contacted you by now, surely?"

"I know of no Captain Sullivan," the man growled.

He stared at me with the same intensity with which he had looked at Ryan before dismissing him.

"You Irish are known to be a lot of rabble-rousers and law-breakers, aren't you?" he sneered. "Bunch of anarchists, the lot of you."

"Anyone who was an Irish anarchist would have his work cut out for him driving the English from our land," I said. "We'd have no need to travel abroad to find a cause."

As I said this I realized what a hornet's nest of trouble he'd stir up for me if he decided to contact Ireland. Nobody in America knew that I had fled from Ireland after I killed a man. I would just have to bluff it out. My eyes held his.

There was a long moment of silence, during which the clock on the wall ticked loudly. Then the older of the two detectives opened the door. "Go on. Get out of here," he said.

"I'm free to go?" I asked hopefully.

"Not by a long chalk," he said. "I'm not satisfied with any of this. It smacks of an anarchist plot to me. We'll be checking up on you and Mr. O'Hare very thoroughly—and that might just take days or weeks. Harris!" he barked. "Take this woman to a new cell, away from Mr. O'Hare. We'll see which of them cracks first."

He grinned at me unpleasantly as I was led from the room.

The new cell had a plank against one wall and a bucket for a commode. I desperately wanted to go, but as there were only bars at the front of my cell, and I was thus visible to anyone who walked past, I sat on the plank with grim determination. After the heat of the day, I couldn't stop shivering. What would happen to me? It was obvious that Daniel was still away and hadn't received my letter. And even if he did finally get it, what good could he do? He had no authority in Buffalo, and these men seemed to be determined to find me guilty.

I sat in half-darkness. A small barred window opened onto the street outside and I could hear an angry crowd milling out there. They were ready to riot, which must be why the police were so anxious to conclude their investigation quickly and needed to produce scapegoats. I hugged my arms to myself and wished I had a shawl. There would clearly be no mercy for someone who shot the President of the United States. I felt almost sorry for Leon, but even more sorry for Ryan and me. This is what I get for meddling, I told myself. What stupid idea had ever convinced me that playing at detective might be a suitable profession?

Then a small voice whispered that I didn't want to be safe and secure and bored. I wanted to know I was alive and independent. I knew I was alive at this moment, but for how much longer?

I could see daylight fading in that small square of barred window. A uniformed policeman came by and poked a tin mug of water and a hunk of bread and cold meat through the bars, as if he were feeding the lions at the zoo. I sipped at the water but felt too sick and worried to eat.

More hours went by. I tried to sleep, but couldn't. Then heavy footsteps came down the hallway. My cell door was unlocked.

"Look lively. You're wanted again. The chief wants a word with you."

I was hustled down the same tiled hallway and into another room, brightly lit with an electric lightbulb. This time a large mustachioed man in shirtsleeves sat at a desk, with other policemen standing around him.

"Miss Murphy, sir," my escort said, thrusting me toward the desk.

"Ah yes, Miss Murphy. The one who uncovered the plot single-handed." The man at the desk had several chins and was leering at me. "I understand you are one of our more promising detectives, Miss Murphy. I should keep you on here, to give my boys some lessons." Chuckles from those standing around him.

"No, sir, I'm very much a novice detective," I said. "But I worked for a man who was one of the best and he was killed. I thought I owed it to him to find out who killed him. It was only by luck that I stumbled upon a picture of the man who shot the President this afternoon, found that he was on his way to Buffalo and put two and two together. I left a message with a captain at the New York Police Department and came straight to Buffalo in the hope of preventing this tragedy."

He was still looking at me through piggy eyes with a leer. "Friend of yours, Captain Sullivan?"

"An acquaintance," I said, lowering my eyes.

He smirked unpleasantly. "Acquaintance, huh?"

"Yes, sir. But if you could contact him, he'd vouch for me. He knew I was trying to find Paddy Riley's killer. And I sent him the photos—"

He held up his hand to quieten me. "It seems he has friends in the right places, this Captain Sullivan. You've been given a glowing testimonial. I'm to understand Miss Murphy is true-blue and has been instrumental in helping the police before. We've had a message from the governor's office and been instructed to let you go."

A great wave of relief swept over me.

"Now?" I stammered. "I'm free to go now?"

He spread his hands in a gesture of futility. "You will, of course, leave particulars of where you can be contacted with us, and you will not think of leaving the country. Who knows what might come out when this investigation digs further."

The feeling of relief was incredible. "It won't uncover anything that implicates me," I said, "or Mr. O'Hare. We risked our lives just now, trying to stop your assassin, and all we got for our pains was bruises and torn clothing."

"Yes, well . . ." my interrogator began. "Our lads were just doing their duty, you know."

"For what it's worth, I'm very sorry indeed for what happened to the President," I said. "Was he killed?"

"He was still alive last time I heard," he said. "Able to speak."

"Well, that's good news, isn't it." I attempted a smile. "We'll just hope and pray for the best."

Then I made my exit.

I came out of police headquarters into the dark street. A large crowd was milling around, still in an ugly mood by the look of them. I hesitated, not sure what to do next. Should I take the next train home? Should I wait and see if I could do anything more for Ryan? I didn't know whether he had been released before me or whether he was still locked in a cell somewhere. The least I could do was to tell his theater company the news. And I had left my overnight bag in his green room. I tried to slip through the crowd unnoticed and find myself a cab, since I had no idea of the layout of this town.

At every step I was afraid someone might recognize me and raise the alarm that I had been somehow involved in the assassination attempt. I sensed that this crowd was in a mood for revenge and I had no wish to be strung from the nearest lamppost. The police should really have given me an escort. It occurred to me that the officer who released me knew this full well. Perhaps he was hoping that the mob would execute the justice he felt was denied him. I moved into the crowd, head down, and wished for once I had a bonnet to hide my features and not such prominent red hair. Gradually I inched my way through and I was almost at the other side, with freedom stretching before me, when I heard the words I had been dreading. "Wait a minute—you were one of them, weren't you? I saw them putting you in the paddy wagon at the Temple of Music." The voice was raised. "Over here, boys. Here's one of 'em trying to slip away."

Before he could grab me, I lashed out and ran. I didn't for a moment think that I could outrun a mob, but I was going to give it a darned good try. Footsteps clattered behind me on the cobbles. I found it hard to move fast in my pointed shoes and with all those skirts swishing around me. I picked up the skirts, revealing what was obviously an improper sight of undergarments, but at this moment I didn't care. Then, over the noise of the pounding feet, I heard the clatter of hoofbeats gaining on me and the next moment a black vehicle drew up beside me.

"Molly, jump in. Quick." I looked up at the sound of Daniel Sullivan's voice. He held out his hand. I grabbed it and was swung inside.

"The railway station, as fast as you can," Daniel commanded the driver and we clattered away just as the first of the mob pounded on the cab door.

I sat there gasping for breath, too overwhelmed to speak. "Are you real?" I asked, gazing up at him. "I'm not imagining you, am I?"

"Quite real." He was looking at me with great tenderness.

"How in God's name did you find me?"

"They wouldn't let me see you before and they didn't make me too welcome at police headquarters either. So I was left kicking my heels outside, hoping that they'd release you as soon as they read the message from the governor."

"You brought a message from the governor?"

"When I first found they had arrested you, they were not willing to release you based on my word alone. I had to summon the heavy artillery and telegraph the governor."

"It was a miracle," I said. "I thought I was done for this time."

"That was a rather impressive sprint you put on back there," Daniel said, giving me the wicked smile I had found so hard to forget. "And a pretty pair of legs revealed, too."

"Don't joke about it, Daniel," I gasped. "It's not funny. In fact, it's all been so horrible that—" Without warning I burst into tears. I had never cried in front of anyone in my life before, and I fought to master myself but I couldn't help it. My whole body shook with sobs. Daniel's arms came around me. "There, there. It's all over now. You're safe," he whispered, stroking my hair as if I were a little child.

In his arms I felt safe. My cheek was against his shoulder. I could have lain there forever.

"You saved my life," I whispered. "That's the second time you've saved me."

"I'm hoping it won't become a habit," he said. "If only you'd stay home and act like a sensible woman, I wouldn't have to rescue you from these harebrained schemes of yours. What in God's name were you doing at that Temple of Music? It's that O'Hare person, isn't it? A damned anarchist if ever I saw one. He got you mixed up in this!"

"No, you've got it all wrong. Ryan was helping me." I didn't say that my own suspicions had echoed Daniel's. "If you want to know what got me into this, it was hunting for Paddy's killer." I sat up. "You got my letter, didn't you?"

"You are fortunate that I did," he said. "I had planned to spend the week at a house party out on Long Island. When I got there, I discovered to my dismay that there was to be a formal ball and I had left my white tie and tails in the city. So I had to race back to get them and found your note."

"So you should have been attending a ball at this moment," I said in a small voice.

"Yes. That's correct."

"I'm sorry I took you away from such a pleasurable occasion," I said, as a picture of Daniel with Arabella, looking exquisite in a ball gown and jewels, flashed across my mind.

"Don't apologize. I am the world's most hopeless dancer, so you have saved me from considerable embarrassment," he said. "But I wish you'd explain to me what on earth you've been doing and what made you come here. Your scribbled note and the photos have left me completely bewildered. I take it this has something to do with Paddy Riley's death?"

"I was obviously too upset to make myself clear," I said. "And at that time all I had were suspicions. Now, of course, I know. Leon Czolgosz killed Paddy."

"Leon—you mean the man they say shot the President? He killed Paddy? Are you sure?"

I nodded. "Paddy overheard him telling Ryan about his plans to disrupt the exhibition. Leon and Paddy lived in the same boardinghouse and Leon found out that Paddy had been snooping in his room." I paused. "He tried to kill me, too."

"He did?"

"He broke into my house and came at me with a knife."

"And you managed to escape?"

"With the timely arrival of my friends."

"My dear, you never cease to amaze me." He shook his head.

"You never went to the police with this?"

"I wanted to make sure of my facts, and by the time I did make sure, Leon had already left for Buffalo. I put all the information in a letter to you and followed him."

"Well, I'll be—" He broke off before he uttered a profanity.

"Daniel, those photos—did you get a chance to look at them? Did they mean anything to you? I know Paddy took the pictures of Leon with Ryan O'Hare when he overheard Leon telling Ryan his plans. But there was also that picture of Sergeant Wolski, talking to a man I didn't recognize. Is it possible he was involved in the plot too?"

Daniel sighed. "Paddy had been working for me for quite a while. But nothing to do with this. We've known for some time that someone in the police force was in the pay of one of the biggest gangs. Information was being leaked to them too often so that they could keep one step ahead of us. I asked Paddy to look into it. I had my suspicions about Wolski all along. And to be frank with you, I suspected that Wolski had a hand in Paddy's killing. That's why I was so adamant about keeping you out of it. If it had been a gang killing, as I thought, and they caught you snooping around, then your life wouldn't have been worth a brass nickel."

"So that's why Wolski seemed so disinterested in solving the case," I said. "He must have suspected that Paddy was on to him."

"Hopefully your photo will give us proof to nail him," Daniel said. "How did you manage to get hold of the pictures, instead of the police?"

"I found Paddy's camera in a room which the police had already searched," I said, giving him a triumphant grin. It was amazing how quickly I had perked up. I felt positively alive and glowing again, but maybe that was just because I was sitting beside Daniel in a darkened carriage while the world slipped by us.

As if to answer this thought, the carriage came to a stop. "We're at the station, boss," the cabbie called down.

Daniel reached up and handed the driver a dollar bill. "Drive around a little longer, will you? We haven't finished our conversation yet."

The driver tipped his hat and we were off again.

"So you did it." Daniel was gazing at me with interest. "You completely disobeyed me when I told you to stay out of this case?"

I nodded. "Someone had to find Paddy's killer and Sergeant Wolski was going to make sure that the police didn't."

Daniel shook his head, smiling. "You said you were going to become an investigator, and you have. Of course, it was unfortunate that Wolski was put in charge of the police investigation, but you got here ahead of us."

"But not in time, regrettably," I said. "I feel so terrible that we couldn't have stopped the President from being shot."

Daniel nodded. "A great tragedy. He's a good man. But he's also a strong man. There's a good chance that he'll pull through."

"I do hope so. If only someone had listened to us at the door and let us speak to the head of security, but they brushed us off every time we tried."

"You did everything you could," Daniel said. "In the police force we know that you can't win 'em all. Sometimes we let the biggest crooks get away or they stand trial and are acquitted. It's all part of the game. You'll learn that if you stay in the business."

"Don't worry," I said. "After this, I'm going to keep well away from criminal cases. Paddy made good money from divorces or embezzlement. I'll stick to those."

Daniel took my hands in his. "You are a remarkable woman, Molly." Then his expression changed. "I can't tell you how much I've missed you. Life has been hell without you. I can't live without you, you know."

"Are you still engaged to Miss Norton?"

"Yes, but—"

"Then you have your own answer, don't you." I pulled my hands away from his. "You can't have us both, Daniel. You'll have to make your choice."

"But you don't understand what is at stake, Molly."

"Oh, I do. She is rich and beautiful. I'm poor and ordinary. When you put it that way, there is an obvious choice, isn't there?"

"You judge me very badly if you think I would be swayed by wealth," Daniel said. "It's more than that. If you'll let me explain."

"Please do. I have all the time in the world," I said.

He sighed. "My parents came to this country starving from the Great Famine in Ireland. They grew up poor. My father moved up the ladder in the police force by hard work and by making the right connections at Tammany Hall. One of the New York politicians who was most helpful to him was Arabella's uncle. He's a very influential man. How else do you think I made captain before I turned thirty?"

Street lamps illuminated Daniel's face as we drove along a boulevard still brightly illuminated for the fair.

"So I have known Arabella for most of my life," Daniel went on. "My parents always hinted that she would be a great match for me and I had to agree with them. After all, she is beautiful as well as coming from a powerful family. What more could a man want in a wife?"

"What more indeed?" I said.

"I was amazed that she said yes to me. After all, I am her social inferior and she cares about these things. I was happy with what I had achieved and all would have been well if something hadn't happened."

I looked up into his eyes. I could just see them sparkling in the light of the street lamps. "I fell in love. I didn't expect to, but I did. The moment you walked into that room on Ellis Island, I knew that I wanted you. I thought you were married to someone else. I thought you were possibly a murderess, but I wanted you more than anything in the world."

"And yet you are still engaged to her."

He put his hands on my shoulders. "I beg you to be patient, Molly. So much is at stake. If I break off the engagement, she'll have me ruined. I'll never get another promotion again. They could even find reasons to get me thrown out of the force altogether. Arabella likes getting her own way and she has a nasty temper when crossed."

"So you will go ahead and marry her knowing that you love me?" My voice trembled a little.

"Of course not. I am paying her as little attention as possible. I want her to become bored and tired of waiting and to be the one who breaks it off. What I pray for is that she finds someone else and learns the meaning of love, as I have done."

His hands on my shoulders tightened as he drew me closer. "I swear I love only you, but I can't throw away everything my parents have worked for. Will you be prepared to wait for me, Molly?"

"Not forever, Daniel," I said. "I won't wait forever. And I'm not prepared to play second fiddle either. I won't go behind her back. It's not fair to her. Come to me on the day that your engagement is broken and I'll throw myself into your arms. But until then . . ."

"I understand," he said. "You're a woman of principle. That's just one of the things I admire about you. As well as that lovely hair and those white shoulders and—" He broke off with a sigh. "Oh, dear God, Molly. I can't be so close to you and not touch you."

Suddenly I was in his arms and he was kissing me. And to my surprise, I was kissing him back. Reason and caution always seemed to fly to the winds when I was in Daniel's arms. I wasn't sure how long we stayed in that cab. I know Daniel handed the driver another dollar at one stage, but time had no meaning. All that mattered was that Daniel loved me and we were here together, and, at that moment, there was no tomorrow.

✵ Twenty-eight ✵

Of course the grim reality of the present overtook us soon enough. The cab deposited me at the station, which was seething with people trying to get out of the city. In spite of the great crush fighting to get onto the next train, Daniel found me a seat and handed me inside.

"You'll be all right now," he said.

"Won't you be traveling with me?" I asked hopefully.

"Unfortunately I'm to stay on in Buffalo on the governor's orders," he said. "He's arriving here himself in the morning to give a briefing. The whole country will be up in arms as the news reaches them. We have to make sure that innocent people aren't killed. Go straight home and stay there, please, Molly."

So I took the night train back to New York. What a difference from the train I had traveled on only a day earlier. Stunned and grief-stricken people sat around me, staring out of darkened windows in silence or whispering occasionally. A woman was sobbing farther down the carriage. I stayed awake all night in fear that someone might recognize me and incite these people to do me harm. But by dawn the high banks of the Hudson came into view and we pulled into New York. I arrived home to find two very angry women.

"How dare you run away to Buffalo without telling us,

Molly," Gus chided as they fussed over me and handed me a cup of tea.

"I didn't want to get you involved in such a risky business," I said.

"But we wanted to be involved," Sid exclaimed. "Now we've missed all the excitement. It must have been very exciting . . ."

"It was horrible." I shivered. "I thought I was going to be kept in jail, and then I was almost torn to pieces by a mob."

"But why? I thought you went there to stop this person from killing the President. Why would they attack you?"

"Because we had to sneak into the theater and climb up onto a balcony to spot Leon. They thought we were his accomplices."

Sid turned to Gus with a grin. "Ryan will never stop talking about this. He must have been thrilled."

"Ryan was as upset as I was. And his play wasn't allowed to open last night."

"Oh, yes, the play," Gus said. "I'd forgotten about that. They've closed all the theaters in New York too. He'll have to wait until things are back to normal and that could be some time, if the poor President takes a while to recover."

"At least Leon is in custody," I said. "He won't be able to hurt anyone else ever again."

"But you're also hurt, Molly." Gus examined my face.

"I'm black and blue all over," I said. "That was when they dragged us down the steps and flung us into a van."

"Is your life always going to be like this?" Sid demanded. "Because if it is, I don't see you making thirty."

I took a welcome sip of tea. Sid had placed a dish of fresh rolls in front of me and there was apricot jam. It was like waking up from a nightmare. "I'm going to try and be sensible from now on. I'll only take uncomplicated, non-criminal cases."

"But you're still going to be a detective?"

"A sensible one. I'll start looking for lost relatives, as I'd planned."

"That sounds much safer," Gus agreed.

"Even so, I'd better start looking for a place of my own." I looked from one friendly face to the other. "I feel so bad that I've put you through all this when you were so kind to me."

Sid put her hands on my shoulders. "My dear stupid girl," she said, "how many time do we have to tell you that we loved the excitement? It has woken us out of our rut. Now I'm back to writing scathing articles on unjust treatment of women and Gus is painting a major canvas on the theme of violence. We insist that you stick around."

I smiled at them. "If you really insist—then I'd love to."

The next day Ryan arrived back in New York and showed up on our doorstep demanding Turkish coffee and sympathy. "I have returned from the black hole of Buffalo and need tender loving care," he said, sinking dramatically into a wicker chair.

"Poor dear Ryan. It must have been awful," Gus said, putting a cup of coffee in front of him. "Were they horrid to you?"

"My dear, I was tortured," he said, raising his arms in a martyr-like pose.

"What did they do to you, the swine?" Sid demanded.

"For one thing, they made me drink out of a tin mug," Ryan said, "and they refused my request for China tea instead of coffee. You have no idea how uncivilized the country becomes the moment one steps out of New York City. I hereby swear that I'll never leave it again."

"When did they let you go?" I asked. "Were you kept in that cell all night?"

"All night and most of the next day too. My dears, I felt like the Prisoner of Chillon. I could actually feel my hair turning gray, though not with years. Then finally a bright young lawyer turned up and managed to persuade them that I would be the last person who wanted the President dead on the very night my play was to have its triumphal opening. So, with great reluctance and many veiled threats, they let me go."

"And the play?" Sid asked. "What will happen to your play?"

Another gesture of great drama. "Let us just pray that McKinley recovers and we can open at the Daley as planned. But in the meantime, think of all the delicious publicity, my dears. I have already agreed to give interviews to the daily paper—My Brush with the President's Would-Be Assassin,' by Ryan O'Hare, brilliant and witty writer of the new play *Friends and Neighbors*. I'll be able to dine on this for a month of Sundays."

They were all laughing. I smiled uneasily. They seemed to have forgotten that at the center of Ryan's amusing tale lay a gravely wounded President. I realized at that moment that Greenwich Village was a small world apart. Life was a huge joke. Cynicism was their creed. And yet Sid and Gus could not have been kinder to me. I didn't quite know what to make of it.

Ryan was true to his word and his story of "My brush with the President's would-be assassin, and my role in apprehending him, by brilliant young playwright, etc." made the front pages of all the New York dailies. These articles garnered him more publicity than the out-of-town opening of his play would have done.

And later in the week, Shamey showed up at my door with a letter for me. "A real coachman and a carriage and all came looking for you, Molly."

I glanced at the envelope. It was from Miss Van Woekem. "I understand you were party to the infamous event. I am dying to hear all about it. Please come to lunch."

Now that several days had passed and the President still clung to life, the mood was changing. The assassination attempt had moved from a thing of horror to a major source of fascination and discussion for most New Yorkers.

"I'll write a reply and you can take it to the lady," I said, ruffling his hair, which was definitely in need of a wash and trim. I felt a sudden pang of guilt. "How are you, boy? How are your father and sister?"

"Not doing too good," he said.

"Your father is worse?"

He shook his head. "He's okay. He's walking around, almost as good as before, and he said I wasn't to bother you with our problems."

"Of course you're to bother me. Just tell me what's wrong."

Shameyboy made a face. "The old dragon is throwing us out."

"Mrs. O'Hallaran?"

"Yeah. She told us we were wrecking the joint and she wants us out by the end of the week."

"But that's terrible. Where will you go? Has Nuala found a new place for you?"

He shook his head. "She ain't got no money, do she?"

"Seamus! Where did you learn to speak like that? You know better than to say 'ain't.'"

"It's how New Yorkers talk. I'm a New Yorker now." He looked defiant.

My conscience was undergoing a silent battle. Much as I loved living with Sid and Gus, I couldn't let these children go back to the slums with Nuala and her brood. After all, I owed my own life to their mother, Kathleen. And I was fond of them.

"I'll stop off and see your father when I come to lunch with Miss Van Woekem," I said. "Don't worry. We'll sort everything out for you."

"Are you coming back to us, Molly?" His face lit up. "It was better when you were there, even though you made me wash."

"We'll talk about it," I said. "Off you go now."

The next day I presented myself at Miss Van Woekem's house.

"My dear child, how very exciting for you," she said as sherry was served. "Do tell me all about it; leave no detail out."

I was in the midst of my tale when Miss Van Woekem looked up and stared out of the window. "Something's wrong," she said.

"What is it?"

"I'm not sure. Go and open the window."

There was the sound of wailing on the breeze. From a window

273

farther down the square, now black bunting fluttered. A newsboy walked down the street shouting, "McKinley dead. McKinley dead."

Miss Van Woekem sighed. "And now that cowboy will take over as President," she said. "I fear the world will never be the same again."

I found I was shivering. How would my world be changed?

❧ Afterword ❧

olly Murphy and most of the characters in this book are fictional, but the events surrounding the assassination of President McKinley are true to historical fact. Leon Czolgosz, the lone assassin, was an enigma. He was not part of any organized anarchist group, although he had hung around at a few meetings, arousing the suspicion of the group's members. His family thought he was crazy and kept him safely out of harm's way on their farm. He didn't work, yet he seemed to have enough money for luxuries like cigars. When he was questioned after he fired the gun concealed in his handkerchief, he claimed he had worked alone and belonged to no group. He admitted to having been inspired by Emma Goldman, although she couldn't remember him.

Historians have not been able to come up with a motive for his deed. I have merely attempted to give him one.

"Irish humor and gritty determination . . .
with more charm and optimism than the usual law
attributed to Murphy." —Anne Perry

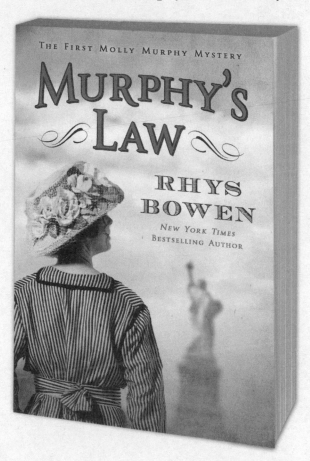

THE FIRST MOLLY MURPHY MYSTERY

MURPHY'S LAW

RHYS BOWEN

NEW YORK TIMES
BESTSELLING AUTHOR

Read the Entire Molly Murphy Mystery Series